Spiteful Spectres

Blue Moon Australia - Book 1

S.C. Stokes, Steve Higgs

Publisher: Steve Higgs

Contents

Murderous Mischief. Thursday, April 20th 1750hrs

On nights like this, James Mooney cursed the fact he'd set up his workshop on Peninsular Drive. The location itself was perfect, a stone's throw from the Gold Coast highway. He just hadn't considered the neighbors or the fact his newfound success would have him working his share of nights.

Shaking his head at the backpacker's hostel, and the evening party just getting underway there, James shut the workshop's roller door in an effort to insulate himself from the distraction and turned his attention to the task at hand.

Why anyone would want to pay to restore a beat-up old Datsun was beyond him. The car looked like it had been through a hailstorm before its owner had backed it into a post, mauling the rear end of the car and preventing the boot from even opening.

"I might be doing them a favor if I just take it to the wreckers now." He laughed as he pressed the button on his hoist. The hydraulics whirred as the vehicle was raised a few feet. He wanted a closer look at the damage.

Sentimental value, the owner had told him when she had insisted on having the old car's dents removed.

"I might be good, but I'm not a bloody wizard," James muttered as he studied the massive indentation in the boot. Trying to fix the workings of it was going to be a pain in the ass, but she'd paid cash up front which bought her a spot at the front of the queue.

Mutter as he might, it was jobs like these that paid the bills. And paid them well. Moving from being a normal auto mechanic to a smash repair specialist had been a branding change that had saved his life, and the business.

After the nasty mess of that court case eight years ago, he'd been on the verge of bankruptcy. But the lawyers had taken care of the allegations as they'd promised. What they couldn't fix was the stigma that had followed him. The Gold Coast was large, but not that large, and some stains were hard to wash off.

Everything had changed the day he'd closed his old garage at Burleigh Heads, moved to Surfers Paradise, and re-branded as a smash repair workshop. Business had literally just started walking in the door. The hailstorm that had followed a few short weeks later had proved fortuitous and the work had just never stopped coming.

Between customers and insurance companies, James Mooney had more work than he could poke a stick at. If things continued like this, he was going to have to expand. If only he could get the owners next door to agree to allow him to take over their lease, he would finally have the extra room he so badly needed.

James looked at his watch. Six o'clock. If he was going to work late, he wasn't doing it without at least wetting his whistle. Making his way into the kitchen, he pulled a stubby out of the fridge and opened it. The carbonation rose to the top and he took a swig of the ice-cold beer. Letting out a pleased sigh, he made his way back to the Datsun.

Trying to ignore the rising racket of the backpacker hostel, he rummaged in his toolbox. Most nights, the street was lively as foreign exchange students and tourists partied through the night. Something whirred overhead and James noted the familiar sound of a helicopter, albeit a little quieter than usual. Scenic tours of the Gold Coast were pretty common with tourists paying top dollar to enjoy the picturesque views. This one sounded a little off though. Perhaps it had a little more altitude than usual.

Not wanting a reminder of the party he wasn't invited to, James flicked on the radio.

The first few bars of Michael Bublé's latest hit rolled through the speakers as James considered where he might start on the hopeless case before him.

Taking another swig of beer, James procrastinated until the workshop's phone spared him the effort of making the decision.

"Saved by the bell," he said to himself as he set down his beer and made his way into the small office adjoining the workshop. He picked up the phone. "Smash repairs, this is James."

There was a metallic click, followed by an awful static that filled the line.

James jerked the phone away from his ear in surprise, before slowly moving it a little closer.

"Hello, are you there?"

He couldn't make out a single word through the roaring static.

"I'm afraid we have a bad line," he said. "You'll have to call back."

James hung up the phone and stared at the handset while he waited for it to ring again.

But the call never came. He shrugged and headed back out to the garage and the forlorn case that was his next repair. As he wandered down the side of the Datsun, he noticed the rear door was ajar.

"I could have sworn I closed that." As he reached for the worn out door, a white foggy haze floated out of the car.

James stopped moving, his feet rooted to the concrete.

The haze had the rough outline of a man but was translucent, allowing him to see right through it.

Not a man, a ghost.

The spirit turned to face him. Just before the ghost's face came into view, the spectre disappeared completely, as suddenly as it had appeared.

A shiver ran down James' spine as he blinked in confusion.

What on earth?

When the spectre failed to reappear, James let out a deep breath. He looked down at the half-finished beer and wondered if that had anything to do with it. It was only his second.

"You've been working too hard, man," he whispered to himself as he pushed the Datsun's door shut again.

A squeak of rubber against the polished concrete floor of the workshop set James' heart racing. The ghost was still here. James started to turn. A heavy weight slammed into him from behind, shoving him into the hoisted-up Datsun.

His head struck the side panel hard enough to leave a dent. Terrified and a little dazed, James pushed off the car with all his might, struggling against his attacker. But whoever it was, they were big. They forced him back against the vehicle, twisting his left arm around until he felt like it might dislocate.

James threw his elbow backwards, but it was stopped by pure muscle. Something thin slipped over his head, dropping to his neck where it stopped.

"Help!" James screamed, but between Michael Bublé, the party raging across the street, and the closed roller door of the workshop, it was unlikely anyone would or even could hear him.

His larynx constricted when the thing around his neck tightened. His last desperate scream died in his throat as the makeshift noose dug into his flesh.

The hydraulics of the hoist whirred, and James Mooney was yanked off his feet, clutching at his neck as his world went dark.

Cultural Confusion. Thursday, April 20th 2100hrs

It was a beautiful night to be out, 20°C with a light breeze that carried a trace of the Gold Coast's night life with it. Stalking toward the half-built commercial complex, I had to admit that everything looked so much more sinister in the dark. Or maybe that was just the trauma of my past, a lingering reminder of my last deployment. I had seen things there that would haunt my dreams forever.

The darkness of night had a way of cloaking the world in shadows and amplifying fear. A twig breaking, something skittering across scrap metal. With the sun shining overhead I wouldn't have given any of those a second thought.

Stalking through the abandoned skeleton of a failed construction contract at night was a whole other matter. Was that my foe? Or simply a possum, hunting about for something to feed its family? Part of me hoped for the latter, but that would be bad news for my client's daughter who had been missing for the better part of two days.

Into the darkness I went. My father had always taught me to face my fears.

"Things are less scary when you look them in the eye, son." I could hear his voice in my head as I approached the temporary fence surrounding the building. It was good advice for the most part, though my dad had never had to defuse an I.E.D in a building where children were playing upstairs.

Sometimes your fear wasn't the danger itself. It was that you wouldn't manage to rise to the occasion and the heavy burden of fear that your failure might cost someone else their life.

Ice water might run in my veins, but sooner or later everyone found their limits. I knew too many good soldiers who had found theirs.

These days, I used my military training to help others in a way I'd never expected. An old army buddy, a man called Tempest Michaels, gave me the idea. At the time I'd thought he was crazy. Now I was starting to see the light. I am six foot two, broad shouldered with a solid jaw. My appearance had been an asset when I was in the service, now in civilian life I found it tended to intimidate folks. My short light brown hair swept tidily to one side wasn't enough to make me approachable and it was far easier to be my own boss than get a job.

Pulling my Swiss army knife from my pocket, I sliced through the flimsy zip ties holding the two pieces of temporary fencing together. The developers really had cut every corner possible on this project. Fortunately, they'd been shut down before they could finish the death trap. Somewhere there was doubtless a pool of angry investors who had lost their fortunes.

I didn't care about their money. Tonight, there was a chance something far more valuable would be lost. Cali Masters went missing two days ago, and this was the first lead of any substance we'd found.

Slipping through the fence, I closed the gap so a casual inspection wouldn't reveal my point of entry. Elsewhere around the compound, my friends would be doing the same. I usually work these cases alone, but given that Cali's mother called with her new lead while I was at the pub, the boys all volunteered to ride along.

A little bit of extra muscle never went astray and tackling the compound from multiple angles would hopefully prevent anyone from sneaking Cali out without us noticing.

The victim was a nineteen-year-old girl with a promising future in engineering. However, when she moved to live in student housing at the prestigious Bond University, life had started to change. She found a group of new friends, and her mother wasn't a fan.

Her mother, Christine, accomplished social stalker that she was, had been following her daughter's university journey, and those she spent time with. Needless to say, her new friends' social media personas had caused some friction in Christine's relationship with Cali.

I'd seen the social media profiles myself while working the case. According to their profile, one of them was the high priest of Beelzebub. Not the sort of things that would help him land a job, but his profile was urging others to help hasten his master's ascension.

From what I could tell, Cali's new friend, the High Priest had a host of hangers-on who followed his every word. When Cali stopped answering her mother's calls two days ago, Christine came to me in a panic.

Christine had gone to the police but received little attention there. This was not unusual. With everything else they dealt with on a daily basis, a college student not answering their mother's calls for two days wasn't going to warrant deploying the cavalry.

So Christine found me, Darius Kane, the Gold Coast's only paranormal investigator. I have an office and everything, Blue Moon Investigations Australia.

Granted, that didn't tend to sway the opinion of the general public who treat me as an oddball, but the resulting news coverage certainly broadcast the presence of someone who could help them solve their paranormal problems.

I've seen my share of oddities in this world, but I still believe that what others perceive or believe to be paranormal is more often than not a mundane problem that can be solved using logic and reason. And I have skills that lend themselves to such problem solving. The federal government spent a considerable amount of money training me; it felt like a shame not to put those skills to use.

A thud echoed through the construction site. It sounded like something striking a concrete slab. Other thuds followed it, until there was a veritable chorus of them drowning out everything else.

I couldn't hear my own footsteps. Which meant my quarry couldn't either. I quickened my pace.

The drumming was joined by a sonorous choir of chanting.

Nothing good ever came of ritualistic chanting.

Racing through the site, I headed for the ruckus, hoping Cali was caught up in whatever was happening here. If I could find her, I could at least tell her mother she was okay.

Christine had called me as soon as Cali's phone was switched back on. It was days like this I was grateful for the 'find my phone' feature, and the fact teenagers tend to have their phones surgically attached to their hands. I was also grateful I'd only just arrived at the pub when she called and therefore wasn't trying to do this with three beers in me.

Less than an hour ago, Cali's phone had come to a stop here. The location was noteworthy because there was no reason for Cali to be loitering at a long-abandoned construction project after dark.

I tucked my knife back into my pocket. It was probably best I didn't have it in hand if I came face-to-face with anyone. Good reflexes saved lives in a warzone. Here they could turn a misread situation into a murder charge.

During my deployments in Afghanistan, I had become all too familiar with close quarters fighting and needed to remind myself from time to time that I wasn't there anymore. I didn't want to send someone to hospital unless they had it coming.

Instead, I settled for my Maglite. It was heavy enough to act as a considerable deterrent should the need arise.

Slipping through the open doorway into the main building, I almost ran right into the people making all the noise.

At least two dozen people in black cloaks carried flaming torches, the haft of which they were beating against the concrete as they chanted in what had to be Latin for all the sense I could make of it. In the middle, a figure in black robes and a gold mask had his hands raised above his head.

If it wasn't the high priest, I'd eat my Maglite. He carried a foot long silver dagger in one hand, so either he was planning a fancy-dress fondue party, or this whole mess was deteriorating rapidly.

My heart raced as I considered my choices. Dozens of men in dark robes plotting murder brought back memories I'd tried hard to put behind me.

There in the darkness I hesitated. I was outnumbered badly.

It's not the same Kane, man up. She needs you, now.

I drew a deep breath and used my phone to send an S.O.S. to the boys as I eyed the huddled masses. In the relative darkness, they didn't seem to have noticed me yet. I couldn't fight my way through two dozen of them alone and even if I could, I still had no idea where Cali was. She could be underneath any one of those cloaks for all I knew.

A set of concrete stairs led up to the second floor. Not that the floor had ever been completed. Instead, there was simply a series of half-finished slabs and scaffolding where the second floor should be.

I raced up the stairs, hoping to get a better view.

When I reached the second floor, I stopped dead.

In the middle of the clearing formed by the circle of black cloaks was a giant red pentagram that appeared to have been painted by hand. It was messy like it had been smeared in blood.

The gold masked menace leading the chanting stood beside an altar in the center of the circle. A woman was bound to it, her hands and feet secured with rope.

It only took me a moment to recognise Cali in the torch light. She seemed out of it, her head lolling about as if in a daze, drugged perhaps. The chanting built in intensity as the high priest raised his knife.

I muttered several expletives; I was out of time. More importantly, Cali was out of time.

The incomplete second floor stopped above the outer edge of the pentagram. It was going to have to do. As I reached the unfinished edge of the second floor, the high priest looked up. His eyes met mine and he paused, the knife raised over Cali's body.

I had no choice. I leapt off the unfinished platform, right at him.

The would-be cult leader dropped the knife as I plunged toward him from the second floor. His hands came up and he caught me like a doomed Patrick Swayze trying to catch a baby elephant. However, it did not go down like *Dirty Dancing*. He buckled under my 110 kilograms of muscle and bone before we both slammed into the makeshift concrete altar.

He got the worst of it, breaking my fall as we tumbled over the barely conscious form of Cali and onto the ground on the other side of it. The chanting abruptly stopped.

I shoved him away, hard and snatched up my Maglite.

"Get him," the leader wheezed, his high-pitched voice breaking behind his gold mask. "He's trying to disrupt the ritual."

The black robed figures closed ranks.

I had no idea just how dangerous these zealots could be, but with my life and Cali's hanging in the balance I couldn't afford to take prisoners.

Swinging the Maglite like a baseball bat, I lashed out, catching the bottom of the torch the closest cultist was holding. It went flying out of her hands, spilling fluid as it fell. The robes of the cultist beside her caught fire instantly.

The man cried out, swatting at the spreading flames. The female cultist who had been holding the torch backed away.

With a swinging boot, I kicked the flaming man out of my way.

"Stop, drop, and roll," I growled, turning a slow circle to see who would be brave enough to come for me. I was badly outnumbered, and if they were bright enough to coordinate their attack I would be in trouble fast. But as I expected they would, the others slowed their approach, sharing glances with each other.

No one prepared them for the ritual to get crashed.

A voice shouted from somewhere in the back of the room. "It's the police—run!"

The tiki torches were cast aside as several of the cultists ran for the hills. From the tone of the voice, I was pretty sure it was my mate Carl adding chaos in the hopes it would turn the ruckus in our favor. Carl was one of the few people I had to look up to in life, at six foot six with blonde hair and blue eyes he'd been born with a natural charisma that had made him a leader in the field, and a womanizer off the clock.

Two of the cultists went flying as someone smashed into the back of the pack. Sonny, another of my friends, emerged, fending off cultists like an NRL line-backer might brush off a defensive tackle. I considered myself a big guy, but the Samoan was almost two of me wide and practically had his own orbit. Grinning like a maniac, I caught only a glimpse of his black hair and pale brown skin as he waded through the masses.

I almost felt sorry for the cultists who got in his way.

"That's Cali!" I shouted, pointing at the altar. "We have to get her out of here!"

"What about them?" Sonny called, clearly meaning the idiots in the robes.

I yelled, "Put down anything that gets in our way! We'll get Cali to safety and let the police sort this lot out!"

One of the cultists jammed the butt end of his torch into my stomach, catching me off guard and knocking the wind out of me. I smacked him in the ribs with the Maglite and he crumpled to the ground, collapsing like a wet paper bag. He was going to hurt in the morning.

Wrenching the torch out of his hands, I cast it aside and shoved him out of the way. In the melee, I'd lost sight of the high priest, and he was the real threat.

He'd snuck around the altar and was picking up his knife. There was nothing quite so dangerous as a true believer.

"Don't you dare," I snarled from the other side of the altar.

As he raised the dagger high, he cried out, "Lord, accept this offering into thy care and bestow thy blessings upon the faithful!"

He drove the knife down, aiming for Cali's chest. There was no chance I could stop it or close the distance to parry his blade, so I did the only thing I could – I threw the Maglite.

Time seemed to slow as the spinning torch smacked him right in his gold mask. His head snapped back, and his mask dislodged as the high priest crumpled to the ground, clutching at his face.

"You broke my nose," he cried, dropping the dagger as blood streamed from both his nostrils. The kid couldn't have been more than twenty-five but that didn't make him any less dangerous.

"It only gets worse from here," I said.

I grabbed the knife on the altar, but something wasn't right. It wasn't heavy enough. It didn't feel solid. I pressed its blade against the stone, and the blade itself sank back into the handle.

It was a spring-loaded prop knife. A convincing one at that.

Oh, dear.

"She switched the knife," the high priest said, his eyes bulging in disbelief. "It's fake."

“Indeed, much like your ascension, your eminence,” I replied, tossing the faux knife aside.

The whole thing was a charade, but he seemed every bit as surprised as I was. Had Cali swapped the blade out? Was she who the priest had been talking about? It seemed unlikely. Cali was out of her mind on whatever they’d given her, and we couldn’t hang around forever. If the lot of them turned on us, our situation could get dicey. I’d seen firsthand what an angry mob could do.

But there was no way I was leaving Cali behind. Willing participant or not, these cases never went to plan. I scooped her up off the altar and threw her over my shoulder. We’d get her back to her mother and the police could sort this mess out later. I’d been hired to recover her; that was my intention.

The cultists were starting to regroup, and I didn't like our chances of subduing those who remained. As soon as they realized the police weren't here, they would come after us.

Carl waded through the masses, laying about with heavy blows, sending cultists sprawling to the floor. One of them I suspected was unconscious.

"Darius, you sure know how to have a good time,” Carl said, laughing over the chaos.

One of the cultists bore down on me until Sonny stepped in front of him. The cultist stopped short as Sonny raised one finger.

"Choose to live,” Sonny said.

Clearly, he’d been watching Star Trek again.

The cultist stood rooted to the spot, unable to move. I was frankly astounded he wasn’t legging it already. Never doubt the stupidity of people in large groups. When he didn't move, Sonny took a step forward, but Carl grabbed his fist.

"Mate, pretty sure the only reason he hasn't complied is that he's too busy crapping himself."

"Get out of here," Carl said to the cultist, thumbing over his shoulder toward the door.

From the pungent aroma in the room there was every chance Carl was right.

"Let's go," I called, stepping over several discarded tiki torches.

Fortunately, here on the construction site there was little but concrete and cultists to burn. I wasn't particularly worried about collateral damage.

"She's a cute one," Carl said. "Seems a bit of a waste to sacrifice a ten."

"Really, Carl? That's what you're thinking about now?" I replied as we made it out of the building.

"What can I say?" Carl replied. "I'm a man of culture and taste."

The cultists might not kill Carl, but syphilis certainly might. He was a relentless womanizer and seldom wanting for female company, though his longest relationships could be measured in hours. Not that I could talk. I hadn't been on a date in months.

Slipping out through the temporary fence, we headed for the car.

My kitted-out Hilux Ute was parked on the gravel lot beside the construction site. It blended in nicely and never looked out of place, particularly in the construction boom sweeping the coast right now. I could park anywhere including a loading bay. It was a practical choice for a paranormal investigator, particularly one who didn't have the cash for a Porsche.

Sonny helped me load Cali into the car before we headed for the Gold Coast Hospital. I dialed Christine, and she picked up on the second ring.

"Christine, we have Cali," I said. "She's alive but I suspect she's been drugged. We are taking her to the Gold Coast Hospital if you'd be so kind as to meet us there."

"Is my baby okay?" she asked, panic ringing in her voice.

"She will be, but a few dozen of her favorite cultists are going to be pretty pissed."

Between the hospital staff and the inevitable police statements it was going to be a long night.

Proper Paradox. Friday, April 21st 1015 hrs

When I started my business as a paranormal investigator, I didn't realize the Pandora's box I would be unleashing in my life. As my old pal Tempest had promised, it was good work. It certainly paid well, but I couldn't have predicted how thoroughly it would affect every aspect of my life.

I spent the first ten years of my working life in the military and knew better than to deal in anything but straight facts. Last night's crawl through the construction site to find Cali Masters was a perfect example of the crazy nonsense I now found myself dealing with on a daily basis. I'd spent half the night with two constables at the hospital providing them with all the details I had on the would-be high priest of Beelzebub.

Funnily enough, it wasn't the strangest night I'd had on the job.

When I opened an office in the heart of Surfer's Paradise and whacked a sign on it that said Blue Moon Investigations, I quickly discovered two things. One, everybody now knew exactly who I was, and two, they were all very interested in what I did.

Some were genuine believers looking for help with Auntie Beryl whom they believe is haunting them from beyond the grave, and others were just local hooligans who drove past while their friend hung his bare ass out the window.

Word got around quickly, assisted in no small part by the notoriety of my first high profile case. Helping the police apprehend the crypt killers, a local group of drug dealers turned murderers, had done wonders for my brand. The case had come to me from the groundskeeper at the local cemetery the gang had been frequenting. He'd thought he was dealing with the living dead, and in the course of my investigation, I'd almost joined the ranks of the actually dead. In the end, I wound up on the Channel 7 news, a fate worse than death though it proved to be good for business.

Like my mate Tempest always told me, the paranormal might be utter nonsense, but that didn't stop people from paying me top dollar to poke around in it.

Pushing open the door of my local coffee haunt, Paradox, I made my way inside, the aroma of freshly brewed coffee and bacon filling the air. Just what I needed to kick off my day after the night I'd had.

Courtney was the barista on duty, and that brought a smile to my lips. I gave a silent nod to lady luck as I made my way to the counter. I didn't saunter, because only douchebags do that, but I did have a little spring in my step. After all, Courtney was at least half the reason I picked Paradox each morning. Maybe ninety percent of the reason, if I was being honest with myself.

Sure, I could have used the late morning coffee as a pick me up, but the lovely brunette had been flirting with me for weeks. One of these days, I was going to manage the courage to ask her to dinner. Or so I kept telling myself.

"Morning, Darius." Courtney beamed as she looked up from the cash register. "Catch anyone interesting lately?"

"Well, I did close a case last night," I replied. "We were kinda badly outnumbered, but we managed to get a missing young woman back to her mother. I'm calling it a win."

I was trying for dashing without the arrogance, but I wasn't particularly confident that I had hit the mark.

"Wow, must have been some night." She smiled before glancing back down at the counter as she unnecessarily reorganized the napkins.

The news had given me some flattering coverage and normally I liked to dismiss the attention, but if it made Courtney think I was that little bit more interesting than her average customer, I figured it couldn't hurt to lean into the notoriety just a bit. I was thirty-five and needed all the help I could get.

"So, are you after the usual?" she asked.

"Yes, please," I replied. "Latte, three sugars."

"You do like it sweet, don't you," Courtney replied as she poured a little milk into the pitcher.

"When you're done, it will still only be the second sweetest thing in here."

A choking sound came from farther down the counter, and I glanced sideways to find her colleague Tommy trying to stifle a smile from behind the case of breakfast muffins. Tommy tried to cover his mouth but when it was apparent he'd failed to stifle his amusement, he flicked his hair with one hand and headed for the kitchen.

"I'd best check on the chef," he called over his shoulder as he made his escape.

Courtney blushed furiously as she slid the steam wand into the pitcher.

Way to embarrass the poor girl, Darius.

The compliment had been clumsy and heavy-handed but then again, I was pretty rusty in the dating game. At least I'd made her smile. Hopefully it was a step in the right direction.

"Want anything with the coffee?" Courtney asked. "A toastie? Perhaps a muffin?"

"I might grab it on the way out," I replied, reaching into my pocket for my wallet. "I'm just meeting a client here first. Probably better if I'm not pigging out on one of those while we're talking."

Courtney perked up. "Another case? It's not the Casper killer, is it?"

Leaning on the counter, I asked. "Casper killer?"

I'd been engrossed in Cali's case the past few days and had no idea what she was talking about.

"I figured you would have heard about a ghost murdering people." As she spoke, Courtney pointed at a stack of newspapers by the register. "It's all over the papers."

"Mind if I take one of these?" I reached for the top paper in the stack.

"That's what they're there for," she said as she finished up my latte.

The front page showed a picture of a vaguely familiar workshop. The headline emblazoned over the top read, "Suicide? Or has the Casper killer struck again?"

Tucking the paper under my arm, I took my latte. Courtney rang the purchase up on the register and I swiped my card.

"Thanks, Courtney, you're a wizard."

I took the latte and the morning paper and made my way to the corner booth. Glancing down at my watch, I found I still had a few minutes before my client arrived. I had recently got in the habit of meeting them outside the office when I could. It gave me a chance to filter out the crazy ones, before allowing them into my safe space. Some people were also a lot better behaved in public. If there was one thing this job had taught me quite quickly, it was that there was no shortage of deluded and potentially dangerous clients.

I flipped open the paper and set it down on the table, reading through the cover piece while I sipped my drink.

James Mooney, a local mechanic specializing in dent repairs, had been discovered dead in his garage in the early hours of yesterday morning. His body was found hanging from the car hoist. No sign of forced entry, no indication that anyone else had been on site.

According to the paper, the local police had refused to comment. And while the paper tried to make something out of that, I knew it was standard operating procedure. Police tended not to comment while still conducting their investigation.

It was unusual for a suicide to make the front page of the paper, so someone must have at least suspected foul play, or perhaps it was the local papers desire to drive sales. It might have just been a slow news week.

The article did conclude that it was the third unusual death in two weeks which was certainly more noteworthy. This was the Gold Coast and while homicides weren't uncommon, they normally had clear connections to criminal activity like biker gangs or drug related crime. Serial killers were something of a rarity here.

According to the article, the two previous deaths included a bank employee and a local lawyer who also died in unusual circumstances. The lawyer, a local criminal defense solicitor, was gunned down in the car park of his law firm, presumably by a dissatisfied customer. Despite the brazen nature of the killing, the police were singularly unsuccessful in their attempts to find any trace of the killer.

The bank manager died in her home, the unfortunate result of an electrocution. Why anyone would try to use a hair dryer in the bathtub was beyond me. Perhaps she'd been under the influence of alcohol or narcotics.

Attempting to link the three deaths was like trying to do a crossword on a Sudoku grid. That led me to believe we were indeed in a slow news week. Serial killers sold papers. A series of unfortunate events did not. The paper chose to speculate that the Gold Coast had a killer who could come and go without being detected, hence the origins of the name, the Casper Killer. A spectre or shade certainly wouldn't leave any trace evidence behind.

Interesting. I sipped at my latte. The article had been written by Holly Draper. She clearly supplemented her journalistic talents with an active imagination.

I pushed the paper to the side. I wasn't in the habit of doing work I wasn't being paid for. On the other hand, if these deaths were making the front page, it might give me an opportunity to continue to raise my public profile.

Still, with the Crypt Killer arrests to my name, I had plenty of paid work in the offing. Cali Masters' rescue was certainly going to help matters. I didn't really need to concern myself with the reckless speculation of the local tabloid journalist.

The doorbell rang as Paradox's front door swung open and a woman in her early fifties strolled into the coffee shop. She continued to glance back over her shoulder. It was almost as if she believed someone might be following her.

Or perhaps the doorbell had startled her. She patted her chest like she was worried she was going to have a heart attack and needed to calm herself down. While I hadn't seen a picture of the client I was meeting, her behavior certainly seemed to fit the expectations I had from our earlier call. I waved to her.

"Mrs. Wheeler?" I called.

Spotting me, she made a beeline across the coffee shop to my booth. When she reached me, she was almost out of breath.

"Mr. Kane, thank you for meeting me on such short notice."

I rose from the table, like a gentleman ought. My parents had always insisted on such things, and military discipline had reinforced the notion.

"Please, have a seat. Would you like me to get you something? A coffee? Or perhaps a muffin?"

"No, no, that's quite all right, thank you. I have my water with me." She reached into her bag and pulled out a bottle of Mount Franklin Spring Water. It was the disposable plastic kind that our resident environmentalists just loved. Her hand shook as she raised the bottle to her lips and managed a small sip.

I gave her a moment to collect her thoughts and her breath. I was in no particular rush, and I didn't want to hurry an already distressed woman along.

"Mrs. Wheeler, what can I do for you?"

"Sally, call me Sally, please," she said as she smoothed her dress. "Mrs. Wheeler makes me feel old, and if there's one thing I'm not, Mr. Kane, it's old."

I smiled. "Then I'll have to insist you call me Darius, because Mr. Kane is my father."

The woman seemed to relax a little. She put the lid on the bottle but still clutched it with a grip that turned the knuckles on her right hand white.

"So you're a paranormal investigator?" Sally managed at last, but not in a tone that made me wary I might be mocked.

"I am, but if it helps, I'm a private detective who specializes in helping those who think they have supernatural struggles in their life. You mentioned on the phone that you thought you were being haunted. Can you tell me more about that?"

My mind flashed back to the Casper Killer. Was it just a coincidence that my first client of the day was struggling with an incorporeal foe?

Sally nodded, the colour draining out of her face a little. "It all started a few weeks ago. Things in the house just started disappearing. They were there one moment and gone the next. I woke up one morning and my husband's prized Origin jersey, signed by Allan Langer himself, was just gone. It was quite valuable, you know."

I did. Football memorabilia had a cult following and game worn jerseys tended to fetch a fair price. Given the State of Origin only played three games a year, it only made the jersey more scarce and naturally more valuable.

"And you're sure thieves couldn't have broken in and taken it? Sports memorabilia is a common target for thieves."

Sally shook her head. "The house was locked up tight, not a window or door left open. I check every night before I go to bed."

I nodded as I made notes on a small pad I always kept in my pocket.

"You said things?" I prompted. "Other items have also vanished?"

Sally nodded before she took another sip of water.

I set my pen down on the pad. "May I ask what makes you think it's a ghost?"

"Not just any ghost," she replied. "My late husband's ghost. He's haunting us."

"Us?" I asked. Judging by her age, I doubted she still had children living at home."

“My new husband and I,” she replied. “It all started after we got back from our honeymoon.”

"New husband? I see. This is your second marriage?”

"Yes, my first husband Gerald passed a few years ago. I met my new husband, Tom, on a singles cruise late last year.” She smiled as she said Tom’s name.

I picked up my pen. “You and Tom have only been dating for a few months then?”

"Ever since the cruise,” Sally conceded “It wasn’t a particularly long engagement.”

"And Tom lives with you? Does anyone else? Children?"

She laughed. "Oh no, Darius, my son and daughter are in their thirties. Too old to be living at home with their mother. I cramp their style.”

“And the children, do they get along with Tom?” I asked, a theory forming in my mind already.

“Holly does,” she replied. “It took Phillip a little while to warm up to him. You see, Tom is a little younger than I am. He’s closer to my kids in age. That caused a bit of a stir when I introduced them. Phillip thought Tom was a gold-digger, but Phillip did take his father's death pretty hard. I don't blame him for that.”

"Do you mind if I ask, how did your husband pass?”

"Prostate cancer.” Sally swallowed as she looked away. “It was quite late when we picked it up. The doctors did what they could but from the day of his diagnosis he only lived seven months. It was all quite sudden.”

“And how were things between you at the time of his passing?" I didn’t put any stock in the spectre theory, but I suspected whatever was bothering Sally stemmed from those closest to her. Understanding the traumatic events that occurred recently might shed light on the matter.

“Well enough.” Sally sniffed. “We had our struggles, like everyone does, but I loved my husband and was faithful to him."

"Then what makes you think he has returned to haunt you?" I asked. It seemed like a little bit of a leap to me.

"The things that go missing in the house, they all belonged to him.”

My disbelief must have been apparent, because Sally continued quickly. “But that’s not all. Each morning when I come down, the leg rest on his favorite chair is up, just like it used to be when he would sit in it to relax. I also keep finding empty bottles of his favorite beer in the trash and Tom doesn't drink.”

Well, that was something. I paused, letting Sally fill the silence.

“It’s been making things with Tom quite difficult. You see, he doesn't believe in ghosts, but I do. And I think my first husband is upset with my new relationship. I worry that if something isn't done, harm might come to my poor sweet Tom.”

“And have you gone to anyone else about this?” I replied. “The police? Your children?”

“The police laughed at me. They don’t do ghosts, apparently. I know what it sounds like but I’m not crazy. You must believe me. I've tried talking to my children about it, but they think I'm just making things up to get their attention. I've even tried going to my husband's grave and talking to him, but nothing comes of it and the spectre continues to haunt us.”

“Well, Sally, I don’t think you’re crazy. But I can assure you that in most instances this sort of paranormal activity proves to be the result of someone close preying on the suspicions and vulnerabilities of the victim. The fact that valuable pieces of your husband's effects continue to go missing is a sign that someone might be profiting from this mischief. I don't think you have a ghost. I think you have a thief. I'm sure the police could assist."

"They snickered when I told them," she replied. "I've never been so embarrassed in my life."

Probably because you told them you have a ghost. Still, I wasn't one to turn down a client in need and the thought of someone taking advantage of poor Sally was starting to upset me.

"I'd be happy to take the case, then," I said.

"Really?" Sally replied. "That's wonderful. When can you start?"

"I'll consult my calendar and be in touch," I said. "There is a chance I may be able to stop by this evening. Is the number you called me on the best way to reach you?"

"It is," she replied. "Why, thank you, Darius. You don't know how much this means to me. I just need some closure and I want my poor departed husband to be at peace."

"Well, I'll see to it. Of course, I am an investigator, and there will be a charge for my services. It includes an hourly rate while I'm on the job, plus a small allowance for expenses I might incur."

I took Sally through my billing and produced a copy of my engagement contract on my mobile phone.

"If you will just sign here on this line," I replied, turning the phone around for her to reach.

Sally scribbled her signature on the contract as if the very act might exorcise her menacing spectre.

"I'll send a copy through to your mobile number. If you have any questions or concerns, please don't hesitate to reach out. I have a few appointments today. My recommendation would be to continue locking down your home carefully each night, and if you hear anything, please don't try to confront it yourself. Dial the police immediately and let them know you have an intruder. Do you understand?"

"Yes," Sally said, screwing the cap back onto her bottle of water.

"Excellent. You'll hear from me shortly."

I rose from the table, an old trick my father had taught me. When you stand up, people know their interview is over.

Sally stood up and tucked her bottle into the bag. "Thank you, Darius."

"One more thing, Sally. Please don't mention to anyone that you've engaged my services until the matter has reached its conclusion."

Sally's eyebrow shot up. "Why?"

"Because if the thief is indeed someone close to you, they might cease activity while they believe me to be on the job, causing the length of the investigation to balloon out and become more expensive for you in the process. The best thing for everybody is if you let me work discreetly and keep our arrangement confidential until the thief has been apprehended."

"You mean the ghost?" Sally replied.

"Sure, if it's a ghost, I will get them too," I said with a smile. "But my fees remain payable whether your apparition is supernatural or simply a scoundrel."

Sally threw her arms around me and drew me in for a tight embrace. The hug caught me a little off guard as she buried herself in my shoulder, coating me in the cloud of the Estée Lauder perfume she was wearing. I tried not to choke as she released me. I still had my pride, and my image as a fearless pursuer of the paranormal to uphold.

Sally departed and I drained the last of my coffee.

Throwing my usual caution to the wind, I peeled a piece of paper from my pad, and scribbled my name and number on it along with a message to call me anytime.

Nothing ventured, nothing gained.

Rolling up the piece of paper, I made my way past the till. Courtney must have been out back, but her colleague Tommy gave me a broad grin. I imagined he might have seen me prepare my note, but I wasn't chickening out now.

"Have a good day, Tommy," I replied as I tucked the piece of paper into the tip jar along with a five dollar note. If anything, I hoped the bribe would stop him from binning my note before Courtney returned.

Leaving Paradox, I paused and basked in the sun. The weather was warm but a light south-easterly breeze took the edge off the heat of the day.

I considered my next move. I wasn't due at the office, and I suspected there was little I could do for Sally Wheeler until this evening.

My mind drifted back to the Casper Killer case. While no one was paying me to explore the matter, I couldn't help but wonder if Holly Draper's article was a work of fiction, or if there was more to the whole affair.

They say curiosity killed the cat, but my father always told me that an idle mind was the devil's playground, so with time to kill, I might as well see what the Gold Coast's serial killing spectre had been up to.

Suspicious Specters. Friday, April 21st 1050hrs

What harm could it do to take a few minutes to look into the Gold Coast's latest bizarre occurrence? If nothing else, it seemed like I ought to acquaint myself with the details lest anyone ask me about it. At least, that was how I justified my curiosity and procrastinated the unenviable task of filtering through my emails.

Standing there on the street, I studied the photo in the paper and found the name of the victim's business. Punching it into my phone, I couldn't shake the feeling that there was something familiar about the address though I couldn't figure out why that was.

It took my phone all of a few seconds to produce the address.

Peninsular Drive. No wonder the case was the talk of Paradox. The site of the possible murder was only a kilometer away.

Perhaps it was meant to be. I made my way to my trusty Ute. Given the thousands of tradesmen working on the Gold Coast, I could blend in just about anywhere. Urban camouflage at its finest.

I had overhauled the vehicle, gearing it up for stealthy surveillance. The toolboxes in the back were laden with all manner of audiovisual gear. Another was packed with tools I might need on a job. You never knew when you might need a hacksaw or crowbar to access those hard-to-reach places.

I'd had the truck kitted out with a hefty bull bar, and the Ute was closer to a tank than a town car. It also meant I seldom had to worry about other cars giving way, which was convenient in the dense traffic of the Gold Coast.

I backed out of the busy coffee shop and pulled out to where the street met the Gold Coast Highway.

Highway—there was a name that was overly generous. Australia had a habit of naming its main roads highways. Whether they were or not was another matter.

The Gold Coast Highway was the original stretch of road running parallel to the beach. It was only two lanes of traffic moving in either direction as they wove between all the apartment buildings and hotels.

Most days, it was closer to a car park than a highway, but it was all we had.

Continued development of high-rises on the valuable real estate around it had left the government no opportunity for expansion. The best they had managed was to throw in a light rail to help ease congestion.

The light turned green, and I cruised across the intersection into Peninsular Drive. The high-rises quickly gave way to residential units and houses, with commercial premises sprinkled throughout. This was the suburbia of the Gold Coast, jammed in between the sand and canals.

It was amazing what proximity to the water could do to a house price. Any house a few streets closer to the water had a price with six zeros after it. Here on Peninsular

Drive, homes were considerably cheaper. They might be the older properties on the Gold Coast, but it was still only a short, fifteen-minute walk to the beach.

All in all, this was a beautiful place to live, or visit for that matter.

My GPS announced my arrival, and I pulled over to the side of the road.

On one side, the smash repair shop was visible, police tape still in place across its entrance. The yard was empty and the lawn on the curb was a good few inches longer than it ought to be. The fences were old and rusted from the salty air. The front gates had been left open, which I took as a sign I ought to take a closer look.

Dozens of cars lined each side of the road, a byproduct of the general lack of parking in the area, and not helped at all by the backpackers' hostel across the road. The hostel occupied a small building, but likely accommodated more than one hundred people a night. This close to Cavill Avenue, the party capital of the Gold Coast, it was the sort of destination beloved by young travelers and rabble rousers alike.

At least four rental vans were parked out front, the ones with the bed in the back that were popular with tourists. There was a lot of Australia to see and if you wanted to get around, you needed some wheels. It wasn't uncommon for tourists to grab a cheap rental van so that they could make use of the many hundreds of caravan parks littering the country's East Coast. You could easily go town to town enjoying all the beauty Australia had to offer and do it on a budget little bigger than what was required to rent the car.

It wasn't a bad idea and if I hadn't spent my youth in the armed services seeing the world, I would likely have done something just like it.

Given the view the hostel had of the workshop, I figured I might start my investigation there.

The backpackers' hostel was an old home that had long since been gutted and expanded. Huge dorm rooms accommodated up to twenty guests in bunk beds with a series of single and double rooms for those traveling on a slightly more accommodating budget. The sign out front announced all the usual amenities: a pool, spa, Wi-Fi, etc. But the real attraction was the bar, which was announced loudly with a sign reading, 'The Party Starts Here.'

A happy coincidence because my investigation might start there too. With the comings and goings at all hours of the night and day, the staff and patrons had to be the most likely to have observed any unusual activity in the neighbour's workshop.

Out front stood a shack serving as the concierge's desk, manned by a young man in his twenties whose brown hair was five or six inches long and swept to the side. It looked damp like he'd just walked out of the water. It was a look I'd never really mastered - messy, but stylishly so.

I made my way over the road and approached the kiosk.

"You're a little old to be backpacking, aren't you?" the young man called in a voice that did nothing to endear him to me whatsoever.

"Probably," I replied. "So it's a good thing I'm not looking to stay."

His face screwed up a little as he worked on processing that, so I let him off the hook.

"I just have a few questions about the goings-on across the road."

His face fell a bit. "Oh, that. Nasty business. Not sure how much help I can be. We already told everything we know to the police."

"I'm sure you did, but I'm not with the police. Just a private investigator checking on a few details. Which also means I'd be willing to make it worth your while."

It was a curious thing just how often money could grease the wheels of justice.

He perked up, a lot more interested in being helpful than he had been a minute ago.

"What exactly do you want to know?" he asked.

"You guys are open twenty-four seven, right?"

"We sure are," he replied. "People come and go at all hours. We've got to be here to assist."

"Who was manning the desk the night your neighbor died?"

I worded the question neutrally on purpose. I didn't want my words to inform his response.

"That would be me," he replied with a sigh. "I'd done the night shift, then got most of the day off yesterday on account of all that mess. Then they rostered me on again today."

I could hardly believe my luck. "You were here, on the night in question?"

"I was, and there are a dozen people who can tell you I never left my post," he added, like someone with a well-rehearsed alibi.

"Relax. I'm not trying to say you were involved, just looking to see if you noticed anything unusual."

"Well, I tried to tell the police, but they weren't interested."

"In what?" I asked, leaning on the counter.

"The night it happened, I saw him close up the shop. He did that whenever he worked late, didn't like the noise we made. But I knew he was still working because his car never left."

"Right," I prompted, looking for whatever tidbit the police hadn't been interested in.

"Well, I tried to tell them a ghost did it. Saw it slip right out through the front wall."

I raised an eyebrow. "You saw a ghost?"

"As clearly as I'm seeing you," he replied, fidgeting on the spot.

"What did it look like?" Perhaps he'd simply misunderstood what he'd seen.

"It was shaped like a person, but like, see-through, you know, like a white fog. It hovered in the front yard, then went right in through the wall. I thought I was seeing things, but a short while later, it drifted back through the wall, hovered there in the front yard for a minute, and then disappeared as it passed through the open gates right there." He jutted his finger at the workshop's gates to drive home his point.

"And it was transparent?"

"Yeah, I could see through it," he replied. "Not clearly, but it definitely wasn't solid. Didn't walk either, just sort of drifted."

I had him take me back over the key details. It was an interrogator's trick. I wanted to see if any details in his story changed.

"And what shape was it again?" I asked.

"Looked like a person, didn't it," he replied. "At least that sort of shape, but it didn't quite touch the ground, if you know what I mean?"

I knew what he was saying, but I wasn't a believer. As far as I was concerned, ghosts didn't exist, and they certainly didn't lynch local mechanics.

"And you told the police?"

"Sure did, but I don't think they believed me."

It was interesting to note that he told the same story to the police, yet those details hadn't made the paper. It felt like the sordid sort of thing that Holly Draper would have grabbed with both hands.

"And why do you reckon that was?" I asked, leaning in to show my interest. "As close as I can tell, you're the only eyewitness who saw anything that night."

"Well, ah..." He looked about like someone searching for their supervisor. "Look, I don't want to get in any trouble."

I reached into my wallet, took out a fifty dollar note, and slid it across the counter.

"I'm not gonna tell a soul, mate. You have nothing to worry about from me."

"Well, I, uh," he stammered as he mustered up his courage. "I might have been a little under the influence at the time."

That made more sense, I thought, kicking myself. I'd just paid a drunkard fifty bucks to tell me what he saw on his latest bender. It could have been something, or nothing. Still, I couldn't entirely write it off. If he had seen something pass through a wall, twice, that was hard to explain away.

"How many had you had?" I asked.

He leaned in like a best mate describing a good night out. "A lot. Don't judge me, man. We had a bus load of Swedish tourists staying the night. They like to party and those Swedish girls, all tens on a bad hair day. Let's just say the drinks were flowing pretty smoothly, if you know what I mean."

I did know what he meant. It meant they'd liquored the whole place up in the hopes of getting lucky with a Swede passing through town. It also meant I couldn't put a great deal of stock in anything he said. Three sheets to the wind and distracted by a group of Swedish girls, I doubted he had much of a clue what happened after the first few drinks were poured.

I left the fifty dollar note on the counter and added my business card. "If you remember anything else about that night, anything at all, just give me a call."

Tapping the note in front of him, I added, "There's more where that came from. Providing it's useful, of course."

He slid the crisp fifty dollar note into his pocket. "I'll keep that in mind, but if there's nothing else, I should really get back to it."

I nodded and was about to head over the road when one last question crystalized in my mind.

"You wouldn't happen to have any surveillance footage of the night in question?"

"Ah, no," he said. "It seems that someone accidentally flicked the cameras off."

Probably the same someone who didn't want to get caught being drunk on the job.

I excused myself and made my way back to the car. Rummaging about in my tool chest, I pulled out a flat-headed screwdriver and slipped it into my pocket. If the garage was locked, I might need a little more leverage.

Crossing the street, I made my way through the open gates. I found that if I acted like I belonged somewhere, I was far less likely to be challenged.

The gates enclosed a car park in front of the smash repair workshop. Several vehicles still sat there, likely customers who hadn't heard what had happened yet, or were still waiting for their keys and vehicles to be returned.

I glanced around to see if I was being observed, but my friend in the backpackers' hostel had made himself scarce. I headed for the front door.

Police tape still crisscrossed the door, marking it as a crime scene. However, with the murder having occurred two nights ago, I doubted there was any evidence left behind.

Nonetheless, having a look around was bound to give me some insight as to what happened. I tried the door but found it locked. The front roller door looked heavily reinforced, so I headed around the side of the building and found what I was hunting for: a rear roller door that allowed vehicles to pass through the workshop into a secondary storage yard out the back. In my experience, they were far less secured than the obvious front entrance, since you would have to drive the car through a wall to get it out of the back yard.

A video camera observed comings and goings in the back of the yard, but I simply slipped beneath its field of view as I made my way along the wall to the roller door. It too was locked, but the mechanism was old and well worn, a small bit of steel passing through a bracket. I tested the door and found it had a bit of give in it.

I lifted the door enough to get my boot under it and then with a little leverage from my screwdriver, succeeded in breaking the flimsy mechanisms holding it in place. Rolling the door up a few feet, I slid underneath it and into the workshop, letting the door slide into place behind me.

The workshop itself was modest in size. A single vehicle hoist dominated the left side of the garage while the right-hand side had a spray booth, vital for any touch up work the owner needed to attend to. Present on the hoist was an old Datsun that had seen better days.

The hoist remained half raised, likely where the police had lowered it in order to remove the body. From the details I garnered reading the newspaper article, the mechanic hanged himself on it, or the scene had at least been staged that way. I figured the hoist had been used as the garage didn't have any other readily accessible beams that might facilitate such unpleasant business.

Running down the side wall of the workshop were several tool chests and a workbench. The only thing sitting on it was a discarded bottle cap. James seemed to run a tidy shop, not the disheveled mess that was all too common in workshops everywhere.

The police had done a thorough job of scouring the site. According to the paper, the victim had been found hanging by a set of cables. Since I could find no sign of them, I guessed the police had taken them as evidence.

I pulled a set of disposable gloves from my suit coat and found some wear on one of the bars. I presumed that might be where James had been discovered. The body of an adult man weighed in at about eighty kilos and was bound to cause some friction as the cables wore back and forth across the painted hoist. If I was right, the wear on the bar was evidence that James had been struggling.

I turned my attention to the vehicle. The Datsun was a blast from the past, a good fifteen or twenty years since its heyday. The car's surface was pitted with damage both from the road and what appeared to be a recent parking issue. A pole sized indentation in the rear bumper showed where the owner had recently failed to park it.

Finding the controls to the hoist, I lowered it to get a better look around the car.

Given its age and state, I wondered if the cost of repairing it didn't exceed the vehicle's actual value. The fact that it was the vehicle being worked on when James died only made me more curious.

The interior of the car was as worn as the exterior. The seats showed evidence of a lifetime of hard use, but the vehicle was neatly vacuumed which surprised me. I checked the glove compartment and found a first aid kit, but little else of note. The console and side door pockets were also empty. Most cars accumulated clutter over time, but this vehicle was conspicuously clean, at least on the inside.

Leaning into the driver's seat, I pulled the lever to pop the boot. The boot mechanism struggled, perhaps on account of the damage from the reversing issue. If I couldn't get in that way, I would have to go through the car.

Climbing into the backseat, I reached for the button that would lower the rear seat and allow access to the boot. The entire right most seat tilted forward, into the cab of the car. It appeared the mechanism holding it in place was broken.

I drew my keys out of my pocket and flicked on the small but powerful penlight clipped to them. With a sigh, I wormed my way through the lowered seat and into the trunk, no easy feat given my size.

Normally, the boots of cars were a repository for all sorts of rubbish. This one was little exception. There was an old gym bag, a couple of loose screws, and a few fading receipts, including one from McDonalds and a meal at the Glades Country Club. I tucked the receipts into my coat pocket and crawled back out of the car.

With the amount of damage to the car, inside and out, it made me wonder why its owner had bothered to repair it at all. The vehicle couldn't be worth much. Perhaps it had other value to the owner, or maybe they were optimistically holding out another decade or two in the hopes it might become a classic. Fat chance of that.

Finding nothing of note, I moved the seat back into place and took some pictures of the car, including the license plate for future reference and then raised the hoist back to where I'd found it.

I headed to the small office at the back of the building. It held an old desktop computer that was probably considered a high-performance machine a decade ago. I fired it up but found it to be locked. Rummaging around the office, I searched the obvious places for a password—a Post-it note on the side of the computer, a paper beneath the keyboard, or a blotter on the desk—but found nothing. I tried the victim's name and a few other common iterations, all without luck.

It was times like this that I wished I had a little more technological expertise, but outside of surveillance gear, I'd never invested much time in that field. My years in the service had involved far more demolition than discrete access, and blowing up James's computer wasn't going to serve any productive purpose other than perhaps easing my frustrations.

Making my way through the workshop, I tidied up after myself, ensuring that I left everything as I found it, before turning my attention to the roller door. I helped myself to a few of James's tools and worked the damaged mechanism back into place. It was still fairly compromised, and I doubted it would hold up to much of a concerted attack. However, it would defeat any efforts to simply lift the door, hopefully keeping the premises secure until the police and investigators could return the vehicles to their rightful owners.

Once I was satisfied that the door was no longer easily accessible, I returned the tools and let myself out through a single door set in the rear of the building. It had a simple locking mechanism that clicked shut behind me. I tested the door to be sure and found it locked.

The fence in the backyard had been replaced with a brick wall, but there was nothing to stop an even modestly fit individual from scaling it. I could do it in my sleep.

If I had intended to kill James, I certainly wouldn't have entered or exited through the front yard. Rather, having scouted my target, I would have leapt the fence, evaded the single camera, and slipped in through the rear. My appraisal made the ghost story all the more interesting. If James had been killed and the attack was indeed premeditated, they would surely have snuck in the back. What had my backpacking friend seen in the front yard?

If only he'd been sober, I would have had more to work with.

Letting out a sigh, I ducked under the camera and made my way back around the building. My Ute was still parked in front of the backpackers' accommodation, and I ducked over the road and unlocked my car. I slipped into the driver's seat as the all-too-familiar wail of police sirens sounded behind me.

Crime Scene Curiosities. Friday, April 21st 1120hrs

I SIGHED AND RESISTED the urge to pound my hands against the steering wheel. I'd thought my little B & E had been entirely too easy. I had looked around before entering the workshop. How had I managed to miss the presence of the police?

My rearview mirror showed an unmarked police car with a band of red and blue lights just inside the cab.

"Sneaky little buggers," I muttered as I turned my engine off and waited to see what my new friends had to say.

Talking my way out of this was going to require a feat of linguistic gymnastics that would qualify me for the Olympics. Good thing I'd had my coffee.

I sat patiently in the front seat of my Ute. Police tended to frown on you leaving your vehicle when they were making a stop. I had a few friends on the force, and I hoped it might be one of them.

Two detectives climbed out of the low-profile Toyota and made their way toward me - a man and a woman in plain clothes. I didn't recognise either of them. So much for that hope. From their clothes, I knew I was dealing with detectives rather than the local constabulary.

The man was of medium height, but thickset. He wasn't wearing a coat, probably due to the heat, and his service weapon and badge were readily visible as he approached. From the look of him, he was in his forties so had the better part of ten years on me.

His companion, on the other hand, seemed to be the junior of the pair. In her thirties perhaps, she wore a sharp cut pantsuit that frankly did flattering things to her figure and was proving a little distracting as I tried to fabricate my story. Her blonde hair was pulled back into a ponytail, clean, efficient, and easy to maintain, and her piercing blue eyes seemed focused entirely on me.

Under other circumstances, I might have found her stare entrancing, but with her hand resting about six inches from her holster, I thought it best not to get too lost in those sapphire pools.

Shifting my grip, I placed my hands neatly on the top of the wheel at ten and two, to look as un-intimidating as possible. Since I was a little over six feet tall and built like a military veteran, it wasn't an easy feat to pull off.

The male detective approached my window and knocked on it gently. His partner took up her position on the other side of the car.

I pressed the button to lower the window.

"Good morning," the detective said in a friendly voice that lacked any sincerity whatsoever.

"Good morning to you too, detective. What can I do for you?"

I was almost certain that they had spotted me leaving the garage, but it never helps your case to volunteer information. What some people misunderstand about the police is that there is almost nothing you can say that will actually help your case, while anything you might say can be used against you in a court of law.

"Do you mind telling us what you were doing at an active crime scene?" the detective asked.

His partner shifted position on the other side of the vehicle.

Glancing back to the detective at my window, I smiled. "Oh, that?"

"Yes, that," the detective replied. His manner appeared relaxed, but even as he leaned in, I could see the tension in his arms. He was like a coiled snake waiting to strike. "At a minimum, I figure it's breaking and entering, but I'm sure with a little bit of thought we could throw some other things on top of it. Tell us what you were doing in there before we slap the cuffs on you and drag you down to the station for a more formal discussion."

"Easy, detective," I replied, not wanting to be baited into saying something that might cause me trouble later. "We're all on the same side here."

"I very much doubt that," the detective said. "But I'll humor you. What side would that be?"

"The side that doesn't think that good man was killed by a ghost like the papers are reporting," I answered calmly.

Seldom were the press and the police friends. I hoped that with a little deft maneuvering, I might refocus his frustrations elsewhere.

"Holly bloody Draper," the female detective said with a groan. "I told you if she kept this up, we'd have every lunatic in town on our case."

"So, you're looking for your own scoop?" the man asked, raising his eyebrow. "Vultures, the lot of you. A man died here."

"Woah, nothing so sinister, detective. I'm a private investigator just trying to help get to the bottom of things."

"Aw hell!" the female detective said from the other side of the car. "He's the crazy one. The one that almost got himself killed by the crypt killers."

The detective at my window nodded slowly. "I think you're right, Hart. I thought I recognised him, just couldn't place where from." He shook his head. "You ought to know better than to interfere with an active investigation. Just because you got lucky once doesn't mean you should push it. One of these days, you're going to get yourself in trouble."

"Interfering in an active investigation only slides in the movies, Scooby Doo," the blonde detective teased.

I pressed the button to lower the window on her side of the vehicle.

"I should be so lucky," I replied, trying to win her over. "Even on a good day, I'm Shaggy at best. Scooby's still asleep on the couch at home."

It wasn't technically a lie, but my partner in crime is Max, an adorable little beagle I tend to take with me whenever I can get away with it.

"Oh, come on, what's the harm in me having a look around?" I added. "You've already cleared out the evidence. I am simply here to try and make sense of the situation."

"Make sense of a suicide?" Hart asked, leaning against the car. "Isn't that a little outside of your expertise? Are you sure you haven't bought into the whole ghostly killer thing that idiot Draper keeps peddling to sell her pointless rag?"

Well, that was a fresh level of animosity. There had to be more to that story.

"You two don't believe it was a suicide any more than I do," I replied. "If you thought James killed himself, two detectives out of the overworked Surfers station wouldn't be whiling away their morning watching an empty garage. You two think there is something else here."

"Perhaps we were just in the area when we saw someone entering an active crime scene and decided to hang around and see what came of it." The male detective's face held firm. He would make a heck of a poker player.

"You can play it as close to the chest as you like," I replied, "but we both know another set of eyes can't hurt. You guys have about half the officers you need. You spend your days run off your feet. I'm not looking to steal your glory. I'm just trying to get paid, like everybody else."

The male detective sighed. "People really pay you to chase ghosts and stuff?"

I didn't figure it would win me any favors to tell him just how well I was paid. Instead, I smiled and nodded. "More people than you'd expect."

"Don't you feel any remorse about swindling honest people out of their hard-earned money?" he asked. "We aren't on the same side. You can't even see our side from where you're at."

"Awfully judgmental, aren't you?" I replied, trying not to let his accusation get under my skin. "For your information, most of my cases are stopping people being taken advantage of by the innumerable con men, crooks, and other scumbags in their sphere of influence. I've never taken a dollar I didn't earn, and all my clients are better off for having hired me."

"And which client hired you for this case?" Hart asked, flashing those pretty blue eyes at me.

"Pardon?" I replied, having heard her perfectly well, but not having a ready answer for her.

"I said, who hired you to look into this case?" she repeated with the distinct air of someone not used to having to ask twice.

I did not have an answer. And what was more, I didn't want to be caught in a lie, so I employed an old trick and let them fill in the blanks.

"I'm not at liberty to say," I replied, "but if you can find someone willing to press charges for breaking and entering, I'll be amazed. Two sharp cookies like yourselves, I'm sure you'll work it out pretty quick."

"You're working for the widow," Hart concluded.

I tapped my hands on the wheel as I gave a shrug. "You said it detective, not me."

Her partner backed up. If I was onside with the victim's wife, they were going to have the devil's job charging me for anything. After all, she would be the likely inheritor of her husband's affairs and she wasn't going to press charges for my presence here. Heck, given I'd gone in through the back door, for all they knew, I had a key. It also meant they were likely stuck with me until they solved the case.

"Look, we've got plenty to do, so we're willing to let you off with a warning," the male detective said. "Just stay out of our way. We don't need an amateur tampering with evidence."

"You're the boss, detective." I gave him my best smile.

The detectives turned to walk back to their vehicle and right as their mind was moving on to the next burden of their day, I called after them, "Say, detectives, what is it you think that links these three recent killings?"

The male detective turned with a wry smile. "I'm not at liberty to disclose the events of an ongoing investigation."

He was clearly pleased to be able to fob me off.

I flashed him a broad grin. "Thanks, detective, that's all I needed to know."

I put up my window as Hart muttered just loud enough for me to hear, "Smart ass."

I doubted her volume was an accident, but I was more concerned with her partner's answer to give it much thought. Not only had her partner not denied it, but he had mentioned an ongoing investigation. If the killings were thought to be unrelated, the police would surely have simply indicated that I was misled. Which meant they at least believed there might be enough of a connection to warrant a closer look.

And that I found all the more fascinating. I was having to reassess my opinion on this case. If two detectives were staking out old crime scenes and there appeared to be an investigation into the three killings, there had to be at least a whiff of something here.

It seemed Holly Draper had gotten something right. That being the case, why was Hart so adamantly against the reporter's article? That sort of attention could drum up all sorts of leads, both the good kind and the bad. The press never failed to bring out the crazies who were more than capable of wasting police resources, but it also tended to focus the public's attention on the case, resulting in tips and evidence that could make all the difference.

I made a mental note to reach out to Holly Draper to see what she knew. I doubted it would score me any points with detective blue eyes, but I seemed to be playing from behind there anyway, so best not to worry on her account.

Last but not least, it was time to consult an expert. I needed to reach out to my friends on the force. First, though, I thought it best to acquaint myself with the finer points of spectral threats and those who believed in them.

Esmerelda was my local expert on all things paranormal. If there was a ghost dropping bodies in Surfers Paradise, Esmerelda would have something to say about it.

Paranormal Palace. Friday, April 21st 1140hrs

The Paranormal Palace is a sanctuary for the supernatural, and those who believe in it.

I happened upon it, quite by accident, only days after opening my office. Two establishments servicing the paranormal community in the same suburb seemed like market saturation to me, and coincidence or not, I couldn't ignore her presence.

Located at the other end of Cavill Avenue, close to the iconic Surfers Paradise arch, the Paranormal Palace is a shop that occupies a basement in which Esmerelda has run wild. It answered the question of what might happen if a gypsy caravan collided with a carnival.

The store is an underground retail tenancy that has been heavily furnished with enough paranormal paraphernalia to make you forget you are less than a kilometer from some of the most beautiful beaches in the world.

I descended the concrete staircase and pushed open the glass door. Bells chimed somewhere deep within the place. I brushed aside the beaded curtain and stepped into the store proper. Incense wafted through the air, though I couldn't quite place the scent.

The shop itself isn't large—rent on the Gold Coast could be quite expensive—but it is absolutely packed with everything a person might need to explore their paranormal or spiritual journey.

Closest to the doors stood displays of crystals, gems, and other spiritual aids. A sign by the display quoted a number of client testimonials and boasted of the establishment's success in hosting the world's foremost psychic mediums.

The further one ventured into the store, the less pedestrian and more niche its supplies became. Bookcases held tomes that looked to be more than a century old. Near the register, a series of glass cases housed truly one-of-a-kind items.

"Darius," a melodious voice called from behind the counter. "I knew you would be in today."

Esmerelda stood behind the counter sorting a small pile of gemstones. She didn't look up as she greeted me though I suspected it was tricks like that which added to her mystique as a medium.

Her wavy black hair ran past her shoulders where it met a crimson red dress cut low in front, offering ample distraction for idle eyes. Her artfully applied makeup hid lines and wrinkles and made it difficult to determine her exact age. I suspected from our previous discussions she was in her late forties, but one could be forgiven for guessing just about anything. In the semi lit store, she could have been thirty or fifty. I could have asked, but that would be considered impolite and there was no telling whether she would give a straight answer to such a mundane question anyway.

I had no doubt Esmerelda sprinkled in a few white lies here or there in the furtherance of her business. I didn't mind. In spite of whatever mischief Esmerelda might use to sell her services, I'd found her to be a reliable source of information on the paranormal. Whilst I might not believe in it, my clients did, and insights into their minds and workings had helped me solve several cases already.

"Esmerelda, you're looking radiant as ever," I said as I approached the counter.

"Flattery will get you far, my boy," she replied, looking up with a twinkle in her eyes. One was blue and one was green, which at times made it difficult to know where to focus. Anywhere but the low-cut front of her dress was probably a safe choice.

"How did you know I'd be by today?" I asked.

"The spirits tell me these things, Darius, you know that," she replied, setting a particularly large gemstone aside.

A slow smile crossed her lips. "Then there are these killings of course. Three bodies drop in our little town and our resident paranormal investigator hasn't even stopped by to consult my expertise. I was wounded."

"Esmerelda, I'm afraid I've had my hands quite full. If I'm being completely honest, the first I heard of these *killings* was this morning when I picked up the paper with my coffee."

"I was beginning to think you'd lost faith in me," she said, "and after my help on the crypt killers' case, too."

Her voice was even, and I found it difficult to tell whether she was toying with me or was genuinely hurt by my supposed oversight.

"Not at all," I replied. "Just had to take a quick trip to London to check in on a colleague of mine. I'm sure the two of you would get along splendidly. Then when I returned, I was engaged to find a young woman who'd been missing for days. I'm afraid I'm a little late to the Casper killings."

She pushed her wavy hair back out of her face. "A holiday? Well, perhaps that explains why this particular spirit has been so active. He knew he had free reign while your attention was elsewhere."

It wasn't criticism; Esmerelda wasn't like that. Instead, she was positing her theory and hoping I would bite. As I was here for information, it did no harm to indulge her.

"You believe the papers then? A malicious spirit on a rampage?" I asked, glancing around to make sure we had the store to ourselves.

"Oh, almost certainly," she replied, "and this latest body only confirms it."

"What makes you think that?" I asked. "I've looked into the case, and I see little to connect the bodies. Granted, they are all bizarre, but related seems a stretch. I see even less reason to believe it's a ghost. Far more likely that someone simply wanted Mooney dead."

"Oh, someone wanted him dead alright. Someone from his past." Esmerelda fixed me with a stare. "Mooney has a few skeletons in his closet. Haven't you heard?"

I hadn't even been back to the office yet, so beyond the signs of foul play at the garage I'd hardly started my investigation, let alone dug into anyone's history.

"Heard what?" I leaned a little closer. "Don't tease me, Esmerelda."

She smiled. "I usually charge for my expertise, Darius. But I like you and you've done a lot to put our industry on the map."

I tried not to let my disagreement make it to my face. Esmerelda made her living promoting the paranormal; I made mine debunking it. We were at opposite ends of the spectrum, but clearly Esmerelda saw all publicity as good publicity so why disagree with her?

"I very much appreciate your assistance, Esmerelda, you know that."

"Yes, but appreciation doesn't pay the bills. Darius, you charge for your services now, don't you?"

"I certainly do," I replied, indulging her. She had an ask and that sparked my curiosity. "What is it that I can do for you?"

She leaned over the counter. "Well, this particular story is already on the front page. If I help you solve it, it's likely to be very good for business, isn't it?"

"Almost certainly," I replied, holding her gaze. "As you said, appreciation doesn't keep the lights on."

"Exactly, so when the media come knocking this time, I'd simply ask that you find a way to mention the Paranormal Palace. In exchange for my ongoing support and invaluable assistance, of course."

She was a shrewd operator to be sure. Beneath the panoply of paranormal and the merchandising of the mystique, Esmerelda had a shrewd mind for business, always angling for anything that could boost her custom. She had seen what the crypt killers' case had done for me and wanted a piece of the action.

I wasn't greedy. If she could help me, it might take another dangerous killer off the street. I didn't see what harm it could do.

"I'd be delighted to," I said. "The only reason I didn't last time, was that I don't make a habit of revealing my sources. If you're fine with me mentioning the store, I'd be more than happy to spread the word. I'm not trying to hog the limelight."

Esmerelda beamed as she brushed a handful of topaz crystals into a small velvet bag and pulled its drawstrings tight. She set the bag beneath the counter and gave me a look that I was sure had encouraged many men to do very silly things.

My heart fluttered just a little in spite of my brain telling me to focus on the case. I feared a different head was doing the thinking right now.

Focus, Darius.

"So, what do you know about James Mooney that I don't?" I asked, folding my arms.

"I know his history. I know why the ghost wanted him dead," Esmerelda replied, her face serious.

"And why might that be?"

Esmerelda made her way to the other end of the counter and pulled on the gold chain around her neck until a key appeared from somewhere beneath the silk of her dress and slithered upward. Lifting the key off her neck, she pressed it into a lock on the back of the glass cabinet and opened the case. She produced a tome that seemed to be hundreds of years old and set it on the glass countertop in front of me.

"Like most of us, Mooney created the spirit that haunted him."

"What do you mean?" I replied, growing increasingly curious.

Esmerelda flicked through the tome to a page covered in handwritten scrawl. "As Tolman writes, ghosts tend to be spirits with unfinished business, Mr. Kane. That's why they linger here rather than passing on. You see, their spirit cannot be at peace until they have settled their affairs. That's precisely what this spirit is doing. Mooney wronged him in life, and now in death, he has avenged himself."

I didn't miss her careful use of the pronoun. "He? What makes you so certain that Mooney's killer was a man?"

"Because I am an avid student of history," Esmerelda replied.

An unrepentant gossip is what she is. If anything happened in Surfers Paradise, you could rest assured Esmerelda knew something about it. Her information came courtesy of the steady stream of men and women engaging her services as a psychic medium. She was more tapped into the gossip stream of the city than anyone else I knew, except perhaps my mother's hairdresser.

The amount of information *that* woman was privy to truly horrified me. I'd only gone there once and what she already knew about every aspect of my life had been so terrifyingly indepth, I'd never been back.

I valued both kinds of information from Esmerelda: the gossip and her insights into the paranormal.

"Enough foreplay. Tell me what you know," I said, my voice deepening a little.

"Typical young man," she replied with a sigh. "Still hasn't worked out that the foreplay is where the fun is. Don't be in too much of a rush, my dear. You'll end up disappointed, as will any lady who finds herself in your company."

I should know better than to rush her. I took a deep breath, as much to remind myself to be patient as to avoid the distracting view presented by being so close to Esmerelda.

"By all means. You were saying?"

"Ah, yes. Before I was so rudely interrupted, I was telling you that Mr. Mooney has a most interesting history. One that is in the public record, if you care to look back far enough."

Esmerelda settled in to tell her tale. "Before he operated his establishment at Peninsular Drive, he was an auto mechanic further down the coast, Burleigh Heads, I believe. He purchased the workshop from his mentor. James ran the workshop for several years until his mentor passed."

"When he did, James was bereft and, in that distraction, it is said he made a mistake while repairing one of his client's vehicles. His client drove the vehicle only a few days before the brakes failed. He crossed a median strip and plowed into oncoming traffic. His client died due to James' negligence."

"You think the dead client was haunting Mooney?" I asked. "Lingering, looking for his revenge? He certainly took his time."

Esmerelda waved a hand dismissively. "Perhaps the ghost might have been motivated by many causes. Anger, resentment, or jealousy. All can be indicators for the kind of unfinished business that would cause a spectre to linger here. Perhaps it is his client's ghost haunting him or perhaps his old mentor was disappointed with what became of the business he sold his protégé. Who can say for sure?"

"Because Mooney closed the business?" I asked.

"Indeed. His reputation suffered as a result of the court case. His late client's wife brought charges against him and, while Mooney was cleared, the court case brought enough public scrutiny that his business never recovered. He closed up shop at Burleigh, moved here, and opened a new business, this time focusing on smash repairs; something in enough demand that people either overlooked his history, or simply didn't know about it. With all the hailstorms lately, I dare say there is more work than there are people to do it. He built a thriving business, one that might stoke resentment in the lingering spirit of its former owner."

Esmerelda tapped the tome in front of her. "Careful though, Darius. If the ghost has found cause to linger, it means further business remains to be seen to. See that you do not add yourself to its list."

Her answer didn't explain why the ghost had dropped two other bodies first, but if the killings were rooted in Mooney's past, I was going to have to dig for answers. At least I had a lead.

I smiled. "You've been very helpful, Esmerelda. As always, your knowledge is surpassed only by your beauty."

"Why, Darius," she feigned a flush, "if I were ten years younger, I would take you out back and do very wicked things with you."

Her sultry voice sent a shiver of excitement down my spine, and I found myself swallowing to remove the lump in the back of my throat.

The bell chimed as another patron entered the store. The tingling charm shattered the moment and I let out a low breath.

Saved by the bell.

The new patron, a woman in her thirties, was carrying her child in one of those fabric sling backpack carriers that seemed to defy physics to me, but then what did I know about baby carriers?

"But alas we shall have to save our dalliance for another day." Esmerelda sighed. "I have other customers."

"Perhaps another time," I replied, the words slipping out of my mouth before my brain had the time to intercede.

"Beware your lips making promises your body can't keep," Esmerelda said as she tapped the old tome in front of her. "If you wish to know more of spectres, Darius, this is Tolman's complete works. There's nothing like it anywhere in the world. I'd be happy to sell you this one, at a discount, even, on account of our strong working relationship."

"And how much would such a prized manuscript set me back?" I asked, more to indulge her than out of any desire to purchase it.

"Twenty-two hundred," she replied. "Two thousand even, if you paid cash."

Ever the merchant, working in cash. I doubted the tax office saw a red cent from the cunning woman. My amazement must have been apparent because she brushed the front of the manuscript.

"It's more than two hundred years old, you know. The only one of its kind, anywhere in the world."

"I'll have to think about that," I replied. "You have been most helpful. Thank you, Esmerelda."

As I turned for the door, I noticed my shirt hanging out of my slacks. It had likely pulled free while I'd been leaning on the counter. I hastily shoved it back in my pants.

"Don't forget our agreement, Darius."

I wasn't sure whether she was talking of my promise to mention the store, or if it was a reference to our proposed dalliance, but I figured it best to play it safe.

"I wouldn't dream of it," I called over my shoulder. I slipped sideways to allow the young mother to pass by more easily.

Slipping through the beaded curtain, I made my way out the door and up the concrete stairs, taking them two at a time. I really did need to put in an appearance at the office at some point. Glenda, my reluctant receptionist, might go rogue on me if I didn't.

As I hit the street, my phone dinged repeatedly in my pocket.

I checked the screen. Three missed calls and a voice message.

The Paranormal Palace is a concrete bunker with notoriously bad reception. The shopping mall on top of it didn't help matters. I imagined Esmerelda had chosen the location on purpose. The one time I'd asked about it, she blamed the spirits' interference rather than the concrete for the poor reception.

Unlocking my phone, I checked my call log. All three calls were from my father.

My heart beat a little faster. It wasn't like him to spam me. Pulling up the voice message, I raised the phone to my ear.

His labored breathing panted down the line. Between gasps he managed only a few words. "Darius, help! Come quickly!"

My heart upped its pace to a heady pounding as the line went dead.

Family Foibles. Friday, April 21st 1215hrs

I RACED ACROSS THE Gold Coast like a bat out of hell, fearing my father's life depended on it. I'd called him back, but he hadn't answered.

He'd sounded panicked, short of breath, almost in pain. As I raced to my parents' home, I hoped that if he were having a heart attack, he'd had the good sense to call an ambulance first. Which begged the question, what was my mother doing?

I made good time, excellent time really, which left me hoping I hadn't collected one or more tickets from the many stationary speed cameras along the way. I hurtled my truck into my parent's driveway and raced for the front door.

My father's voice called out, "Darius, I'm back here."

He didn't sound like he was dying, which was at once both a relief and an irritation.

I followed his voice around the side of the house and found my father working away in the backyard.

My father, Vincent, is a tall man – six-three but lean. Like I had once been before the army packed a good deal more muscle onto my frame. His once black hair was interspersed with gray that ringed his head like a silver crown. He worked away in a t-shirt, jeans, and a set of old work boots. The sheen of sweat on his face told me he'd been out here for some time.

He stood at a trestle table, a slab of timber in front of him, a circular saw in hand as he deliberated on his next cut. My heart pounded in my chest as a series of emotions battled within me. Frustration at the fact that I had raced over here, seemingly unnecessarily. Relief at the realization that there was nothing wrong with my father. He was simply attempting another do-it-yourself renovation and had likely found himself in well over his head.

My mouth dropped open as he lowered the saw at an odd angle.

"Wait, Dad, no," I shouted as the saw blade mauled the timber, sliding along its surface before finally biting into the wood.

There is nothing quite so dangerous as a retired accountant with too much time on his hands and an inflated view of his domestic talents.

Dad pulled the saw back, a look of utter shock on his face as he inspected the damaged timber. He set the saw on the bench, and it whirred slowly to a standstill.

"Dad, what are you doing?" I called, crossing the yard to his side.

"Putting a roof on the patio, son. What does it look like?"

Death by domestic ineptitude.

At least that was what I was sure the coroner would say if I left my father to his own devices.

Dad leaned in, examining the timber closer, perhaps trying to determine if it could be salvaged, or whether he was going to have to start over.

"Keep the blade vertical," I said. "If you need an angled cut, move the timber, not the saw."

He set the saw down and looked up at me. "Don't lecture me, now, Darius. I watched a video on it this morning. This is exactly how he did it."

"I hope not." I laughed, shaking my head. "Dad, a YouTube video is hardly an in-depth education."

Resting my hands on my hips, I surveyed the chaos in the backyard. There were timber offcuts everywhere, as well as half a dozen pieces that seemed to have been cut to size and were sitting neatly on the tiled patio.

"Why don't you pay someone else to do this?" I asked. "It's not like you're short of a dollar and it has to be better than cutting your own hand off."

"Now, son, that's not the can-do spirit I taught you, is it? Why pay someone else to do something I could very well do myself?"

Some free advice: never try to convince an accountant to spend money. They are tighter than Scrooge McDuck at tax time. Rather than argue with him, I made my way over to the bench to assess just how much actual danger he might be in.

"What do you need my help with?" I asked. "Since you obviously didn't call me here to consult me on my carpentry expertise."

"I just need a little help lifting a beam into place." He pointed to a massive piece of timber resting on the back patio. He'd set the braces and support posts that would hold up the load bearing beam. It lay beside them and ran almost the length of the patio.

"Your mother and I tried to lift it earlier with no success, dang near put my back out," my father replied.

"That's because you're in your sixties," I said. "The two of us aren't going to get it up there either. Leave it there. I'll bring Sonny and Carl by. The four of us ought to be able to get it into place without breaking our backs."

"Thanks, son, that would be great." He let out a sigh of relief. "How are things at the office?"

And with that question, the urgency of my father's latest project seemed to fade.

When I'd told my parents what I intended to do on leaving the army, my mother had all manner of concerns. My father on the other hand, had nodded, smiled, and told me it sounded like a good fit for me. In hindsight, I was confident he would have said the same if I told him I was planning to make a living as a human statue.

Dad was great like that, willing to support me no matter what course I charted. He'd had a markedly better reaction than my dear old mum who had been convinced I was taking up witchcraft and was on a direct flight to hell.

"Business is good, Dad. Ever since that last case, my phone and email are going night and day."

"Too many clients and you'll become the bottleneck in your business, son. You'll need staff."

He grinned as he extolled the virtues of employing others. The notion of a growing business had always excited him. It was the sale of his own accounting practice that had allowed him to retire in his early fifties.

"Maybe one day," I replied. "For the time being, I'm just planning to pick and choose the best cases. You know, sift out the crazies, take the people I can genuinely help."

"You always did have an eye for seeing what others can't," my father said. "You'd have made a hell of an auditor."

"Not likely." I scoffed. "I'd have died of boredom by my third day."

"Still," my father replied, "boredom lets you sleep at night. How are you really doing?"

Life had been pretty rough since getting back from Afghanistan. My tour there opened my eyes to just how lucky I was to live in a country like Australia, and just what kind of terrible monsters truly exist in the world. At their hands, I saw things I couldn't unsee—images that still haunted my dreams, or at least they did when I managed to get to sleep. The truth was I worked a lot of nights as a paranormal investigator. The miscreants I hunted didn't come out to play during the day and it stopped me having to face my demons, or at least postponed the meeting.

I leaned on the table. "Well enough, Dad. Keeping busy helps."

"Darius!" my mother Sue's excited voice carried from the kitchen. The patio door swung open, and she bustled through it, a glass of lemonade in each hand.

Wearing a summer dress, she looked younger than her age, not least because her hair was kept pristinely blonde by her hardworking stylist. Perhaps that was why her hairdresser knew so much about me. I was fairly confident that a gray hair constituted an emergency and an immediate visit. Mum cared about the little things. It was how she managed to take care of the house, dad, and me.

"I thought that was you, dear. That car of yours has a very distinct rumble."

"It certainly does," I replied. There were few vehicles on the road with the kind of horsepower installed in mine. You never did know when you were going to need a little more juice under the hood.

"Hi, Mum." I wrapped my arms around her, taking care not to bump the drinks. "Don't you dare let dad talk you into trying to lift that beam again."

I let her go and she handed over one of the drinks. "Oh. I won't, dear. Merely the thought of it threw my back out, it did. Chiropractor won't be pleased at all."

"And how is Doctor Fielding?" I asked, before draining half the lemonade in a large gulp.

"He's well, dear. You ought to pop in and see him from time to time. Adjustments are good for a man your size. Keep that spine nice and healthy. Dr. Fielding says he hasn't seen you since you got back."

That was Mum, always worried about my wellbeing, but in the past few weeks I'd had far more pressing concerns than my spinal health. Like getting murdered by a bundle of drug dealers masquerading as the walking dead. There was no way I was going to tell my mom that though.

"One of these days, Mum, when I have a few minutes."

She handed the other glass to my father and surveyed his handiwork.

"How is the patio going, dear? Still determined to put it up yourself or can we throw in the towel and call a qualified builder?"

There was a subtle barb in the way she lingered over the word *qualified*. My mum had a wicked glint in her eye; she did enjoy ribbing my father. I suppose it was her way of ensuring he finished the project.

"Over my dead body. We have made quite good headway today. This patio will be up before one of them even comes by to give us a quote, or my name isn't Ian Kane."

He was as stubborn as a mule, a trait which was likely to be the death of him. Particularly if we continued to let him play with the power tools.

"Okay, dear, I'll leave it in your capable hands." Mum smiled, mission accomplished. She turned back to me. "What brings you by?"

"Dad called me, all short of breath. I figured he was having a heart attack, so I rushed right over. If I knew he was just trying to lift that beam, I would have brought the boys with me."

"I told you not to leave a message, dear," mum berated my father, shaking her head. "You know your father. A man of few words."

My father shot me a conspiratorial wink.

"I never needed them," he said, "on account of marrying a woman of so many words."

I laughed. Seeing them entangled in their usual dance brought a smile to my face.

"While you're here, dear, I've been meaning to talk to you about Saturday," mother began.

"Saturday?" I racked my brain, trying to recall what I had committed to.

"Bingo at the church," she replied. "The barbecue. Remember, you promised the pastor you'd be able to lend a hand."

My, that had come around quickly. Mum asked me for a hand weeks ago. In all the excitement of my caseload, the event had slipped my mind.

"Of course, Mum. I'm working a few cases at the moment, but it shouldn't be an issue."

Bingo wasn't really how I wanted to spend my Saturday. I enjoyed the time with mum and dad, but their church friends could be a mixed bunch. I wasn't sure I was in the mood to spend a whole day with them.

"A new case already?" My mother fixed me with a look like she'd caught me with my hand in the cookie jar. "I hope it's not that dreaded killer the papers are talking about. That one sounds dangerous."

I didn't want to worry my mum. She stressed a little too easily. And I wasn't technically working the Casper killings case on account of the fact no one had hired me, so a little lie of omission seemed the order of the day.

"No, I just took a case for a lady whose possessions have been disappearing. I suspect that someone close to her might be taking advantage of her."

"That's dreadful," mum replied, hands resting on her hips.

"Exactly. I have to put a stop to that kind of thing."

"I don't understand why she doesn't just call the police."

I mopped my brow with the back of my coat sleeve. It was far too warm to be dallying about outside in a suit coat. "She did, but she told them she thought it was a ghost, so they gave her about as much attention as you'd expect."

My mother laughed. "What use would a ghost have for such trinkets anyway?"

It was the combination of sense and nonsense that perfectly summed up my mum. She was a believer in all things spiritual, including ghosts, while retaining a healthy dose of common sense and practicality she'd drummed into me from a young age.

"That is the question, isn't it, Mum?" I replied with a smile. "Don't worry, I'll take care of it."

"Good, good..." her voice trailed to a whisper, before she cleared her throat. "And stay away from that Casper killer, will you? I know that mess at the cemetery has been good for business, but there is no need to push your luck."

"I'll do my best, Mum." I planted her a kiss on the forehead. Given the police didn't want my help, it was unlikely to be too difficult to accommodate her request. It was mostly my curiosity leading me to pursue it, anyway. Perhaps that or a little ambition for some more notoriety. Or maybe it was just the fact I didn't like to think a killer might be prowling the same streets I frequented.

"How are things going in the dating department?" my mother asked, fixing me with a look that was all business.

I glanced down at my watch.

"Look at the time, Mum. I really must be going," I replied, unwilling to endure another round of my mother's dating advice.

"Darius, don't you dare. This is important."

I could see her gathering momentum like a hurricane about to make landfall.

I pressed my glass back into her hand. "Thanks for the lemonade, Mum. It really hit the spot, but I must be getting back to the office."

Turning to my father, I pointed at the timber beam laying on the deck.

"Don't touch that," I called as I backed away. "I'll be by with the boys later to fit it in place. Frame up the rest, if you will, but leave the heavy lifting to us."

I was almost at the side of the house when I called over my shoulder, "And try not to take your hand off with that saw."

"Take my hand off," my father scoffed, "never. I'm a natural."

Naturally likely to end up in hospital.

"You can't avoid the discussion forever," my mother called after me as I made my way down the side of the house.

"Oh, don't worry, Mum," I muttered, quietly enough that she couldn't hear me, "I remember the high notes. Marriage, good companionship, grand babies before you die, got it."

Of course, I could have mentioned Courtney, but that would have been like sinking my own ship before I even had a chance to brave the storm. Mum would have hunted through every coffee shop on the coast looking for my prospective date. I wouldn't wish that on anyone, and I certainly wasn't going to let her mess things up with Courtney. I was perfectly capable of doing that all by myself with a hastily scrawled note and a heavy-handed compliment.

I climbed into the truck and headed for the office. It was high time I put in an appearance and saw what mischief Glenda had gotten up to this morning.

The Iron Lady. Friday, April 21st 1300hrs

WHERE A PRIVATE INVESTIGATOR sets up shop says a lot about the kind of person they are. I went where the money was, at least so I thought. The Gold Coast, the jewel of the sunshine state with plenty of wealthy patrons, misbehaving millionaires, and wandering wives.

Wanting to be in the heart of the action, I'd set up my office on Cavill Avenue, next to the famous open air Cavill Mall. However, calling it an office is a little generous. It was more of a filing cabinet, but paying rent on the Gold Coast felt like I might need to auction off an organ to avoid breaking my lease.

When I pushed open the glass door, Glenda had her feet on an ottoman as she reclined in her office chair. The latest John Grisham was open in her lap, a steaming cup of coffee resting before her. She looked like work hadn't bothered her all day. That made one of us. Her gray hair was cut short at the shoulder, her glasses rested low on her nose. She didn't have a care in the world, other than what might happen in the final chapters of the legal thriller.

It was the kind of behavior most bosses might fire an employee for, but in Glenda's case it was a part of her contract. I'd started Blue Moon's Australia branch on a shoestring budget. What money I had saved in the service had gone into my car and house. So when it came to the business, I had needed to make a few compromises. One of those was not hiring a proper secretary.

I simply couldn't afford it.

Mum had introduced me to Glenda, one of her book club's more senior members. She'd long since retired, her husband having passed many years ago. With no family left, time was heavy on her hands. After a little haggling, we'd come to an agreement. Glenda would man the office and answer the phone, taking messages in exchange for a token salary. Of course, she was free to read as she pleased and, provided she looked after her two duties, I left her in peace and made sure there was a quality coffee maker in the kitchen and enough coffee supplies to last her a lifetime.

Not that I could rankle Glenda, even if I tried. She was the kind of Australian whose iron backbone had been forged during World War II. Short of a bomb going off beneath her chair, I doubted you could so much as raise Glenda's blood pressure a single digit.

All that aside, she did the job and kept me on my toes. We got along well enough provided no one made the mistake of asking her to get them a coffee. She might answer the phone, but she was no one's lackey.

"Morning, Darius," she called, her eyes never leaving the page. "Nice of you to come by. I was beginning to think you'd forgotten where the office was."

"How could I forget, Glenda? I pay the rent and your salary," I replied, repeating the steps to the dance we enjoyed each day.

"Boss or not, in my day, men showed up for work at eight, sharp."

"That's because in your day they were still riding a horse and buggy, Glenda. If they didn't start at eight, they might never get home in time for dinner."

That one got her eyes out of the book, and she fixed me with a stare.

"One of these days, that smart mouth is going to get you knocked on your arse."

I laughed all the way to my office. One point to Darius.

"And when it does, I will be in familiar territory," I called, as I paused in the doorway to my office. "Any messages I should be aware of?"

Glenda looked across her desk at the pad she kept by the phone and shook her head.

"There were a few calls. Most of them were a few French fries short of a happy meal, if you know what I mean."

"I certainly do, Glenda. That's why you're here, to sort the wheat from the chaff. What were the others?"

"Others?" Glenda asked, her eyes already drifting back to her book.

"You said most of the callers were crazy. That implies there were others that were not. What did they want?"

"Oh right," Glenda replied. "There were two that had some promise. The first was a psychologist who thought you might be able to use her services."

"Hard pass," I answered. I was in no mood to be psychoanalyzed. I would face my demons on my own terms, thank you very much. "And the other?"

Glenda turned a page. "Oh yes, she was a reporter of some sort. Wanted your comment on the Casper Killings."

My ears perked up at that. "What was her name?"

"Molly, Dolly ... something or other." Glenda adjusted her glasses that were almost falling off her nose.

"Holly Draper?" I asked, recalling the morning's article.

"Yes, that's the one."

"Did you get her number?" I replied.

"Of course," Glenda said, shaking her head a little. "What do you take me for?"

I wanted to say, distracted, but I could ill afford to answer the phone myself. I would never get anything done.

"Marvelous. Call her back and let her know I would love to discuss the case, perhaps tomorrow over some morning tea. I have bingo with Mum and Dad in the afternoon so the morning would probably be best."

"And the other one?" Glenda asked.

"Just leave it for the time being."

"You really should talk to someone," Glenda replied. "It'll be good for you."

"That's why I have you, Glenda. Look at that. I'm feeling better already."

One of these days, Glenda's stern demeanor was going to turn away a genuine client. In the meantime, she was doing the Lord's work saving me from wasting hours locked in polite conversation with people who were convinced the wind spoke to them.

In my haste, I realized I'd forgotten to mention Mrs. Wheeler. Taking off my coat, I slipped it over the back of a chair and poked my head out of the office.

"Oh Glenda, I did meet with Mrs. Wheeler this morning. She seems genuine enough. Could you please send her contact details through to me? While you're at it, if you could forward her a copy of the signed engagement letter and let her know that I should be over this evening to help her with her ghost problems."

Glenda smiled. "Certainly, right after I finish this chapter."

I glanced at the book. She was more than two thirds of the way through it, and it wouldn't surprise me if Mrs. Wheeler didn't get her engagement letter until Glenda finished the novel. But I didn't see the harm in that, so I retreated into my office.

"I'm going to sort through my emails, then catch a drink with the boys. If you need me, you know where to find me."

Glenda was already back in another world, so I closed the door.

My office was a simple affair: a timber desk I'd picked up at an auction that helped convey the illusion of success, a row of filing cabinets, and a bookcase loaded with old law cases. I'd read them in a previous life, but lawyering hadn't suited me at all. It was one of many reasons I'd enlisted in the first place.

I made my way past the leather seats I reserved for clients and fired up my computer.

While I waited for the old government surplus machine to boot, I set about gathering supplies for the Wheeler case. As a private investigator, I didn't have any authority to arrest people. There was the odd occasion that I had made a citizen's arrest, sitting on miscreants and thugs until the boys in blue arrived to cart them off. My real role tended to be largely surveillance and gathering the evidence my clients required to resolve their concerns.

Exactly what form that took depended on the case, so it never hurt to be prepared. I gathered up a series of small surveillance cameras. They were portable and recorded straight to the cloud so there was little chance of losing the footage. I checked their batteries before loading them neatly in a small Samsonite case.

When I finally reached the desktop, I opened my emails. Many of my cases came straight through that inbox, but so did every nutcase on the Gold Coast. I scanned through the headings, dispensing with the obvious spam, then aggressively culled the list to a few possible contenders.

A woman at Southport complained that a werewolf had taken her cat. Another claimed a Bigfoot sighting in the hinterland to the west, and there was a man who swore he'd seen a mermaid swimming at night at the Spit. The Spit was a thin stretch of beach at the northern point of the Gold Coast. It was where the seaway passed between the beach and South Stradbroke Island. That particular stretch of water was home to a vast host of oceanic wildlife. It wouldn't surprise me if he'd seen a dolphin, but a mermaid? SeaWorld was next door, and they would have been all over that.

Chasing missing cats felt a little below my pay grade. If the cat had vanished, it either didn't want to be found or it had fallen afoul of one of the many dangerous natural predators that actually existed here. We didn't need werewolves, not when a feral dog, dingo, or fox could have found it.

Bigfoot sightings weren't uncommon. Australia had literally hundreds of them, on account of the vast wilderness and national parks that could be found literally everywhere. For a country almost the same size as the continental United States, it had only a tenth of the population.

Which meant plenty of vast empty spaces that quickly became fodder for paranormal phenomena and conspiracy theories. Of the two, the mermaid case seemed the more promising, so I sent a follow-up response asking for a more detailed outline of what had occurred. There were certainly both dolphins and sharks in the bay, but the ocean was a big place, and you never could tell what you might find there. In a sea of email sewerage, this case was the most promising option. Or at least the corporate email it came from led me to believe they might actually pay for my time.

As I hit send, my phone vibrated with one new message.

It simply read, *Where are you taking me to dinner?*

I didn't recognise the number, and figured it had to be Courtney. I didn't tend to get many unsolicited dinner invitations, so I tried to play it cool. I took a moment to do a search for restaurants in the area and found some promising candidates. The problem was, I didn't want to take her to any of the pubs I usually frequented, but neither did I want to go too fancy on the first date and send a message that I was flush with cash. I didn't want to have to disappoint her later when she discovered the truth.

Would you prefer Chinese or Italian? I texted back.

Italian, came the speedy reply.

I texted her the details of the restaurant I had in mind and offered to meet her there at seven. Having not dated in some time, I wasn't sure if that was too early, but I took my chance. I was going to have to cut drinks with the boys short, but it was a worthy cause. They would give me hell about it, but ultimately they would understand.

See you there! Came the response along with a winking emoji. It was cute and brought a little smile to my face. Perhaps I hadn't messed things up too badly.

I was still grinning when Glenda came through the door.

"What are you so cheery about?" she asked. "A worthy case perhaps, or just a funny cat meme?"

I didn't know which surprised me more, that she noticed the smile or that she knew what a meme was.

"No, even better," I replied. "I have a date."

"It's a miracle," she said. "Shall I tell your mother?"

I leaned across the desk, pointing my finger right at her. "Don't you dare."

"I figured you'd say that, but Hilda will be most unimpressed if she is the last to find out."

"And I'll be most unimpressed if she runs this one off with talk of grandbabies. Now, Glenda, what can I do for you?"

"Oh yes, that. I almost forgot. There's a woman waiting for you in the lobby."

I looked down at my calendar. "I don't have any appointments in my schedule."

"She was a walk-in," Glenda replied. "But I figured you might be able to make a little time for her.

I still had a few minutes to spare before I needed to head home to get changed. "Who is it? Did they mention what they wanted to speak to me about?"

Glenda shrugged. "She didn't tell me about her business, but her name is Wendy Mooney."

I bolted upright. How many Mooneys could there be in the Gold Coast? Was she related to the victim? There was only one way to find out.

Wronged Wives. Friday, April 21st 1400hrs

My afternoon had certainly taken an unexpected turn. If Wendy Mooney was related to the latest victim, she might be able to shed some much-needed insight into the case. The real question was, why was she here?

Wendy stood in the lobby of my office, dressed in a crop top, yoga pants, and sneakers. Her face was a little flushed. Either she had recently been crying or she had just finished exercising. Given everything I supposed she might be going through, it could well have been either, or both.

I met her eyes and found the white of her eyes was streaked and bloodshot. From her age and the diamond ring, I was confident I was dealing with James Mooney's wife rather than a sister.

"Mr. Kane, I'm Wendy Mooney. Thank you for seeing me."

I crossed the room and stretched out my hand. "Darius. Please, I'm sorry for your loss."

She took my hand, her lip trembling as she sniffled. She seemed likely to burst into tears at any moment. I wasn't particularly good at dealing with grief. Exposure to death hadn't made me any better at dealing with it, or those scarred by it, either.

Her grief certainly seemed genuine enough, but I took nothing for granted. I had learned in this game that appearances could be deceiving. More often than not, when a body dropped, it was statistically likely to be someone close to or known by the victim, usually spouses, who played a part in the mischief.

"Would you like to step into my office? We can talk more comfortably there. It's this way." I motioned toward my office door but felt a little awkward. In this human filing cabinet, there was literally nowhere else it might be.

"Thank you," she whispered. "I wasn't sure if I'd need to have an appointment. I wasn't expecting to just interrupt your afternoon. I guess I, uh, I don't really know what I was expecting."

"Don't worry about that." I guided her toward the office. "Please, I have a little time and you've made the effort to get here. I'm happy to see you now."

I motioned the chair across from my desk. She slipped into it as I took mine.

"Mrs. Mooney, I must say I am surprised to see you here," I started slowly, trying to gauge her response.

"The police called me," she replied. "Told me someone had been snooping around the garage. I think they wanted me to press charges. They asked if I had hired you. Why would they ask something like that? And what were you doing there?"

I nodded. "All good questions, Wendy. I'm an investigator of sorts. I became aware of your husband's death and was in the area, so I swung by the garage to see what I could turn up. I look into these sorts of unusual occurrences all the time. I was wondering if there was more to your husband's case than made it into the paper."

"And what did you find?" Wendy asked, taking a tissue from the box on my desk.

"Nothing substantial yet, I'm afraid. But that doesn't mean there's nothing to be found. Like I said, I only just became aware of the case."

I didn't want to give her any false impression. I understood what it was to lose someone. People were easy to exploit when they were at their most vulnerable. The last thing on earth I wanted to do was take advantage of a widow's grief.

"So it is the sort of thing you would look into, though?" she asked, her hand shaking as she clenched the tissue.

"I work all sorts of cases here," I replied. "In spite of what the sign might say, I don't hunt ghosts. I find the information my clients need to put a matter to rest."

I noted my word choice and kicked myself internally. Wendy looked to me to fill the silence, so I decided to make the most of the unexpected interview. Given I had no idea what the police had gathered from the scene, I hoped Wendy might be able to fill me in on the status of their investigation. Or at least what detail they might have given her.

"What did the police think?" I asked. "The case seems to have garnered considerable attention. They appear to still be watching the garage. They must have a working theory."

"They won't tell me anything." She sobbed. "All I get is the same line. It's an ongoing investigation. I know it's only been a day, but they don't seem to have any suspects and I'm tired of learning about my husband's death in the paper. The only reason they even called today was to see if I would press charges."

"What exactly did they say?" I asked, wondering what I'd done to raise their ire. Other than traipse through their crime scene.

"The detective, she said you were interfering in their investigation and had broken into James' garage."

She? So it was Hart that had made the call. Interesting. Either her partner had delegated that delightful task to her, or she had taken the initiative of her own accord and was trying to sink the boot in while she had an opportunity. Leads must have been thin on the ground if they had time to pursue me.

"We've had an increase in unusual activity of late. It wouldn't surprise me if the police are playing this case close to their chest," I replied. "It's not you. It's fairly standard operating procedure."

"But close to their chest doesn't help me," Wendy replied, her voice rising an octave. "I've lost my husband. I have three small children and every day that goes by, my situation is only getting worse. Only this morning the insurance company told me the earliest indications are that my husband took his own life, and they won't be paying out on his life insurance policy until the police prove otherwise."

Everything made a lot more sense. That was what had brought her to my office so quickly. Not only was she grieving her husband, but she was facing the loss of his income and the safeguards that had been put in place to provide for their family.

"Unscrupulous bastards," I muttered. "Excuse the language."

"Oh, I have called them far worse, most of it right down the phone at them."

I swept my hand across the surface of my table. I didn't want to appear overeager, and I also needed to hedge my bets. If the police weren't trusting Wendy with any of the details of their investigation, there was a reason, one I certainly wasn't going to mention to her, and that reason was that they might be withholding the information because she might still be a suspect. The last thing I wanted was to have my time wasted by a black widow trying to collect a quick insurance payment. I was nobody's patsy.

"Tell me this, Wendy. If your husband didn't take his own life, and we discard this ridiculous notion that a ghost might have done it, who killed your husband?"

"I don't know," she replied. "I have been asking myself the same question. James has been working too hard to have time to make enemies."

"Well, let's have another think about it together," I replied. "If we want to know who did this, we need something to go on. Any detail, no matter how small or insignificant it might appear, might help me."

"Well, there was the matter of the accident," she replied. "But that was ancient history."

Esmerelda's gossip seemed to be right on the money.

"Accident?" I replied, intentionally playing coy. I wanted to hear the story from her perspective.

"Yes, my husband was a mechanic by trade. Years ago, he fixed a car that ended up in an accident. Everyone believed he'd made a mistake that resulted in the driver striking another car in an intersection when its brakes failed. It turned into a media frenzy. There was even a criminal case, but my husband was acquitted. At first, I thought that might have something to do with his death. But the man in the accident died and his wife who had led the crusade against my husband passed almost three years ago. They had no children so unless you believe that their ghost killed my husband, I don't think they had anything to do with this."

I nodded as she spoke.

"Does your husband have any other acquaintances or business associates? Anyone he owed money to?"

"No, the court case drained our reserves. We had to sell our house to pay the legal bills and used what little we had to open the new workshop here, but we didn't go into any debt. We've been renting a home ever since but business has been picking up. We have cash in the bank and were even considering a new house. Of course, that's not going to happen now."

I couldn't help but feel sorry for Wendy. I knew what it was like to start over.

"And you can't think of anyone who might have wished to harm your husband?"

Wendy paused, racking her brain. "Well, there were some men that came by the workshop a few weeks ago. James mentioned it to me because they wanted to buy him out. Made him a cash offer. We talked about it for a few nights, but with the money he's been making, we'd be better off keeping the workshop. If anything, we needed to expand it and take on some staff. So James turned them down."

That was a more promising lead. Certainly more concrete than a ghost.

"A cash offer?" I asked. With interest rates being so low, it was a little unusual. "Any idea why they wanted the property?"

Wendy shook her head. "James didn't say that much about it other than that they'd been back, and he'd politely turned them down."

Money was so often a motive for murder that I wanted to understand who'd been behind that decision.

"Turned them down." I nodded slowly. "Whose idea was it to say no?"

Wendy didn't hesitate. "Both of us. Business has been good. After the last garage failed, we never expected things to go this well. But we could both see the promise here. Like I said, we wanted to expand, and with how crazy the real estate market is here on the coast, if we did sell, we'd never get another workshop in such a good location. As it is, we'd actually been working on trying to acquire the neighboring premises so we could expand. The last thing he wanted to do was sell."

Expansion. Well, that would certainly put them into competition with whoever was trying to acquire their garage. That seemed like motive to me.

"Did he mention who these men were? Did he get a name?"

"I'm sorry." Wendy shook her head. "He didn't give them to me. All he mentioned was that they were local businessmen. I'm not sure that helps at all."

"Everything helps." I replied, trying to reassure her as a potential theory formed in my mind. There were characters in this world that didn't take no for an answer. Murder seemed a stretch, but it wouldn't be the first time someone had acquired property from a deceased estate to further their own ambitions.

Property prices were certainly on the rise. The workshop land was probably worth two or three times what James had acquired it for only a few years ago. Such was the boom-and-bust nature of the cycle. With new developments going up every few weeks, even a small footprint could allow for a new apartment building. I made a note on my pad to check the air rights and other relevant factors on the properties around the workshop.

Commonly, developers would buy up as much air rights and land as possible and put up the largest building they could manage. Anything with a view of the water fetched a considerable premium. Peninsular Drive wasn't far from the canal but with the right position it could likely see the beach and breakers too. It was the most concrete motive I could think of, but it was going to take some research into property acquisitions in the area. Hopefully, I could find who was buying up land on Peninsular Drive.

"Okay, Wendy, I'll tell you what. I'm willing to work your case, if that's what you're looking for. I'll need access to the workshop to take another look around and hopefully this time without being disturbed by the police, I might turn something up. But there is still the matter of my fees."

"Mr. Kane, I have a little money in the bank saved, but I'm not working right now. The cash I do have is all we have, and I have the children to consider. I am not sure what you charge but I fear my budget might not allow for it. I came largely in the hope you'd found something, but I don't know that I can afford your services."

I didn't like to work for free, but I also couldn't sleep at night if I turned away a woman in such clear need of help. If she was innocent, and my gut told me her grief was genuine, then I was leaving her at the mercy of an insurer who didn't want to pay out and facing life as a single mum with three young children. And that wasn't something I could do and still be satisfied when I look in the mirror each morning.

"I don't work for free, Wendy."

Her face fell, and she blotted at her eyes with the tissue. "I understand."

I held up a hand. "But on the proviso that you tell no one about this arrangement, I'm willing to structure my fees a little differently. You've mentioned the insurers are withholding payment because of their doubts about the case. My deal is this—if I can prove without a doubt there was foul play and your husband indeed did not take his own life, they'll be forced to pay out his policy. I'm willing to wait on payments until the funds are released. If I find nothing, and they don't, then you pay nothing. No risk on your part, but should we succeed in clearing your husband's name, you would pay my rates as normal. They're set out in our fee agreement. Glenda out front will take you through them."

"You would do that?" Wendy asked.

"Not normally," I replied, "but I find myself wanting to help you, and you didn't dob me in to the police and because of that I'm willing to make an exception. Also, if you could, provide me with a key to the garage in case I need to take another look around."

"I have a spare here." She reached into her bag and drew out a key before placing it in my outstretched hand.

"Excellent. I will continue my investigation. In the meantime, I do have another appointment I must attend to, so I will take you out to Glenda who will guide you through how the retainer works. If you have any questions, simply ask. If anything comes to mind, please let me know as soon as you think of it."

She nodded as she rose from the seat. "I will, thank you, Darius. I can't tell you how much I appreciate it."

"Not a problem," I replied. Stepping out into the lobby, I found Glenda waiting, her book almost done.

"Glenda, could you please take Mrs. Mooney through our fee agreement and have her sign an engagement letter? I'm late for my next appointment."

"Late? You only just got in." Glenda raised an eyebrow.

"Indeed, but these cases don't solve themselves," I replied as I headed to the door. It wasn't technically a lie. I was heading to another appointment, but it was at the pub, and my main concern was about just how much the boys were going to make me pay for the fact I was ditching them early for a date.

I'd probably be safer chasing Mrs. Wheeler's ghost.

Pub Priorities. Friday, April 21st 1530hrs

I RACED HOME. THOUGH the day had started rather slowly and had promised an abundance of time, it seemed the fates had conspired to change that in a matter of hours. I'd gone from no cases, to two. First, Mrs. Wheeler, and now Wendy Mooney with her husband's high-profile murder. I'd also almost been arrested. Hopefully, with Wendy's backing, that particular obstacle would be a thing of the past.

Detective Hart certainly wasn't my biggest fan, which was a shame because under other circumstances I wouldn't have minded getting to know her a lot better. In my gut though, I had the distinct impression the only cuffs she planned to put on me weren't the fluffy kind.

Her dogged resistance to my involvement was only one perplexing element of the Mooney case. The more I learned, the more concerned I got. Esmerelda's gossip hadn't turned up anything about new developments, but then again that wasn't really the sort of tidbit that crossed her table.

The prospect that someone wanted the land the garage was on was a promising lead. I made a mental note to look into the other two killings. A lawyer and a banker. Perhaps they were also somehow involved in the expansion for whatever undertaking was being planned for Peninsular Drive.

Reaching my home, I pulled into the driveway and opened the garage door. Normally, I would have headed straight to the pub, but if I was going on a date, I figured I could use a little bit of polish. It wouldn't send the right message to show up in the same thing Courtney had seen me in this morning.

A series of feverish barks echoed behind the internal door that divided the house from my garage. I put down the roller door to prevent my eager puppy from shooting past me and into the street.

Max was the other reason I'd come home. He'd been promised a walk, and it wouldn't do to keep him cooped up all day and all night. If I was headed to the Wheelers after drinks with the boys, I wasn't going to have time to walk him later. I grabbed his leash off the hook on the garage's wall and opened the internal door. Max, all twenty pounds of him, tore through the crack and leapt excitedly at my legs. He was little, perhaps not the manliest of breeds, which my mates liked to give me no end of trouble over.

I squatted down and gave him a good pat, rubbing my hand along his back and ruffling his ears.

"Hey Maxie, how are you doing, boy?"

I never intended to have a dog, but life had been pretty lonely when I got out of the service. Overnight, I'd gone from a barracks full of brothers in arms, to a lonely two-bedroom house. Then one night, I'd come home and there was Mum with Max in her arms. One look at those big brown eyes and I just couldn't say no. His previous owner had moved to a unit that didn't allow pets and Max was destined for a shelter.

There was no way I could let that happen. We've been partners ever since. He's proved to be a great companion, often accompanying me on my cases. At times, he can be a little bit of a distraction, but he seems to possess the power to drag every woman within a hundred feet over to meet him and thus me. As far as wingmen go, Max is simply the best. I've taken him to Paradox more than once. Shameless, but I can use all the icebreaking help I can get.

The more I thought about Max, the more wisdom I saw in my mother's machinations.

"Ready for that walk, boy?"

He scampered as I fixed the lead around his collar. I snapped up a baggie on the way out the door – just in case.

Normally, we would head for the dog park, or on a weekend even down to the Spit. The Spit is one of the best dog beaches nearby, which makes it the perfect playground for Max, who loves to play in the sand and surf. Though he does frequently misjudge his abilities and end up submerged in the salty waves.

With the limited time I had to work with this arvo, we instead took a loop of the boulevard. Max, sensing time was short, decided he wanted to sniff every pole and letterbox on our walk, but I did my best to keep up a fair pace without short changing him too much of his promised play.

"Come on, boy," I said. "Dad has to get home and have a shower. I promise we'll do better tomorrow. Plenty of time to play."

Two thirds of the way home, Max spotted a cavoodle being walked by its owner, a haughty woman in her late forties that seemed capable of looking down at me, even though I was a good foot taller than her. She didn't think a lot of me, which was a shame because Max quite liked her companion and was prancing about trying to get her cavoodle's attention. I held tight to his leash as the pair approached.

About fifteen feet before she reached us, she turned and used the pedestrian crossing to make her way to the other side of the road, hellbent on avoiding us.

"Well, that's a little rude," I muttered to Max as I rubbed him behind the ears. "Don't worry, buddy, pretty sure it's me, not you."

Some of the local people didn't approve of my profession and frankly, while it had bothered me at first, I was quickly developing a pretty thick skin. If you wanted to snob me fine, but don't wrong my little Maxie.

We made it home, much to Max's dismay. He would have happily walked another two or three laps. I pulled some of his dog food from the fridge, filled his bowl, added some biscuits, then refilled his water before I raced for the shower.

Fifteen minutes later, I was standing with a towel wrapped around my waist, busily trying to wrestle my mass of sandy brown hair into something resembling anything other than a possum's nest. Giving up, I found a set of slacks and a decent open collared shirt in the cupboard. Throwing everything on, I took one last look in the mirror and raced for the car.

I noted just how much time had got away from me. The boys would already be on their first round. Beer waited for no man.

I cruised down to the pub and pulled in behind the historic building. If there was one thing I'd missed while on operational tours with the army, it was quality pub grub. The second I cleared the door, I spotted my mates carousing at a table in the corner.

I made my way through the throng of patrons and ignored the thrum of pokies coming from the room next door. The good old one-armed bandit was a fixture of pub life. I wasn't much of a gambler myself, at least not when it came to money, but the fact many others were served as the reason the food and drinks were so cheap here. Aussie pubs had learned their lesson well from Vegas. Bring them in with their bellies, run them dry at the tables, or in this case the pokies.

"Darius, you're late," Carl called as I approached.

It was a miracle Carl had beat me here, on account of the fact I was confident he didn't own a watch. Carl was a good few inches taller than me, and built like a brick dunny, all straight lines and sharp edges. He worked as a laborer in construction, largely so he could get out early enough to sneak in a surf at the beach before or after work. His tangle of sandy blond hair always looked like it was drenched in ocean spray and, with his big blue eyes and muscular form, Carl never wanted for female companionship.

If he wasn't a hulking giant, I was sure his exploits would have got him in trouble with the enraged spouses of women who had succumbed to his charms. Not that Carl really had to try. It seemed like most women threw themselves at him, each of them aspiring to be the next Mrs. Hannigan. Unfortunately, Carl was about as likely to settle down as Barney Stinson.

"Hey buddy, big day at the office, what can I say." I looked around the table. "Thanks for your help last night, chaps. Things got a little hairy with that lot."

"Don't mention it," Carl replied. "Saving a damsel in distress ... I should be thanking you. That story is going to get me more action than Hugh Heffner on a good day."

"You're a beacon of selflessness, Carl," I replied, "and as a thank you, next round is on me."

A cheer went up from the table as I sat down.

"Need any other help?" Sonny asked. "I could use a few more hours moonlighting."

He was drinking his usual lemon lime and bitters. Sonny would barely reach my shoulders on a good day, but he was at least two of me wide. He spoke in a quiet tone that was entirely at odds with the rest of his appearance. I was confident he could have had a dazzling career in the NRL but for the fact they tended to play on Sundays and Sonny didn't do that for the same reason he didn't drink.

Fear of God, or perhaps the more immediate threat of his wife Lucille that seemed to keep him in check. Sonny was a good sort. If anything, I got him in more trouble than he would ever have gotten himself in whenever he helped me on cases. His presence was certainly a powerful deterrent. Most troublemakers took one look at him and reassessed their life choices on account of how much they enjoyed having front teeth.

Not that Sonny often lost his cool, but if you did manage to rile the islander, heaven help you, because no one else would willingly get between you and him.

"A couple of new cases," I replied. "You boys heard anything about the Casper Killer?"

"The ghost running around offing people?" Doug asked. He was the last in our little band of brothers. Doug was on the skinny side, still waiting for a growth spurt that would never come, but made up for it with a thick mop of brown hair. Doug was a gamer with a love of magic and an infectious enthusiasm for a good book. It didn't surprise me one bit that he'd bought in to the ghost angle on my latest case.

"That's the one, and due to the fact we don't have any resident Ghostbusters in Surfers, one of the victim's wives has asked me to look into it."

"Is she hot?" Carl asked without any hesitation.

I hadn't noticed, but decided to spare her Carl's attention by dodging the question. "Carl, one of these days thinking with the wrong head is going to get you in trouble."

"If you did a little more thinking with it, buddy, you'd be a good sight happier," Carl replied. "Let me take you out tonight. We'll hit Cavill and find some young ladies eager to meet Surfers' most eligible paranormal investigator."

"I'm Surfers' only paranormal investigator," I replied. "Certainly the only one with an office."

"To-mah-to, to-mae-to," Carl replied. "You worry about the details a little too much. If anything, you get in your own way."

"Is that what you told yourself before bedding that constable's wife? I would have thought spending the night in lock-up would have given you plenty of chance for reflection."

"Nah, he's got his suspicions, but he can't prove a thing. If I'd known she was married to a cop, though, I might have steered clear. Only two kinds of people around here carry guns—cops and criminals. I try to avoid them both as much as possible."

So Carl did have a line, though if you asked me he was playing pretty close to it at times. If you believed him, danger was his middle name, but he was a good friend, never reticent to lend a hand.

My mates and I laughed for a few minutes, sharing stories from our day. I told them what I knew of the cases, or at least what had been reported by the paper. I trusted them all, but the last thing I wanted was for them to share a potential lead with the wrong person. Not that they were gossips, but it wouldn't pay to spread any misinformation either. As the time for my date drew nearer, I leaned on the table.

"Boys, I hate to break up the party early, but I have to head off. Let me grab another round."

"What? Leaving early?" Carl asked. "Have you got a hot date?"

I paused, probably a second too long.

"Oi, you do!" A broad grin spread across Carl's face. "Who's the lucky lady?"

"Early days yet, boys," I replied. "I'm not saying a word."

"Why? I might have met her," Carl replied. "Maybe I can help."

"That's exactly what I'm afraid of," I replied as I headed for the counter.

Leanne was working tonight. The attractive bartender was on the shorter side, but she was a curvy lass with dyed red hair that went past her shoulders. She sported a set of low waisted jeans and a spaghetti strap tank top that did its level best to distract me from holding her gaze. I suspected the owner had hired her to ensure a steady stream of male patrons eager to buy their next beverage.

"How are you doing, Darius?" she called as I approached the bar.

"Pretty good, Leanne. I was hoping I could buy the next round for the table. Two of whatever Carl and Doug have been drinking and a lemon lime and bitters for Sonny."

"And a rum and coke for you?" Leanne asked as she gathered the glasses. "You haven't ordered anything else in months."

Her smile robbed me of my witty response, so I resorted to tweaking my usual.

"Just a coke for me," I replied. "I've got to hit the road and I need to stay sober tonight."

"Where's the fun in that?" she replied with a wink as she got to work fixing the drinks.

Her words, I was sure, had gotten many men three sheets to the wind. Not that she'd ever let them drive afterwards. Anyone that frequented The Wave knew she had almost lost her best friend to a drunk driver. She did her darndest to ensure none ever left from her bar drunk. Once I'd seen her pull out a nine iron from under the counter to threaten a man who'd tried to leave when he'd barely been able to walk.

She was not to be trifled with.

"You're looking sharp this evening." Leanne took in my pressed shirt. She fixed my coke and set it on the bar. "Seeing a client, or maybe someone else?"

She raised an eyebrow when I didn't answer.

"Uh, the latter," I replied a little sheepishly. "First date."

"Congratulations. Who's the lucky girl?"

"Someone I finally had the guts to ask out," I replied, still playing my cards close to the chest.

Leanne set all four drinks on a small serving tray. "She'll be lucky to have you. Go get her, tiger."

I paid with my card and carried the drinks back to the table, Leanne's encouragement still ringing in my ears.

By the time we downed the drinks and I extricated myself from the boys, it was twenty to seven and I was hard pressed to make it to the Green Olive in time.

By the time I reached the restaurant, my heart was pounding. I looked down at my watch. Five past seven. Were my hands shaking? It was the first date I'd been on in months and while Courtney was flirty at Paradox, I was losing confidence in my ability to make meaningful small talk.

I brushed a trickle of sweat from my brow. I could diffuse a bomb; surely this couldn't be any harder than that.

"Late, nervous, and sweaty," I mumbled. "Come on, man, get it together."

I grabbed a tissue and wiped my brow, before brushing my clammy palms on my pants.

I took a long deep breath. "You've faced down terrorists, insurgents, and a mob of cold-blooded killers in a graveyard at night. You can do this."

As a cold sweat ran down my brow, doubt chose to set in.

Dinner Dalliance. Friday, April 21st 1910hrs

I HAD MADE A terrible mistake. Waiting to meet a date was more stress inducing than diffusing an IED.

My heart pounded steadily as I made my way into the restaurant hoping I hadn't kept Courtney waiting.

The Green Olive was a neat upmarket restaurant, all wooden tables with white tablecloths and red and white serviettes. The dining area was split into two sections, one for families, the other filled with smaller two person tables more suitable for a date.

A small bar ran along the side wall and a large kitchen stood out back.

I scanned the restaurant, looking for any sign of Courtney, while I tried to remember what the best etiquette for this situation was.

She wasn't in the waiting area, or at the bar. Had I beat her here? Should I wait in the lobby? I didn't want to appear impolite and part of me was starting to fear that I might get stood up.

What if she'd had second thoughts? I was a few years older than her.

Get it together, Darius.

I approached the maître d's station.

"Can I help you?" A middle-aged man in a pressed white shirt and black slacks asked.

"Table for two, please," I replied. "The reservation is under 'Kane'."

He looked at my distinct lack of companion and gave me a sympathetic smile. "Of course, sir, right this way."

He guided me through the restaurant, set me down at a table, and spread the napkin over my lap.

"I'll keep my eye out for your guest, sir. Might I have their name?"

I was just about to open my mouth when the chair on the other side of the table slid out, its legs dragging across the timber floor before a young man sank down into it.

It took me a moment to recognise Tommy, Courtney's partner in crime from Paradox. He was wearing a red collared shirt and jeans, and had a broad smile. At least this one didn't feel like it was at my expense.

"Good to see you, Darius," Tommy called as he spread a serviette over his lap.

"Here are the menus," the maître d' said, whipping them out from under his arm and setting them before us. "Would you like anything to drink?"

"I'll have a glass of the house red," Tommy replied.

"Lemon, lime and bitters," I added. Best to be sober given I was clearly being ambushed.

"Very well," the maître d' replied. "I'll be back with your drinks shortly."

An awkward quiet settled over the table.

"Courtney isn't coming, is she?" I asked.

"No," Tommy replied.

What was his game?

"You saw me write the note."

"I did," he answered, playing a little coy.

"Well, we both know that note was meant for her."

"Of course it was, but Courtney gets hit on relentlessly and the poor dear is too kind to say no. The last weirdo she went out with had five ferrets. Five, Darius. And that was the least unusual thing about him. The poor girl went on three dates with him. They're not even legal here in Queensland. What sort of nimrod has bootleg ferrets?"

Ferrets were a little outside of my wheelhouse, but I could certainly see the picture he was painting for me.

"So you thought you would come and vet me, huh? Make sure I wasn't hiding any exotic pets, or have a closet full of skeletons literal or figurative?"

"You catch on fast," he said. "If Courtney won't look out for herself, someone has to."

Tommy's deception might have bothered others, but truth be told, it was kind of nice to see him looking out for his friend. It was the sort of thing I could get behind.

I might not like the way he'd inserted himself into my night, but on the other hand, he could have just turfed it into the trash.

In a roundabout way, his presence was a compliment. I was in with a chance.

The maître d' placed the drinks on the table. "Are we ready to order, gentlemen, or do we need more time?"

"I'm good to order," Tommy replied. "I picked out mine while I was waiting at the bar."

He was presumptuous but not obnoxious. I looked down at the menu, deciding what I might do.

"Unless, of course, Mr. Kane has somewhere else to be?"

If he wanted to play first date chicken with me, he was going to need more than that. I shook my head.

"I've been looking forward to this all day. Order away. I'll work out mine momentarily."

Tommy leaned forward across the table. "You're serious? You're not going to kick me out, or head on home?"

I laughed. I remembered what it was like to be young and living on a shoestring budget. "I invited you to dinner and I'm a man of my word. I won't be sharing a plate of spaghetti or anything like that."

"You should be so lucky." Tommy grinned as he picked up his wine.

"I wouldn't dare to be so presumptuous," I added, "but there's no reason we can't enjoy a nice feed and get to know each other. You want to look out for your friend. You'll do that best by getting to know me a little better, and we can enjoy a great meal while we do."

"You're alright, Darius," Tommy said. "The town might think you're mad as a hatter, but you're alright."

"Let's not rush to judgement," I replied. "The night is young, and I'm starving."

"In that case, I'll have the fettuccine, thanks," Tommy said to the maître d'.

"Make that two," I replied, holding up two fingers. "My friend here is clearly a man of taste."

"An excellent choice, sir," the maître d' replied. "Would you like anything to start?"

I shook my head. "I'm happy to wait for the main attraction."

"That makes two of us," Tommy replied. "Hard to interrogate my suspect with a mouth full of garlic bread."

The maître d' headed for the kitchen to place the order.

"How long have you been working at Paradox?"

"About six months," Tommy replied. "Courtney got me the job. We're old friends from school."

"Nice. What do you do when you're not making lattes and laughing at customers' clumsy attempts to flirt with your colleagues?

"I'm studying a double degree, law and justice," he replied.

"Heady stuff. What are you going to do with it?"

Tommy smiled. "I'll probably work a few years in a firm here on the coast, then perhaps open my own practice. Not sure what area of law yet though."

I was just about to follow it up with another question, when Tommy raised his hands. "You might be the investigator, but I'll ask the questions here.

I picked up my lemon lime and bitters. "By all means, I'm an open book."

"Paranormal investigator? How does one get into that line of work?" Tommy leaned forward in his seat.

I took a long swig of my drink. "To be honest, I kind of just fell into it. Before this I was in the army. Ever since I left, I've been trying to find my feet. A friend of mine suggested I give it a go. He runs a similar agency in the United Kingdom. He sorta showed me the ropes."

"So you believe in ghosts and witches then?" Tommy asked, clearly trying to measure my sanity.

"Not really," I replied, "but my clients do, and so I'm here to help look into things others might overlook or flat out ignore. The police are busy. They don't have time to chase ghosts, even if those ghosts are ripping off pensioners. So if people are convinced they've got a ghost, and the police don't have time to spare on that sort of thing, I take a look around. It's that simple. More often than not, I find a mundane cause at the root of the matter. My clients think they have paranormal problems, hence paranormal investigations."

Tommy nodded. "Interesting. So you don't feel like you're bilking people out of their hard-earned cash?"

"Not at all," I replied. "They bring me a problem and I fix it. I don't play into their paranoia or talk up their superstitions. They have a problem. I solve it."

"If you're dealing with criminals, surely it's dangerous?"

"Most of them are more bark than bite," I replied, trying to play the danger down.

Tommy stroked his chin. "I read about the Crypt Killers."

"There is always an exception, Tommy. But when I served, I was in the SAS. I met far worse than them."

"So you're a badass?"

I laughed. "I acquired skills that have come in remarkably useful now that I have repurposed them to helping others. It's turned out to be a good fit. I help people move past what's bothering them and at the end of the day, I can look myself in the mirror and feel good about what I do."

"Sounds dangerous," Tommy replied. "You're not worried one of these loons will hold a grudge? The way I see it, you're lucky the Crypt Killers didn't put a bullet in you."

"Some people call it luck. I like to believe it's the intersection of preparation and opportunity. Sure, I didn't know quite what I was getting myself in to, but I walked in there with my eyes open, mindful of what was going on around me, and we took a group of killers off the street."

"You're like Batman but poorer," he replied with a laugh.

"I'm no vigilante. I can't just go beating people senseless, but I do defend myself. At the end of the day, I usually end up presenting facts and evidence, either to my clients, or to the police. This isn't Hollywood. You can't go around cracking skulls and expect to carry on a business."

"But you could," Tommy replied.

"I don't understand."

"Crack a skull. You could defend yourself, if push came to shove."

I didn't know what he wanted to hear, so I gave him the truth anyway.

"I did two deployments in Afghanistan," I replied. "We went door-to-door hunting for insurgents, protecting civilians and disarming weapons that would have killed dozens of innocents. I have no trouble defending myself or those I care about."

"Fascinating." He set down his glass of wine.

The maître d' brought our meals, and we tucked in. The interrogation seemingly over, we exchanged small talk about the news, including the Casper killings. I didn't tell Tommy I was on the case. I didn't want him thinking I might put Courtney in danger.

The meals were delicious and as the clock rolled past nine-thirty, it was almost time to head to the Wheelers. Given I wasn't going to be getting up to anything more exciting, there was no reason I shouldn't make a start on the Wheelers case, before this would-be ghost caused any real problems.

As he finished his fettuccine, Tommy set down his napkin. "Most men would have spat the dummy the moment I sat down, upset that Courtney hadn't showed, or worst still be embarrassed to be sitting here, seemingly on a date with another man."

I shrugged. "I needed to eat and so did you. You're certainly pleasant company. I guess I'm surprised you didn't have anywhere more interesting to be."

If I was being honest, the whole affair had been far more relaxing than a date would have been. Perhaps I'd needed this more.

"Don't you be flirting with me," Tommy replied, goading me.

"I wouldn't dream of it. Incur the wrath of your boyfriend? No, thank you, but seeing as you have a little time on your hands and you clearly have a mind for finding answers, I was considering offering you some work." I leaned forward. "If you're up for it."

"You want me to work with you? Catching ghosts?" Tommy asked, raising his eyebrow.

"The next ghost I see will be my first," I replied. "But for now, I could use someone who knows their way around the law, is handy with a computer, and knows how to find information others might want to keep hidden."

Tommy straightened up in his seat. "Tell me more."

"I need a researcher who can garner information without getting into trouble. I'll pay you for your time, of course, and you'd be free to do it around your other commitments."

"What would I be researching?"

"I'll give you a current example," I took out a small notepad and a pen to jot down details for Tommy. "I'm working a case. One potential angle involves a party that is buying up land in and around Peninsular Drive, potentially for a development. I know they're approaching landowners, but I don't know who they are. Their transactions should leave a trail. But digging around will take time I can't really spare right now."

"Peninsular Drive, that's where the Casper Killer's last victim was, wasn't it?" Tommy looked at me sternly.

"Indeed, it was," I replied. "The victim's wife came to see me today. She gave me the lead, but she doesn't know who approached her husband. Now that he's dead, they are hardly going to come out of the woodwork while the police are investigating the murder. They could be responsible, or they could be unrelated."

"And you want me to do what exactly?" Tommy asked, setting his fork down on his plate.

"I want you to find out anything you can about transactions in the area," I replied. "Anyone buying land, any development applications that have been filed, and anything else you might think relevant. Put that fine legal mind to work. Bundle up your findings and send it over. If you feel like researching the other victims too, it might help me build a profile."

"And you'll pay me for my time?" Tommy asked, eyeing me closely.

"I certainly will. And it won't be minimum wage."

Tommy mulled it over. "It does sound interesting..."

"If there's one thing I can assure you, Tommy, there is seldom a dull day."

I tore off the notes I'd made and slid the page across the table.

The maître d' came by the table. "Is everything to your satisfaction, gentlemen?"

"It was excellent, but I'm afraid I've got to be going so if you could bring the bill, that would be marvelous."

He returned a moment later with a small vinyl folder. I slipped my credit card into it.

"You don't have to pay for dinner," Tommy said, reaching for the bill. "I always intended to pay my share."

"Don't worry about it," I replied. "This one is on the boss. Future wages will be cash, at least until I get my payroll sorted properly. Are you in?"

Tommy smiled and pushed his knife and fork together on the plate. "When do I start?"

I pulled out my business card and set it on top of the note page. "Start as soon as you're ready."

"It's that easy?" Tommy asked.

"That easy," I said. "In the meantime, I hope you'll excuse me. I have a case I'm working this evening."

"Working the case after a date?" Tommy replied, waggling his finger. "You were expecting to strike out, weren't you?"

"Uh, it's a flexible case," I replied, trying not to sound like as much of a bucket of nerves as I had been on my way into the restaurant. "I don't like to be presumptuous, and I'm a little old fashioned that way. Besides, there is a lovely lady who will rest a little easier without a ghost pilfering her possessions."

"And what are you going to do if it's a real ghost?" Tommy asked.

Taking my credit card back from the maître d', I slipped it into my wallet. "I'll cross that bridge when I come to it."

"Darius," Tommy said, getting out of his seat. "I, uh, know your pretty into Courtney...but she's single because she wants to be. Not for lack of choices. She collects nice guys like you, has some fun, and then she moves on. She doesn't mean to, but she leaves a bit of damage in her wake. You seem like you're looking for more than that. Just thought I'd give you a heads up."

"I thought she was your friend," I said, a little confused.

"She is, and she's lovely, Darius, but the lovely ones can break your heart too. Trust me on that. I've found that out the hard way."

He was warning me.

And I wasn't quite sure what I wanted to do with that. On the one hand, part of me wanted to go for it and have my fun while I could. Another part of me knew I wanted more than that from life.

"Thanks for the warning, Tommy. I'll keep that in mind. In the meantime, I have a ghost to bust."

I headed for the door, wondering what exactly waited for me at the Wheelers.

Ghostly Ganders. Friday, April 21st 2215hrs

On reaching Sally Wheeler's house, I had to reconsider my approach. I'd expected a small, four-bedroom house in suburbia, but the address she gave me led to an impressive property at the edge of the hinterland.

I should have expected that anyone with the cash to burn on valuable sports memorabilia likewise had the means to purchase a nicer home. The Gold Coast hinterland stretches into the hills to the west. Away from the coast, the woodland landscape became green and lush.

The increased elevation also gave many of these homes a view of the water they might not otherwise enjoy. If Australia had landed gentry, this was where they would live.

The trip took longer than I'd planned, and I stashed my car several houses away to avoid arousing suspicion in whoever might be taking advantage of poor Sally. I didn't for a minute believe she had a ghost, but someone was stealing from her, and I resolved to discover who it was.

I slipped my pack over my shoulders and hiked up to Sally's property. It was after ten and Sally and her new husband would likely already be in bed. Hopefully I would be able to set up my surveillance and find a position to wait for their sticky-fingered spectre to arrive.

As I walked through the dark and sparsely wooded yard, a bird warbled from somewhere beyond the tree line. At least, I figured it was a bird. The sound was awkward, and unpleasant enough to cause the hairs on my neck to react.

"Easy, Darius," I told myself. "There's no such thing as ghosts."

Some places I'd visited had given me the creeps though, whether genuinely haunted, or simply possessing the unpleasant atmosphere that seemed to attend places with a history of human cruelty. It was as if the air itself was tainted with misery. Or perhaps that was my imagination.

Here, the air was crisp and clean. Drawing a deep breath, I tried to put such unpleasant thoughts from my mind.

The Wheelers' home was a beautiful Queenslander, a raised two-story home. The bottom floor was an open garage and storage area, whilst all the living space was on the second floor. A beautiful veranda wrapped right around the house, allowing the Wheelers to enjoy spectacular views in almost every direction.

Sally had left a key in the garden for me, but if at all possible I wanted to avoid having to enter the house where I would disturb the people inside – I didn't want to cause them any further trauma.

Moving through the yard, I found her rose bushes and identified the gnome she mentioned in her text. Flipping it over, I pulled the key from inside and slipped it into my pocket, just in case.

I had changed out of my date attire and was wearing a simple outfit intended to help me blend into the darkness. The black and green camouflage covered as much skin as possible, and a black beanie pulled down tight helped to keep my hair in check. I moved through the woodlands around the house putting my training to best use to stay out of sight.

If any neighbours saw me, they would almost certainly call the police. But here on the Wheelers' property the nearest neighbors were a good half a kilometer away and spotting me through this much brush in the darkness would require a sheer fluke. On the downside, anyone else sneaking into the Wheelers' home would likely benefit from the same coverage.

I moved through the woods and did my best to guess where my quarry might approach from. A firebreak behind the property was wide enough to fit a vehicle down it. I suspected they were parking there and slipping through the brush to the house.

I checked the approach myself. Confident that I was alone, I made my way up onto the patio. Circling the house, I set cameras as I went, tucking them in discrete locations behind plant pots, and pointed at the stairs and other avenues of approach. Several were positioned in windows facing the house's main internal thoroughfares.

I did my best to avoid creaky timber slats, but on the patio, it was next to impossible.

Queenslanders were largely timber constructions, and I imagined every breeze that blew through it contributed to Mrs. Wheeler's belief that she was being haunted by her husband. The creaking of anyone moving around out here certainly wasn't going to help.

I had to be careful to ensure the cameras were not easily identified by our thief, so I couldn't place as many as I might have liked.

I also had a camera strapped to my chest. My investigations frequently got me involved with the police, and to avoid unpleasant 'he said, she said' scenarios, I liked to have recorded evidence of what actually transpired.

With my cameras in position, I retreated off the veranda to wait. I found a small stand of trees that provided an excellent view of the house, but was off the beaten track for anyone sneaking in from the fire trail. From my place here, I could observe the rear of the house and its eastern front.

I hunkered low and pulled a camouflage blanket out of my bag to spread over me. Someone would have to just about step on me before they realized I was here.

The real danger in these parts was the wildlife, though. Australia was home to the world's most venomous snakes and most of them could be found here in southeast Queensland.

Most common perhaps was the eastern brown snake or the red belly black. Both were distinctive and quite dangerous should one find themselves in close proximity. I'd spent my youth and teenage years hiking these trails and considered myself fairly competent as an outdoorsman.

It was the love of nature and the outdoors that had taken me into the army. A desire to see the world. Unfortunately, the parts of it I had seen weren't the kind they showed you in the brochures.

I hunkered a little deeper into my nest and waited. Most people hated waiting, but I found it gave me ample opportunity to think and plan. If anything, I was grateful that I was still awake – it's easier to avoid nightmares if you manage to avoid sleep. Not an entirely sound long-term strategy, and certainly not one any qualified therapist would recommend, but it would do for now.

And it was going to come in useful for helping Sally Wheeler deal with whatever miscreant was praying on her superstitions.

Minutes turned into hours, the temperature dropping steadily as the clock passed midnight. I was grateful I'd set up shop here in Queensland and not in the colder southern climates. The cities down south might be bigger, but the weather was infinitely worse.

Here, in winter it would drop to freezing, and we might get a little frost on the ground, but I couldn't remember the last time it actually snowed here. Snow days never happened at school, though flood days did, when the torrential rain would swell the rivers, cutting us off from making it to school.

All was quiet in the Wheelers' yard, but in spite of myself, a sinking feeling settled in my gut. I hadn't seen so much as a mouse approach the house, but the second it crossed my mind to question if this was a waste of time, I thought I could make out something moving in the darkness.

Having long since learned to trust my instincts, I pulled out my phone and flicked through the cameras, cycling from screen to screen. As I flicked through the kitchen camera, a black silhouette passed out of the camera frame right as I switched to it. I rustled back through the cameras, flicking from one to the next as quickly as I could until I reached the living room. The black shape passed by the camera again, humanoid but hazy, as if the camera was struggling to get a good view on it. The darkness didn't help, and my current earnings couldn't spring for night vision.

One thing was certain: something was moving around the Wheelers' house.

"How did you get in there?" I whispered.

I'd been watching the approaches to the house. No cars had come or gone that I'd heard.

Since the moment she gave me the case, I'd been convinced one of Mrs. Wheeler's children were making off with their father's possessions. Probably in an ill guided attempt to save them from her new husband.

Now I was forced to reassess my thinking. If they'd passed through the yard, I would have caught them, or I had underestimated my foe.

Stashing my pack, I made my way to the house. Rather than try the front door, I headed around to the laundry, on account of the fact it was a simple timber door rather than a screen that was likely to clatter as I opened and closed it.

I slid my key into the well-oiled lock. Slipping inside the house, I eased the door shut behind me.

Something was definitely moving around. It was quiet, but it was there. Slipping off my shoes, I set them aside. I didn't want the heavy soles to give me away.

My thick woollen socks moved silently on the polished timber floor as I made my way through the house. My heart rate picked up as my body anticipated the hunt.

I stalked quietly through the house, making my way to the lounge room. I perched in the hall, capturing what I could on my bodycam.

The thief was no ghost, that much was clear. For one, both its feet were on the ground, and it was walking, not drifting idly about.

The intruder moved confidently, bending over the recliner and fiddling with an unseen lever to raise the footrest. He slid about the room, relocating simple objects like the TV remote, perhaps part of his ploy to terrorize Mrs. Wheeler into believing her husband had truly been there.

He continued the charade before stopping in front of a cabinet full of assorted collectibles. Reaching inside, he grabbed a hand full of gold commemorative coins and other knickknacks and loaded them into a small fanny pack. Then he picked up a football and tucked it under his arm.

From the way he worked, it was clear this wasn't the thief's first visit. He moved with familiarity, picking out the trinkets with the greatest value.

As he loaded things into his pouch, I hit the light switch, flooding the room with light.

The thieving ghost leaped like a frightened cat. Of course calling him a ghost was a misnomer; he was as human as I was, and dressed in similarly black clothes, though he wore a stocking cap to obscure the details of his face.

"What the...?" he started, but I was already moving across the room toward him. Hefting the football, he hurled it at me.

I swatted it aside and dove forward, crash tackling him into the recliner. The recliner tilted back, slamming into the floor where it pitched us onto the carpet. The sound of it striking timber echoed through the house and I suspected it would soon rouse Sally and her husband from their slumber.

The thief was fast, rolling to try and get on top of me. His first blow was aimed straight for my chin, and it was only instincts born of training that had my arms high enough to deflect the blow. His second blow went into my stomach, forcing some of my wind out of me.

Catching his wrist, I twisted it hard and kicked off the timber floor, throwing him off me. He hit the coffee table hard, letting out a grunt of pain.

He tumbled across the floor, scrambling for his footing. Reaching into his bag, he pulled out a small knife. I looked at him and looked at the knife.

"You ought to put that down, or one of us is going to get real hurt," I said. I was gambling heavily that only one of us had spent the better part of a decade practicing close quarters combat in the army.

"Get away from me," he said as he brandished the knife.

"What kind of ghost needs a knife?" I taunted as I took a heavy book off the coffee table. He shuffled around the other side of the table as I continued to circle. I wanted to stay between him and the door. There was no way I was letting him out of here. Then I realized I'd discounted the window.

He lunged forward, the knife racing at my chest.

Raising the book, I realized it was a photo album. I jammed it into the path of the oncoming blade. The knife pierced the pages, and I yanked the album to the side, twisting the blade out of his hand. I let both clatter to the floor and dove across the coffee table, crash tackling the man. He hit the couch, and I landed on top of him. Before he could move, I delivered two hard blows to his ribs. I say hard, but if I'm being honest, I was holding back. I had the advantage and wanted to stun him, that's all. When the fight left him, I gripped his left arm, twisting it behind his back. With my weight pressing into his back, the fight was over.

Just to be sure, I applied enough pressure that if he continued to struggle, he would dislocate his own shoulder.

"You are going to want to stop moving before you break something," I advised.

The idiot flailed a little, but with all my weight resting on his back and only the soft couch to try and leverage against, he didn't succeed in getting any real momentum. For good measure, I found his right arm and twisted it behind his back to join his left and held them down with my knee.

I reached into my pocket for a pair of zip ties. They were already preformed into loose circles which I slipped over his wrists and pulled them tight. In the absence of a set of handcuffs, zip ties can be remarkably effective. A trained operative would know how to break out of them, but most civilians were more easily detained.

"Tom," Sally cried from down the hall.

"It's just me, Sally, Darius," I called back. "We're in the lounge. Come and take a look at your ghost."

Her slippers padded down the hall. She appeared in the doorway, in a dressing gown that had been hastily pulled tight and tied at the waist.

She took one look at me, one look at the ghost and muttered, "Tom, what's going on?"

"You know him?" I asked.

"Yes, Darius, that's my husband," she whispered. "What on earth is going on?"

I sighed. I'd expected it to be her son, but I'd been off on that one. Turned out, her son's instincts for his new stepdad had been right on the money.

I patted Tom on the back. "You, sir, are going to have some explaining to do."

Sally's hands went to her head. "I don't believe it! I just don't believe it!"

"Sally," I said. "If you'd be so kind as to call the police, they'll take him into custody, and you can decide what to do next."

I pulled the stocking off her husband's head. He looked decidedly ashamed as I patted his cheek.

"Don't worry, Sally, I caught the whole thing on video. There will be plenty of evidence should you wish to press charges. But for the time being, at least you know there's no ghost to contend with."

I sat him up on the couch before leveling my finger at him.

"Don't you move. We already have you for theft and assault with a deadly weapon. You won't want to do anything else the police might take an interest in."

Sally took three steps across the room and slapped her husband hard enough his head whipped around.

I couldn't help but smile. The woman had spirit.

She shook her finger at him. "You!"

"Sally, the police, please."

Sally stomped out of the room and dialed the police.

"Who the hell are you?" Tom asked as his soon to be ex-wife left.

"Just a guy that makes a living stopping con men like you from taking advantage of people. I hope you've got a good lawyer. You're going to need it. Two, perhaps. A criminal and a divorce lawyer might be necessary, though I'm not sure there's much the second one can do for you."

We waited in awkward silence until the slow but steady wail of sirens grew. Patrol cars were making their way up the hill. It wouldn't be long now.

As I watched their lights flash from the window, I found myself muttering, "Anyone but Hart please. The night's been long enough already."

Robert's Retirement. Friday, April 21st 2330hrs

Robert Minders startled awake, his throat hoarse from the piercing scream that echoed through the room. A cold sweat rolled down his face as he kicked at the thick doona that felt like a weight pressing down on his chest.

Only as he saw his bedroom coming into focus did Robert breathe a sigh of relief. The nightmare had felt so real. The ghosts had been everywhere, and try as he might, he couldn't outrun them. Whenever he'd changed rooms, they'd simply drifted through the wall, their terrifyingly transparent forms haunting his every move.

As the nightmare faded and clarity returned, Robert panted for breath. Leaning back on his pillow, he rubbed his eyes and tried to breathe to calm his nerves. His heart pounded a relentless rhythm as he tried to come to terms with the awful dream. Why had the ghosts been after him in the first place?

Guilty. Guilty. Guilty. Their relentless rasping cry had harried his every move.

Guilty of what? Robert had never done anything to them. Robert considered himself an upstanding citizen, he didn't even jaywalk.

Robert reached for the glass of water he kept on his bedside table, his hand bumping the glass and spilling a little as his tired fingers flailed for it. Wrapping his hand around the glass, he lifted it to his lips, spilling a little down the front of his nightshirt.

Setting it down, Robert shook his head.

"I'm going to need something much stronger than that," he muttered as he swung his legs over the side of the bed and into the slippers he kept there. "This is what I get for watching the news."

He groaned as he made his way out of the bedroom. News of the Casper Killer was everywhere, some ghost killing innocent people all over the Gold Coast. First it was in the papers, now the nightly news was carrying the story. Normally these things wouldn't have affected Robert, but he'd first taken note of the story when Victor Sellers was brutally murdered.

The news always seemed so cold and distant, but it became a whole lot more real when you knew the victim.

Robert hadn't known him particularly well. They crossed paths in a courtroom years ago. Sellers was eloquent and fast spoken, and his argument had been quite compelling.

Robert tried to put the case from his mind as he made his way downstairs and into the kitchen. He pulled a few ice cubes from the tray in the freezer and tossed them into a glass before heading for his study.

After all, that was where he kept his best liquor.

The death of James Mooney the other day had made the Casper Killer impossible to ignore. The premature demise of a once acquaintance was something Robert could set aside. After all, Victor Sellers must have argued hundreds of cases in his time.

James Mooney's death shattered all notions of coincidence.

Robert's decanter was sitting right where he'd left it, on his mahogany bookcase. The glass stopper was ajar, resting on the lip at an awkward angle, but Robert pulled it off and set it down before pouring himself a whisky. Without hesitation, he threw his head back and downed the liquor in a few heady gulps.

James Mooney. There was a name he would be happy to never hear again. The whole affair had wasted months of his life, and for what? Nothing. Nothing had come from the entire sordid matter. Now eight years later, it was robbing him of his precious sleep.

Robert sighed as he poured himself another scotch. If nothing else, he wanted to sleep through the night. Surely these nightmares were simply the function of an overactive mind. Now that he was retired, time weighed heavily on his hands.

"You've got to get yourself a hobby, Robert," he muttered to himself. "Take up gardening, or lawn bowls."

He laughed. He didn't know where to even start on either hobby.

A rasping whisper carried through the house like a restless breeze. The hairs on Robert's neck stood on end.

At first, Robert thought he was simply imagining it, but the sound came again. Only this time it was closer.

"Did I leave the window open again?" he asked himself as his heartbeat grew faster.

The haunting whisper came again, only this time it was louder and clearly coming from inside the house. His house.

"Justice." The word was clear in spite of the wheezing rasp that attended it.

Robert picked the phone off the receiver and dialed 000 as quickly as he could. The phone rang as Robert raced to the door of the study.

“Guilty.” The wheezing rasp was even closer now.

It was the same voice he’d heard in his dream. He knew what he would find.

A white translucent shape, bigger than he was, drifted down the hall toward him.

It had a form, like a man, but moved unnaturally, hovering over the ground as it made its way inexorably towards him. It didn’t rush; it didn’t need to.

Robert’s voice caught in his throat as he tried to scream. His heart pounded relentlessly as if beating in sync with the frenzied crescendo of an orchestra.

"Operator,” the voice in the phone announced. “Do you need the police, fire, or an ambulance?"

"G-Ghost," Roberts stammered as the ghost reached the door of his study.

"I'm sorry, sir, could you repeat that? I couldn't quite understand you. It sounded like you said ghost?"

Robert Minders felt a stabbing pain in his chest. He bent over his desk, his eyes rising to the decanter on the bookshelf. His breath came in short, ragged bursts as his head swam.

What was happening?

"Sir, are you there?" The operator called.

Robert dropped to the floor, clutching his chest, unable to breathe. The phone slipped out of his open fingers, bouncing across the carpeted floor.

As Robert's eyes closed, footsteps thudded down the hallway, but before they could reach him, Robert's heart seized up.

A Familiar Face. Saturday, April 22nd 0100hrs

THE SQUAD CAR PULLED into the long driveway and made its way up to the house. I waited on the front timber steps, praying that fate would be kind to me.

As the two police officers climbed out of the vehicle, I breathed a long sigh of relief.

The familiar face of senior sergeant Fitzgibbons was a welcome sight. The sergeant and I met when I'd been working the crypt killers' case and my fortuitous timing built considerable goodwill with the veteran sergeant when I'd shown up at a most opportune moment.

He was in his forties, of medium height and build with his blond hair cropped short. His uniform was well worn and faded from hours spent outside in the sun. It was a good two or three shades lighter than his partner's, a young constable whose eyes possessed that eager 'fresh out of the academy' look. One hand rested on her heavy belt, laden with the tools of the trade as she took note of me in my all-black attire.

Her mousy brown hair was pulled back in a bun: tidy, efficient, practical.

Fitzgibbons must have recognised me by the porch light because he let out a chuckle. "When a woman called the station rambling about a ghost, and a thief, I ought to have known you would be involved."

"You know me, Fitzy," I said. "I can't just sit idly by while a gold digger swindles his unsuspecting spouse. Going to have to let you down on the ghost front though; she married the man. He didn't slip in through the walls as some spectral apparition. He's packaged and waiting for you in the lounge."

"The rest of the officers on shift are going to be disappointed," Fitzgibbons replied, pausing at the bottom of the stairs. "There was a pool going as to just how crazy she was."

"I hope you didn't pitch in," I answered. "I'm afraid she's rather sane. Just superstitious."

"Superstitious enough to hire a ghost buster," Fitzgibbons said. "Things have a way of working out in your favor, Kane."

"Good fortune is often found at the crossroads of preparation and opportunity." I looked down at my watch. "You two made good time, getting out here this quickly. Quiet night in town?"

Fitzgibbons glanced at his partner before responding. "Between you and me, anything with the word ghost in it is getting priority attention at the moment."

"The Casper killer," I muttered, kicking myself for overlooking the possibility. "I should have figured that might trigger an alarm."

Anyone or anything that drops three bodies in as many weeks is going to have the unfettered attention of the Queensland police service.

"Indeed. Now that it's on the front page even the mayor is putting pressure on us to get something done."

Interesting. Fitzgibbon's words confirmed what Hart and her partner had alluded to earlier. The police were treating the cases as connected. But why? What did they know that I didn't?

"Poor old Mayor Tom." I chuckled. "At times, I think he cares a little bit too much what the newspapers say, and not enough about what the people in this town really need."

"The paper drives the votes," Fitzgibbons replied, "and if there is one thing the mayor cares about, it's getting reelected. I've never seen someone so adept at turning the media to his own end."

"And we remain stuck with him, I guess. Lucky us. One of these days we'll end up with someone who cares about fixing things for the community rather than the next election."

"From your lips to his ears." Fitzgibbons nodded toward the sky.

"So what do you know about the Casper killer?" I asked.

Fitzgibbons rested his hands on his hips. "Why do you want to know? How did you come to be involved in that mess?"

Fitzgibbons was proving a little more guarded than I expected. I wasn't sure whether that was because of the case itself, or the presence of his rookie. Talking about an active investigation was usually frowned on.

"The victim's wife came to see me," I said as I rose to my feet and stretched my back. "She wants me to investigate. It would seem the insurers are trying to call it suicide. They don't want to pay out on Mooney's policy. She's staring down a future without her husband, no source of income, and three young kids."

"So you took the case," Fitzgibbons muttered. "Of course you did."

"You know me," I replied with a shrug.

"A sucker for a damsel in distress. One of these days, that's going to get you into trouble."

"Perhaps, but for the time being I'm doing my best to get others out of trouble."

"Why don't you just leave the policing to us?" his partner asked. I could almost feel the disdain born of her newfound authority in her voice.

Fitzgibbons turned to her. "Easy, Hitchens. The coast has its share of problems, but Darius Kane isn't one of them."

"A glory hound with an appetite for fame. At best he's in the way, and he'll get himself or someone else hurt," she replied.

Fitzgibbons held up his hand. "Slow your roll. There aren't nearly enough of us to go around, so you can dispense with that us-versus- them mentality. You need to recognise that we have a lot of friends and allies in the community. Valuable resources that can save lives."

"But he—"

“But nothing.” Fitzgibbons shook his head. “I almost died last month. I was alone in a graveyard looking at a hole that a bunch of murderers planned to dump my body in. My family would have never found me. I'd have been dead, and they'd have never got any closure.”

Hitchens went still as Fitzgibbons recounted our harrowing experience with the Crypt Killers.

“As I knelt there, unarmed and waiting for a thug to put a bullet in the back of my skull, Kane showed up, thirty meters away and in the dark. He's a hell of a shot and the only reason I'm standing here today."

"Everyone gets lucky from time to time," I replied, growing a little uncomfortable as the sergeant laid it on thick.

"Screw lucky," Fitzgibbons replied. "You solved the case before we did, and you had the stones to take that shot. It gave me enough reason to look up your service record. That was no lucky shot."

I shifted my weight from one foot to the other and leaned on the rail running down the stairs. "I hope we never have to find out. Is there anything you can tell me about the case? I've only just taken it and the third scene was scrubbed down pretty well. I haven't checked the others, but with the time that's lapsed, I imagine they'll be clean too."

Fitzgibbons folded his arms. "I'd love to give you a head start, but this one is being handled by the Surfer's station. Best I can do is make a few calls to see what I can find out."

"Appreciated," I replied. "I wouldn't mention me though. They didn't appear too accommodating when I ran into them today. That Hart, she's a piece of work, huh?"

I was on a fishing expedition, so I led with my most promising bait. I didn't even know the other detective's name. Given her disposition and striking looks, I figured Hart would be well known.

"The detectives at Surfer's are a bunch of hard arses on a good day," he replied. "And Hart is right at home there."

"I see." I made my way down the stairs.

"That's not on her though. Surfer's can be a hard beat and I'm sure she's weathered her share of crap from inside the department and out."

I didn't doubt it. With the figure she cut, I imagined she'd copped some serious flack on her way through the academy. I'd hoped for a little more information to go on, but sometimes those were the breaks. I would have to start from scratch in the morning.

"So what's waiting for us up there?" Fitzgibbons asked.

I pointed up at the house. "The wife, Sally Wheeler, engaged me to catch her ghost. She believed her ex-husband was haunting her and pilfering his more expensive possessions. Turns out it was the new hubby playing on her superstitions and flogging the stuff off for whatever cash he could get."

"That's just low," Hitchens chimed in.

"On that we agree," I replied. "You'll find him in the living room, ready for pickup. Don't take any nonsense from him. I have oodles of footage of him being caught in the act. I'd be happy to send a copy over to assist in his prosecution.

"Very good, Darius. We'll take it from here."

"Have a good night, sergeant," I replied, stepping off the stairs to make room for them both.

"Get some sleep, Kane," Fitzgibbons called after me. "You look like you need it."

I waved him off with one hand as I headed for the stand of trees I'd left my backpack in. I slung my pack over my shoulder and started the hike back to my car. Despite the late hour, I had a spring in my step. It might not have been the night I was hoping for, what with Tommy's date ambush, but I'd closed Mrs. Wheeler's case in record time.

Given how things turned out, I suspected she was going to be a little upset with the outcome. No one liked finding out their spouse was a scoundrel. Once widowed, now soon-to-be divorced. She was having a rough run in that department.

I would wait a day or two before sending my invoice, just to be sure she'd had time to calm down.

The trip back to my car was uneventful, something I was grateful for. With the adrenaline of the fight behind me, I was running out of steam. Climbing into the driver's seat of my truck, I fired up the engine.

By the time I pulled into my garage and closed the door, it was just after 0200hrs, which made for a much later night than I had intended. I was glad Mrs. Wheeler's husband was an impatient thief. I'd expected to spend a few nights staking out the Wheelers' house.

I set my pack down in the study. I would download the footage tomorrow. For now, I needed sleep.

In my bedroom, I changed into boxers and a T-shirt and found Maxie curled up in a ball on my bed waiting for me. My little partner was already asleep. There was a faint little wheeze as his stomach rose and fell. I snuggled in beneath the covers and dozed off.

Sleep came swiftly. In a fortunate mercy, my dreams stayed at bay, or perhaps I was too tired to remember them.

All too soon, a pounding racket carried through my house.

The thumping was followed by Max's frantic barking.

I looked at my alarm clock. Seven-forty-five am. It was too early for chuggers, the charity muggers that went door-to-door championing whatever cause was paying their salary this week.

I dragged myself out of bed. My body could function on less sleep, but I really shouldn't make a habit of it. I might have become accustomed to it over the years, but as my mother liked to remind me, I was getting older.

The knocking continued.

Rubbing my eyes, I headed for the front door.

My faithful hound was leaping at the window, messing with the blinds as he tried to see who was out front.

"Quiet, Maxie," I called. "I'm here now."

I paused with my hand on the timber door. "Who is it?"

A familiar feminine voice called back, "Queensland Police Service, Mr. Kane. We would like to ask you a few questions."

Unwelcome Houseguests. Saturday, April 22nd 0745hrs

I WASN'T IN ANY state to receive visitors. But from the insistent pounding on the door, I doubted my on-again off-again friends at the Queensland Police Service were going to take a rain check. I could almost smell Detective Hart's disdain through my front door.

"What now?" I grumbled as I grabbed a pair of pants from a basket of unfolded laundry I'd been successfully ignoring for two days. I slid the shirt over my head and scooped up Maxie, running my hand down his flank to calm him down.

"Easy, boy," I whispered as I turned the lock on the timber door. "Let's see who it is."

I swung open the front door so that I could look through the external security screen.

Sure enough, the two detectives from Mooney's workshop were waiting on my front step. The burly veteran wore the same faded grey slacks and white pressed shirt with a few wrinkles in it. Either he had a wardrobe full of the same outfits or he'd not changed since yesterday. Either seemed just as likely.

His partner Hart, on the other hand, was wearing a different power suit. This one was navy blue and well pressed. Her hair was pulled into a high ponytail, and not a hair on her head was out of place.

"Well, this is an unexpected delight," I muttered. "Detective Hart and, sorry, I didn't get your name yesterday?"

I looked at the veteran who stared past me into my home.

"Gibson," the detective replied, his eyes not meeting mine.

I did my best to play nice, despite them waking me. It wouldn't do to antagonize them, particularly not now that I was working the same case they were.

"Detective Gibson, delighted to see you. May I ask what you're doing here on my doorstep at such an early hour?"

"We have a couple of questions we would like to ask you, Mr. Kane," Hart chimed in. "Is now a good time?"

A loaded question, if ever I'd heard it. Were they really going to take a walk and come back later if I said no? Not likely.

"I guess it's as good a time as any," I replied. "Now that you've woken me up."

Gibson ignored the remark, but he did meet my eye for the first time since I'd opened the timber door. "May we come in?"

"Well, I dunno about that, detective. That depends if you brought-"

"A warrant?" Hart cut me off. "Do we need one? Are you hiding something, Mr. Kane?"

Her smile showed her polished white teeth and was about as genuine as a used car salesman.

I sighed. "I was going to say coffee, detective. But it seems you left that at the station, along with your sense of humour. Not to worry, I'm sure I can rustle something up."

Hart's smile faded. Clearly, she wasn't used to being made light of. In fact, I was confident men often fell over themselves to see that she got what she wanted. Not this man. I knew well the dangers of dating above the line on the crazy-hot matrix.

I flicked the latch on the screen door and pushed it open.

"By all means, come on in."

I led them into the lounge room. My furniture wasn't much to look at, just an old leather sofa and a recliner that faced toward the TV. I'd inherited both from my parents when they upgraded a while back. The furniture was worn, but more than good enough for me and the boys to watch the game on. In hindsight, I was pretty sure my mum had used the opportunity as an excuse to make sure I had some furniture. I was something of a minimalist.

I motioned to the sofa. "Grab a seat."

"Cute dog," Hart said. waving at Max, who let out a low growl.

I took my seat on the recliner and gave him a reassuring pat behind the ears. "Yes, he is. And an excellent judge of character. Usually. He's probably just a little cranky that he hasn't had his breakfast yet. He can get a little hangry in the mornings."

The two detectives looked at each other and something passed between them. The three of us sat there in an awkward silence and given they were in my home, I waited for them to fill it.

Yesterday they threatened to arrest me for trespassing. If they had, I might have been in some strife, but now I had a signed engagement letter from Wendy Mooney. I was well-positioned to answer any follow-up questions they might have come up with.

"It's an interesting thing, Mr. Kane," Gibson began, "but when I spoke to Mrs. Mooney, she gave the distinct impression she had never heard of you,"

"That is interesting," I replied. "Or at least it would be if it were true."

"You're saying she was lying?" Gibson countered, this time a little faster.

I shrugged. "Perhaps she wasn't sure what to say. You two come off a little gruff and intimidating. And she is grieving, detectives. You really do need to take that into account."

"So you're going to continue with this charade?" Hart asked, leaning forward in her chair.

"I'm not sure what you mean?"

They were going to need to do better than that. I'd been interrogated by the finest trainers in the armed forces. They were considerably less gentle and played by a different set of rules to the detectives.

"This charade that you're working for the widow when she had no idea who you are." Hart's voice rose. "What were you doing at the garage?"

"As I said yesterday, I am simply working the case."

"Working it for whom?" Hart asked, drumming her fingers against the armrest of the couch.

"I told you, I'm under no compulsion to disclose my client's identity but seeing as it's clearly causing you some distress, I have a signed engagement letter from the victim's wife."

I made my way across the room and plucked up the key she'd given me the day before.

"I also have this key to the garage that she gave me to further my investigation."

Hart was first off the mark. "You smug bas-"

"Please, detective, there are children present." I patted Max's head as Hart fell silent. I tried not to smile, but was failing miserably, so while I was up, I grabbed the container of Max's biscuits and poured some into a bowl before refilling his water. I set him down and he raced out of my hands to dive into his breakfast.

When neither of the detectives said anything, I pushed a little. "I hope you didn't travel all the way out here just for that. I could have told you as much on the phone."

"Uh..." Detective Gibson started as he framed his next line of attack.

"Not to worry, you're here now. Are there any other questions I can assist you with?"

"Mr. Kane, you appear tired," Hart chimed in.

"A natural byproduct to having been woken up," I replied. "What of it?"

"The bags under your eyes," she added. "Indicative of someone who hasn't had enough sleep for some time. I would have thought you had the freedom to choose your hours, Mr. Kane."

"I do choose my hours, detective. Unfortunately, so do the criminals I deal with and most of them tend to be nocturnal."

"Yes, far easier to break and enter under cover of darkness. Less chance of being caught," she replied a little smugly. "Though it can wreak havoc on one's sleep schedule. Or maybe that's just a guilty conscience keeping you up at night."

I sank back into my armchair, trying not to let the barb get under my skin. "Look, detectives, I feel that I've been rather patient with this nonsensical expedition you two seem hellbent on exploring, but you are quickly running out of runway, so get to the point."

"Or what?" Hart replied. "You seem a little irritable. Did I touch a nerve?"

Her pillowy lips parted slightly as she smiled.

"No, detective," I replied, meeting her stare. "It's your ignorance that bothers me."

Her mouth snapped shut, her eyes growing a little wide at the insult.

I ploughed on. "If you'd bothered to do your research, you would know that in my previous career, I served with distinction in our Armed Forces. While you were picking what you'd wear to your high-school formal, I was preparing for deployments in Iraq and Afghanistan. I've seen things that would haunt your dreams for the rest of your life like they do mine."

The room went deathly still.

"So, detectives, while I've done my best to humour this excuse for an interrogation, I will not have the scars of my service mocked by those who weren't there to see the price we paid for them."

I let that linger. Hart might have been pretty to look at, but the more she spoke the more irritating I found her. She had the ability to get beneath my skin and I couldn't quite put my finger on why.

"Watching an empty garage yesterday, hassling returned servicemen today? Is it just me or is it a slow week for you guys? I thought there was a serial killer on the loose and here you are in my living room, and for the life of me, I can't figure out why."

Gibson cleared his throat. "Mr. Kane, my partner is clearly unaware of your history and meant no disrespect. I believe what she meant to ask was where were you last night between the hours of ten and two?"

Hart shot a look at her partner, her fingers balling up into frustrated fists as he put words in her mouth.

I'd been at Sally Wheeler's catching her new husband before he could pilfer all her remaining possessions.

"Working a case," I replied, finally realising what this really was.

"Can anyone corroborate your whereabouts?" Hart asked, turning her attention on me rather than her partner.

"Certainly, why?" I replied.

"I'm afraid we're going to need to speak with them then," Detective Gibson replied with a steady matter of fact tone.

"And why is that?" I asked, glad that for once I had a rock-solid alibi for my whereabouts.

It was Hart who broke first. "Because there was another death last night."

Distracted Detectives. Saturday, April 22nd 0800hrs

I STARED AT THE detectives, not sure whether to laugh or be offended. The silence in the lounge room grew increasingly awkward by the moment.

Eventually, I couldn't help myself. "So let me get this straight. Your serial killer has dropped another body and instead of running down that fresh lead, you're here questioning me? Why? Because I happened to visit the scene of a crime?"

"We are running down every possible lead," Hart replied. "You didn't just visit the scene of the crime. You gave us a dud story about being hired by the victim's wife when clearly, she'd never met you."

"She's hired me to investigate her husband's murder," I replied coldly. "We've been over this already."

"Now, perhaps," Gibson added. "But that wasn't the case yesterday, was it? You might have been able to suck her into your story, but we won't be so easily manipulated."

I shook my head. "Are you out of your collective minds?"

Both detectives stared at me.

"Discard all the other reasons that this is mental and look at the killings themselves. Can you identify a single solitary reason I might have for any of this? What motive do I have for killing James Mooney or any of the others for that matter? Until I read about them in the paper, I didn't know they existed."

"Perhaps you're a sociopath and you just enjoy the hunt," Hart replied. "The killer is clearly disciplined, well trained, and growing bolder by the day. Answer the question. Where were you last night between ten and two?"

"Working a case. Where was the body found?"

"We'll ask the questions," Gibson replied, all pretense of friendliness gone. "Can anyone corroborate that?"

"Easily," I replied. "I was at a client's home in the hinterland. It was a surveillance job. I have extensive footage of the case and it just so happens that I closed it shortly after midnight. So at the time in question, I was handing over a scumbag to two of your colleagues. They'll corroborate my story in its entirety."

"Is that so?" Hart straightened her suit coat. "And their names?"

"Constable Fitzgibbons and his new rookie. Have a long talk with them. Perhaps they'll be able to disabuse you of this ridiculous notion that I'm involved. I'm an investigator. I'm only doing my job."

"And we are only doing ours," Gibson replied, "running down every possible lead. No matter how tenuous it might be."

"Tenuous is the word for it," I replied. "Speak with Fitzgibbons. If after that you want to have an intelligent discussion about who is dropping bodies in our town, I'll be all ears. But for the time being, detectives, I have work to do."

The detectives looked at each other. Hart rose from the lounge first.

"Stay away from our case," she said, fixing me with a stare. "We don't need your antics costing anyone else their lives."

"As I've said, I've been engaged to solve this case. I'll not be intimidated into idleness. You know where the door is. See yourselves out."

Gibson nodded along. "We'll see you later, Mr. Kane."

I sat in silence. There was nothing to be gained from antagonizing them further, though it certainly took every ounce of self-restraint I had not to.

The officers strode to the door, Gibson trailing behind the overzealous detective Hart. Irritating though I might have found her, I couldn't help admire the shape her figure cut in that pantsuit as she stormed out of my house.

"That's the kind of thinking that's going to get you into real trouble, Darius," I muttered to myself.

As the screen door swung shut, I got up and locked it behind them. The ridiculous interview had disrupted my morning, and I couldn't help but wonder why the two detectives were so fixated on me. I couldn't have been the first PI that had run across one of their cases.

I pushed the thought aside as a more harrowing realization settled over me.

If they were focused on me, it meant I was the best lead they had. Which wasn't promising.

The killer was more capable and dangerous than I'd anticipated. Four crime scenes and no evidence to go on.

Were we dealing with a genuine ghost? My logic and reason pushed the proposition aside, yet still the thought lingered there at the back of my mind.

Picking up my phone, I found a message from Glenda.

The journalist would like to speak to you over morning tea at the surf club.

Hopefully, Holly Draper could shed a little light on the case. I was eager to see what she might have turned up at the other two crime scenes. Seeing as Fitzgibbons had nothing, and Hart and Gibson weren't sharing, I needed something to go on. Something told me when Fitzgibbons spoke with Gibson and Hart, they weren't going to be particularly forthcoming. At least not after this morning. If I wanted evidence from the other scenes, I was going to have to go elsewhere to get it.

Making my way into the kitchen, I threw together a quick protein shake. Plenty of blueberries, frozen banana, spinach, peanut butter, and linseed all blended up with a few cubes of ice. I wasn't much of a breakfast eater, but the healthy snack was my compromise. It tasted better than you'd expect, perhaps because I left out the kale. I always left out the kale because no one needed that kind of punishment in the morning.

Downing it, my thoughts returned to the case - a fourth victim in such a short time frame. If the murders were all related, and I had good reason based on the detective's behavior to believe they were, then the killer was accelerating his timeline.

The gap between James Mooney and this latest victim was only a matter of days. Whatever the killer's agenda, more blood would surely be spilt if they weren't stopped.

I sat down at my computer and opened my email, fully intending to start researching the other victims as soon as I cleared my inbox for the day. To my surprise, there was an email there from Tommy.

It stood out because the subject line read, "Thanks for dinner, dear."

The incorrigible young man made me laugh.

Out of curiosity, I opened the email expecting him to be having another poke at my expense. Instead, I was confronted with dozens on dozens of attachments and a text wall that could have passed as a PhD thesis. At the top was a short note.

Dear Darius,

Thanks for dinner and for the job opportunity. I've never been an investigator before so I'm not sure which of these will interest you. I included everything I could find. Let me know if you need me to dig deeper into anything in particular. Four and a half hours worked.

Regards,

Tommy

I scrolled down to find a small dossier on the first victim. Charlotte Stanley. She was forty-two years of age at the time of her death and working for one of the country's leading banks.

According to Tommy, her specialty was lending and finance, and she had been well regarded both by the bank and her peers until her untimely demise twelve days ago. Tommy's research matched what I had read in the paper.

Charlotte had died of electrocution when her hairdryer fell into the bathtub. The police hadn't found any evidence of foul play and the scene had little to lend itself to the theory of a serial killer.

According to Tommy, she was single, and her social media profile revealed she hadn't dated anyone in recent months.

Her death was clearly unusual, but there were no readily apparent motives for why anyone might have wanted her dead.

I moved on to the second victim, criminal defence lawyer Victor Sellers. Victor had been gunned down in the car park of his firm. Police believed it to be the act of one of his clients. A few newspaper clippings had been scanned into the attachments and neatly referenced in Tommy's notes. In red text was a line that read: Possible connection to Peninsular Drive.

I read on. Tommy's dossier on James Mooney didn't add anything I hadn't already come across. Having spoken with his widow and been through the garage, I was familiar with the publicly available information regarding his death.

I scanned Tommy's notes again and began to notice a pattern.

Charlotte Stanley was found locked in her house. No sign of forced entry. It was one of the reasons the police had initially ruled it an accident. Victor Sellers died in a locked parking structure that should have been inaccessible to the shooter. Shot several times in the stomach; it was an ugly way to go.

James Mooney died in his garage.

If it was one and the same killer, then that person had a proficiency for getting into and out of areas both undetected and without regard for locked doors. I made a note on my pad. Security specialist?

At the bottom of the email was the name of a fourth victim. At least that was what I thought it was until I realised that Tommy, who had worked half the night, wouldn't have even heard of the latest victim yet.

Which made me wonder who on earth Benjamin Marino was.

The name seemed familiar. I pulled up a search engine and punched it in. Up came a page full of results, including pictures of a man in his forties with jet black hair swept neatly to one side, his thickset arms wrapped around two impossibly attractive models. Some sort of party was raging behind him, and I realised where I knew the name from.

Benjamin Marino was the self-styled party-magnate of the Gold Coast. He ran a string of nightclubs and ruled his empire from its headquarters, a strip club down at Broadbeach. Marino had been a person of interest suspected of participating in a number of crimes, though none of them ever seemed to stick. Like water off a duck's back, evidence, witnesses, and compelling testimony always seemed to disappear long before he got a day in court.

If I had to guess, I would stake every dollar to my name that Marino ran at least one of the organized crime rings on the Gold Coast.

Beneath his name and occupation, which Tommy had listed as 'sleaze bag', there was another note. Marino was discreetly buying up land in Peninsular Drive through a number of companies he controlled.

According to Tommy, Marino wasn't a director of any of the companies, though Tommy had attached a government search showing that Marino, or entities he controlled, owned a majority of the shares in the companies doing the acquiring.

Marino, it seemed, was trying to hide his growing interest in Peninsular Drive. Interesting.

Attached to the email was a development application that had been filed with the city, along with a series of contracts for deals settled along Peninsular Drive already. The development application showed his intention to erect a series of residential buildings along one entire side of the street. More than a dozen properties had already been acquired, including properties on both sides of the commercial unit James Mooney operated out of.

If his current progress continued, Benjamin Marino would soon own the entire street. The undertaking was massive, and the potential revenue from that many properties was staggering.

How had no one noticed this?

The police ought to have been banging down his door, not mine.

Money was a powerful motive and hiding behind some fictitious spectral killer certainly seemed to be keeping the town distracted. I considered the other victims, and the situation made more sense.

How many of the mortgages in the area had been written by Charlotte's bank? I suspected more than a few of them. Victor Sellers could well have represented Marino or some of his goons. Perhaps Sellers had grown greedy as the massive project got underway. Was Marino silencing him in preparation for taking over the town? If Sellers had secrets that could damage the mob boss's reputation, it would explain why he'd wound up dead.

James Mooney was in the way, that much was clear from the map. If Marino had intentions to develop the area, then Mooney's own dreams of expanding his workshop fell right in the middle of Marino's proposed domain.

A theory was forming swiftly. I had no idea who the fourth victim was, but I was willing to wager they had something to do with Marino's scheme to take over Peninsular Drive. If I could find out their identity, I might just be able to work out what his next move was before he made it.

I smiled to myself and murmured. "Way to go, Tommy."

Hitting reply, I pounded out a response.

Great work. Very thorough. Send me your bank details. I'll get you paid today. Also, are you able to track any connection between Marino and Sellers? Is there anything in the court records?

For a day that had started off as a dumpster fire when the detectives chose to stop by, things were starting to look up. I had found my first solid lead on the Casper killings. Unfortunately, if Marino was responsible for this mess, it upped the danger factor considerably. Marino wasn't a lone wolf; he had an entire organization behind him.

I doubted he was doing the work himself. Someone like Marino would hire a professional. An individual with the skills to bypass the security precautions these victims had taken. I wasn't going to be dealing with a jaded lover here. There could well be a hitman working the Gold Coast and if I wasn't careful, I was going to end up square in his sights.

I archived the email for later reference and skimmed through the rest of the box, my gaze landing on one with the subject, YOU HAVE BEEN WARNED.

I clicked on it. The email address was a nondescript Hotmail account with a series of letters and numbers.

The body of the email was a few short sentences.

You should not have transgressed in our affairs. My lord Beelzebub is coming and at his arrival you will burn. You purloined our sacrifice. We shall find another.

The email had no signature, but I hardly needed it. The cultists I'd rescued Callie Masters from were holding a grudge. Outnumbered on the night, I hadn't had much choice but to withdraw and tell the police what I'd found at the construction site.

Given the fake ceremonial knife, I had assumed they were more bark than bite. Considering the email, perhaps I'd misjudged them.

The most surprising element of the entire matter was that they appeared to have identified me in the chaos and darkness. I scratched my scalp as I considered this unwanted escalation.

If nothing else, they had shown a willingness to kidnap. So they weren't entirely benign and deluded. On the plus side, I was single. If they intended to sacrifice someone in my circle of influence, it was a narrow field to choose from.

It really had to be my parents, Max, or one of my friends. I laughed at the thought of them trying to apprehend Carl or Sonny but sent them a warning text anyway.

Perhaps I ought to spend the night at my parents tonight, just in case. I doubted the lunatics would try anything during the day but come nighttime, who knew what they were capable of.

There was a slim chance that they were simply trying to scare me, but I wasn't in the habit of taking threats lightly. I would deal with the cultists in due course, but I had more pressing issues to tackle first.

I needed to know if Marino and his goons were the Casper Killer, or whether there were multiple problems brewing in Peninsular Drive. Once I cleared the case, I would track down my old friend, the high priest, and see if I couldn't break his nose again for good measure.

I knew I shouldn't, but I hit reply anyway.

Simmer down, Cinderella. I'll deal with you shortly. If I were you, I'd clear out of town. I hear the police are looking for you.

I didn't wait for a response, I shut down the computer and threw on something more suitable for being outdoors: jeans, t-shirt, and boots. I grabbed my leather jacket off the coat rack, topped up Max's bowl, and made for the door. Max let out a pining bark and I stopped.

"Hey, don't be like that. I'll be home soon, I promise. And tomorrow you can spend the whole day with me."

He looked at me, begging me with those big brown eyes.

"I'd take you with me, but things are getting a little dangerous and I don't want anything to happen to you, buddy. I'll see you soon."

I ruffled his coat and then slipped into the garage, closing the door behind me. Moments later, I rolled out of the drive in my Ute.

Reading Tommy's email had given me some ideas. I'd assumed that the killer had snuck into the garage to commit the murder. But if I was dealing with a professional, there was another option. James Mooney had been inside the garage and would have heard someone trying to break in. I wasn't putting any stock in the drunk hostel operator's account of the ghost. No, I had a better idea.

Given that I'd found the back seat of the old Datsun down, I now wondered if I had given it the proper consideration it deserved.

What if the killer had been inside the garage the whole time?

What if he had been smuggled into the workshop inside the car? It would explain the damaged boot, and how the killer had taken James by surprise so easily.

It also meant that my skepticism about the old car being repaired was on the money. It could actually have been the vehicle the killer used to get inside the garage.

Had a similar strategy been employed at the law firm? I would run that down later. For the time being, I was operating on the premise that the Datsun had been used by the killer to smuggle himself into the scene.

I needed to take another look at that car and find out what, if any, paperwork James Mooney had on the owner. It was possible they'd left a fake identity, but at this point anything could help. All I needed was a connection to confirm my growing theory that Marino was behind this. If I could find it Benjamin Marino was going to have a horrible day.

I tapped my hands on the steering wheel. Hiring Tommy had been a spot of genius. The mass of information spoke to his work ethic, and his turnaround had been sensational. If he kept this up, I was going to have to steal him from Paradox.

I arrived at the surf club a few minutes early, eager to compare notes with Holly Draper. Part of me was rather looking forward to meeting her. I was bound to get along well with anyone who irritated Detective Hart.

The surf club was an old two-storey brick building overlooking the sand dunes and the Spit. As far as meeting places went, it was one of my favorites. The salty sea breeze and view of the water was quite relaxing.

I took the stairs two at a time, until I was struck with the realization that I had no idea what Holly Draper actually looked like. At the landing, I was just pulling out my phone to do a search on the journalist when a hand came to rest on my forearm.

"Darius, so nice of you to meet me for lunch."

Lunch Liaison. Saturday, April 22nd 1130hrs

THE FAMILIARITY OF THE hand on my forearm made my heart beat a little faster. A woman stood at my side. Her striking red hair was cut at her shoulder and curled in toward her face. Her piercing green eyes were hidden poorly behind wire-rimmed glasses. She wore a white blazer with those big shoulder pads over a black dress with a gold belt that seemed to serve little function other than to draw attention to her slender waist.

I swallowed to clear the lump forming in my throat. "Miss Draper, lovely to meet you."

One of the woman's eyebrows shot up, her head cocking to the side ever so slightly.

“Darius, I believe there has been some sort of mistake,” she said slowly. “My name is Mary Baker. Your assistant said I should meet you here?"

Baker, Baker, Baker. Glenda hadn’t mentioned anyone called Mary Baker.

"You're sure you spoke with Glenda?" I asked, trying to work out what was going on.

The woman smiled. "Yesterday, twice."

It took me a moment to realise what had happened, and when I did, I tried not to let the disappointment register on my face.

Glenda, distracted by her latest book, had confused the two messages. I tried not to groan audibly as I realised that meant she had palmed off Holly Draper and instead booked me in for morning tea with a psychologist. As I stood there in the door of the surf club, I wondered if it had indeed been an accident. She had been recommending I speak with someone. Was this her way of making that happen?

I started to get a little indignant at the thought of Glenda presuming to know what was best for me. I would get help on my terms, not have it thrust upon me.

Mary patted my forearm. "Shall we find a seat?"

Mary might have had a year or three on me age wise, but she was undeniably attractive. The more I looked into those deep emerald eyes, the more I struggled to come up with a good reason not to go along with her. I wasn't in the mood to be psychoanalyzed, but Mary had as yet made no attempt to do so.

"We shall," I replied with a smile.

As I led her through the lobby of the surf club, I couldn't help but think that this was the second time in twenty-four hours I'd ended up sharing a meal with the wrong person. Though one glance at Mary had me inclined to believe she might be the universe making things up to me for Tommy stealing my date with Courtney. Good karma if you believed in that sort of thing, and I certainly did.

Mary smiled at me, and my nerves eased a little. It couldn't hurt to spend a few minutes with her. It was still early for lunch but when we reached the counter, Mary ordered a serving of fish and chips for each of us and reached for her bag.

"Oh, please, let me. I insist," I replied, going for my wallet. "It's the least I can do after this mix up."

"Mix up?" Mary asked. "What do you mean?"

I glanced back at the door. "Uh, before, when I called you Holly. Glenda was meant to be organizing a meeting with a potential source for a case I'm working on. She appears to have mixed up her messages."

"Dare I ask what she was meant to do with mine?" Mary asked, looking at me over the top of her glasses.

I swallowed as I led her to a table. I wasn't in the habit of lying so I leveled with her.

"I told her to throw it in the rubbish," I replied.

Mary slid into the seat, seemingly unperturbed. "Is that so?"

"Yes," I began as I sat down opposite her. "I thought you were going to try to treat me, and I'm not in the market for a psychologist."

Mary laughed. "Then it's a lucky thing for me that she didn't. You can relax. I'm not looking for a patient, just some insight."

"Into?" I asked leaning on the table toward her.

"We'll get there." She reached for a pitcher of water a staff member had placed on the table. "Would you like a drink?"

"Yes, please," I replied, moving my glass a little closer. "I must say, you aren't what I expected."

Mary filled my glass. "And what is it you were expecting?"

I laughed. "Well, for starters, most of the people who call my office are a little bananas. You, on the other hand, seem entirely in possession of your faculties. Which makes you something of a rarity."

"Well, that makes us a pair of rarities," she replied. "A paranormal investigator. I was more than a little curious to see if you're a superstitious fruitcake who lucked into the limelight with the Crypt Killers, or whether there was something more substantial to you."

Her eyes lingered on me as she spoke, her emphasis conveying the impression that she'd drawn a favorable conclusion, though from what I wasn't quite sure. I'd shown up expecting someone else and fumbled my way into lunch.

"Ah yes, the investigator thing." I tried to play it cool. "It does tend to give a certain impression, but it really is the best explanation for what I do. To be clear, I spend far more time disproving the paranormal than dealing with it."

"You don't say." Her grin told me that she'd surmised as much. I got the distinct impression she didn't subscribe to paranormal paranoia, which only served to further increase my opinion of her. Somehow, I'd lucked into lunch with an intelligent woman, overlooking one of my favorite beaches. My day was picking up by the moment.

"Your sign says Blue Moon Investigations. What led you down this line of investigation? I mean, there are plenty of PIs out there. Few of them brand themselves for the supernatural."

"That's probably why the work just keeps flooding in. You wouldn't believe how busy I've been."

Her smile widened. "Oh, but I would. I don't investigate bizarre occurrences, but I meet with genuine believers every day. I have clients who consult a horoscope before venturing outside. Another stops by their psychic on the way home from our appointments. At first, I wasn't sure how to take that, but you get used to it with time."

"I feel your pain." I laughed as our fish and chips hit the table. It was early in the day, but the lightly battered piece of fish looked incredible, and the chips had already been lightly dusted with chicken salt. My mouth watered as I stared at my plate.

"You wouldn't believe the stories I get told," Mary replied, picking up her cutlery. "The part that always gets me is just how intensely people believe in them. People are just so willing to set aside logic and reason and place both the responsibility and blame for their lives at someone else's feet. Ghosts, horoscopes, fortunes. Belief is a powerful force, Darius."

I couldn't argue that. I'd seen it firsthand with the cultists. One's beliefs could readily drive a man to acts of barbarity that boggled the mind or shaped one's soul into an instrument of peace and healing. Belief was a more potent influence than most realized.

"So you wanted to see if I was crazy too?" I replied. "It wouldn't be the first time someone has wondered. What's your professional opinion, doc?"

"Far too early to tell." There was a glimmer in her eye as she cut into her fish. "I think I might need to spend a little more time with you."

Was I imagining the sultry tone in her voice? Perhaps I really had been single for far too long. Or maybe Carl was right, and I just needed to get laid. The thought that Carl's stance on relationships might be valid wasn't a worldview I was ready to embrace.

I popped a piece of fish into my mouth, savoring it before picking the slice of lemon off the plate and squeezing it over the rest of the fish. That would do nicely.

As I chewed, I couldn't help but wonder why Mary was here in the first place. She didn't seem to be wanting for clients and I was quite sure I wasn't ready to see a psychologist. To be honest, I wasn't sure I needed it.

Sure, there were the nightmares, but I figured they would go away on their own. All I needed was time. Time and a world where everyone and everything wasn't trying to kill me. My last tour in Afghanistan was a trial by fire. I had seen the good and the bad, but in the end, it was the paranoia that got me. I was a coiled spring that just needed time to unwind.

"If you're looking for a client, doc, I don't want to disappoint you, but I don't think I'm in that sort of head space right now."

"Brutal honesty," she replied. "Fascinating. But don't stress on my account. I'm not on a recruiting drive and I think my professional body might have something to say about a 'flirt to convert' strategy for finding clients. They tend to frown on that sort of thing."

So she had been flirting. Was I really that rusty? My word, I needed to get out more. However, my investigator's instincts were firing at the back of my brain. If she wasn't here looking for clients, why was she here? She'd sought me out after all.

"So why did you call my office?" I asked. "You don't appear to be wrangling with a paranormal problem, and you aren't looking for clients. To what do I owe the pleasure of this lunch?"

Mary pushed a piece of fish around her plate. "I find people fascinating, Darius. I'm writing a paper on what drives successful people. After seeing your face on the news, I couldn't help but wonder what drove you. By all accounts, the Crypt Killers weren't idle thugs, they were killers, and yet you persisted. You showed remarkable courage."

I wasn't sure that I was the stuff academic papers were made of.

"I was just doing what needed to be done." I picked up a chip and devoured it.

"But what makes you do it?" she asked. "Is it the money? Is it curiosity? Or is it something else?"

I found myself nodding along as she spoke. I eagerly devoured another few chips before answering. Being the center of the discussion made me feel a little self-conscious. I didn't consider myself a hero. I was just doing what I knew how to do.

"Well, it all started when I got back from the service."

"The service? You were in the military?" Mary asked, seemingly surprised.

"Fourteen years. Did multiple deployments. I decided my most recent needed to be my last." I dug into my chips as I tried to think of how I could steer the conversation away from where it was headed.

"So not an accidental hero, a trained one." She shook her head as she spoke. "Fascinating."

"I didn't say that," I replied, worried that she might put that in her paper. "I just needed work."

"Modest too." Mary smiled. "Reports say you saved a police officer's life in that graveyard."

Try as I might, I couldn't discourage her from singing my praises. "Right time, right place."

"A pattern it would seem," she replied with that full smile. "Makes me wonder why a man like you is still single."

She was driving the pace of the discussion and part of me, the investigator side of me, realised I still knew almost nothing about her. She had an easygoing nature that made her easy to talk to.

"Who said I was single?" I asked, challenging her diagnosis.

"The lack of a ring on your finger, for one." She set down her knife and fork. "There is also how willing you were to come to lunch with a woman that you never intended to meet with."

"Perhaps I'm just a philanderer," I replied, testing her.

Mary laughed openly. "Darius, you could more easily pass yourself off as the pope. I would know. I've met my share of the former."

We ate quietly as her words hung awkwardly in the air between us. I was tired of being the topic of conversation. I wanted to know more about her.

"What made you want to be a psychologist?" I asked, hoping to revive the discussion with something a little more interesting than my obviously unsuccessful dating life.

"I love helping people," she replied. "Much like you. I just have a very different skill set."

She certainly was a good listener. I'd opened up more than I'd expected in the time we'd been eating.

"I love to know what drives people. I enjoy working out what makes them tick. Then if they want to change, I try to help them gain closure and move on with their lives."

I picked up another chip. "You study success. How do you measure yours?"

"Oh." Mary leaned back in her seat. "That's a good question. The healing process can be a tricky business. I suppose it is when my clients are finally able to put the past behind them and move on."

Moving on. That sounded nice. Unfortunately, in my case, it seemed far more easily said than done.

"And hypothetically speaking, how long does it take your clients to leave the past behind them?"

"Each case is different, Darius," she said, and I felt like she could see right into my soul. "But for those who work at it, they always get there in the end."

There was a momentary silence, before she spoke again.

"But when they do, I find it hugely fulfilling."

She had a passion to her that kept me on the edge of my chair. Or perhaps it was just watching her lips move. Those soft pillowy lips. I wondered how they might feel on mine.

Glancing down at my watch, I realised it was almost half past twelve. Somehow, we'd talked away an hour and a half and it felt like a matter of minutes.

Part of me wanted to stay, but I had an appointment with my parents this afternoon and still wanted to swing back past Mooney's garage.

Much to my chagrin, I needed to leave. I wiped around my mouth with my napkin.

"Mary, it has truly been a delight, an unexpected one perhaps, but a delight nonetheless."

“You’re not leaving already, are you?” she asked.

“I'm afraid I have other engagements this afternoon. I promised my parents I would join them for bingo and I’m a man of my word. Perhaps we could catch up again another time?” I heard the hopeful inflection in my own voice and prayed it didn’t come off too needy.

Her lips perked up into a smile. "Oh, I'd like that very much, Darius. I might linger for a little while. I do like to watch the water.”

I followed her gaze out to the beach where dozens of people went about their life.

"Watch the water? Or the people?" I asked.

"You caught me, Mr. Kane. Very perceptive. I’ve been watching that man on the striped towel, down there. In spite of the fact he’s clearly with his wife, he’s been unashamedly checking out those two fetching young ladies down by the water. I’m just wondering when his wife will catch on.”

I followed her gaze. Sure enough, he was staring after the two young women while his wife read a novel.

“I don’t know, but when she does, there is going to be hell to pay. So you don’t mind if I call you for dinner sometime?”

"Not at all. Your dear Glenda has the number. Call anytime." Mary smiled, and I resolved to call sooner rather than later.

I set my card on the table and slid it across to her. “You can also feel free to call anytime. No need to chat with Glenda unless you feel the need.”

Part of me felt a little guilty. Courtney may not have known it thanks to Tommy, but I had tried to ask her out, and here I was already looking forward to my next meal alone with Mary.

There was something different about her. I just couldn’t put my finger on it, but whatever it was, I liked it.

I nodded to the window. “Enjoy the show.”

Mary laughed and I made my way out of the surf club, a little spring in my step as I went.

As I raced down the concrete steps, I couldn’t help but laugh. An hour ago, I was ready to chew into Glenda for ignoring my instructions, now I wanted to give the stern old bird a hug.

She set me up with a psychologist, and it had gone better than I'd ever imagined.

There was a part of me that very much wanted to linger here. Returning to the scene of Mooney’s murder wasn’t nearly as enticing as another hour or two in Mary’s company.

But my gut was telling me I’d missed something at the garage.

Workshop Worries. Saturday, April 22nd 1400hrs

Armed with Wendy Mooney's key, I returned to the garage on Peninsular Drive. Rolling down the street, I searched about, curious to see if the detectives were still staking out the property. The unmarked car they'd been hiding in yesterday wasn't anywhere to be seen.

Parking in the workshop's carpark, I climbed down out of the cab of my Ute and made straight for the front door.

As I walked, I couldn't help but wonder why the police had been staking out the garage in the first place. Their technicians had already cleaned out the site. Had they found something of note? Had the police already come to the same conclusion I had - in a garage whose average customer seemed to drive expensive SUVs, the battered old Datsun was an anomaly.

Too old to be worth anything and too young to be an antique, it really didn't justify Mooney's time or expertise to repair. With the amount of work on his plate, I would have expected it to be relegated to the end of the line. But it had been up on the rack being worked on.

I suspected whoever dropped it off had paid cash and handed Mooney enough to motivate him to take a look at it immediately.

If they hadn't, the killer hiding in the boot might have baked to death in the heat outside. The thought also prompted an uncomfortable realisation. Mooney's killing had to be at least a two-person job. One to drop off the car with the second person - the killer - hiding in the boot.

The theory lent further credence to the notion that Marino and his goons might have had James Mooney killed. Esmerelda had floated a theory about Mooney's checkered past, but Marino's acquisition of the surrounding properties provided a far more compelling motive than an eight-year-old disagreement that had already been hashed out in the courts. If Mooney's death really had stemmed from his past, why had the killer waited so long to retaliate? And why the other victims? That didn't make sense unless there was a larger picture I couldn't yet see.

Benjamin Marino was squarely in my sights as the man with the most to gain from James Mooney's demise. If the police had come to the same conclusion, it was possible that they were staking out the garage to see if Marino or any of his goons returned to the scene of the crime. Or perhaps they were waiting to see if whoever dropped off the Datsun returned for it. After all, there could be evidence left by whoever had hidden in the boot. Torching it seemed the obvious solution.

Reaching the door, I looked back at the car park. There seemed to be fewer vehicles in it than yesterday. I supposed Wendy had been progressively returning the keys to the rightful owners. Several vehicles remained, but I doubted that would last long. Word of Mooney's death had spread pretty quickly.

I drew the key out of my pocket. There was no need to be stealthy now and even less reason to break and enter. It felt a little different entering through the front office.

At the receptionist's station, I scanned the vehicle log for the Datsun. As I suspected, it was the last vehicle checked in by Mooney on the day of his death.

Now that I knew the vehicle's significance, I was far more interested in who owned it and where it came from. I took the address from the register and punched it into my phone. The street existed, but the house number was at least twenty too high to be a real house. A fake address, but a carefully considered one.

I wasn't sure what I was expecting, but I doubted someone clever enough to smuggle themselves in the boot of a car was dumb enough to do anything by random chance. I made a mental note of the fake address. The optimist in me had been hoping for a break in the case, but clearly it wasn't going to be that straight forward.

Drumming my fingers on the log, I considered my choices.

As I did, I took heart from the fact that the address confirmed I was on the right track. The car had certainly been a tool. I considered trying to log into Mooney's computer again, but I doubted it had anything more useful than the register, so I left the office and made my way into the garage to take another look at the Datsun.

Only this time as I stared at the car, it wasn't just an odd car; it was the means by which the killer had smuggled himself into the garage. I kept that at the forefront of my mind as I approached the car. Even the best killers left some kind of clue. The perfect murder was a flight of fancy, a pure work of fiction. Reality was far messier.

I strode over to the car, stepping around a jerrycan full of fuel and a siphon hose that Mooney would have used to drain the tank on vehicles before he dropped them. Walking along the side of the pockmarked old Datsun, I looked a little closer.

The first time I saw the car, I thought it was pointless to fix a vehicle so clearly weather-beaten with hail. Now as I looked at those same pockmarked dents, I thought about it a little more. Hailstorms had grown more common, and anything with this much damage was normally written off by the insurer and wrecked. The Datsun shouldn't have even been on the road. If that was the case, then the Datsun had likely been purchased from a wrecker.

I made a mental note to check the nearby wreckers for sale records. Someone had to have sold it to the killer. Perhaps if I was lucky, they might even have some surveillance of the sale.

Opening the back door, I checked the rear seat again. This time I looked closer at the mechanism and noticed it wasn't broken at all; it had been jammed.

Jammed to allow whoever had been hiding in the boot to open it from the inside and make their way stealthily into the body of the car. That had to have been how they jumped Mooney. There was certainly no getting out through that boot.

Sneaking through the car itself was still a risky maneuver. Surely the mechanic would notice the seat dropping forward. Unless of course they waited until the Datsun was raised on the hydraulics. If they were willing to hide for hours in the boot of the car, they would be patient enough to wait for the ideal moment to spring their trap.

If they could slip out of the car quietly enough, they would have a chance to overpower James while he was working.

Looking around the garage, I searched for signs of a struggle. There was plenty of wear and tear—it was a workshop after all—but there were no obvious signs of whatever fight left James Mooney dead.

The death had been staged as a suicide, like Charlotte Stanley. The only real evidence to suggest it was fabricated was the scuffing on the hydraulics where

Mooney's makeshift noose rubbed back and forth along the paintwork as he struggled. Definitely not a suicide, but I still would have expected there to be more evidence of the fight. James Mooney was not a small man.

The killer must have got the drop on him.

I thought of the hostel worker's account of the ghost. It was possible he was drunk out of his mind, but what if he wasn't? What if something or someone had distracted the mechanic? A ghost? Perhaps not. But what if it was an accomplice? What if the same person who had checked the car in, came back that night and knocked on the door. That could have drawn Mooney's attention away from the garage and provided an opportunity for the killer to slip out of the car.

It would also have given the killer a lookout, someone to make sure they weren't interrupted while they staged the faux suicide scene.

Perhaps that was what the hostel worker had seen. The car's actual owner returning. If only they had video footage, we might have an actionable lead to go on. I cursed my luck that the hostel had killed its surveillance the night of the attack. Not for the first time, I wondered just how many murders had gone unsolved because a male witness was distracted by a pretty face.

I circled the weather-beaten car. If it was, as I suspected, an insurance write off, it shouldn't have even been able to drive on the road. It wouldn't have had a registration or a set of license plates. And a vehicle without plates was almost guaranteed to draw attention. The killer and his accomplice drove the car here.

Mooney would have noticed a detail like missing plates. They might have made him suspicious.

I made my way around the front of the car and found a shiny set of newly issued Queensland state license plates. Unlike the car, they weren't damaged at all. In fact, the plates, and the screws holding them in place were in near perfect condition. They certainly hadn't been on the car when the hailstorm wrecked the bodywork.

My gut told me I was onto something. The only problem was, I didn't have the resources to run the plates. It was times like this I wish I had access to police resources. I was confident that somewhere in their system was the answer for how the car came to be here, with these plates on it. Even if the plates were stolen, and I suspected that might be the case, knowing where they'd been stolen from might give me a chance to catch the killer. After all, there were cameras everywhere nowadays. Our ghost couldn't evade them all forever.

Fortunately, I had learned a few tricks in my time as an investigator. I couldn't run a license plate check, but every new vehicle sold was listed on a different registry, one that gives public access in order to facilitate private vehicle purchase and sale transactions. It's called the Personal Property and Security Register or PPSR. It wouldn't tell me who owned the plates, but it could tell me what type of vehicle they had belonged to and whether or not it was encumbered by any financial institutions. And that was a start, a lead I could potentially run down.

Working on my phone, I punched in the registration, paid the search fee, and waited while the site processed my request.

The screen flashed up a result.

I punched the air in triumph. According to the PPSR, the license plates didn't belong to a beat-up old Datsun, but to a much newer 5 series Beamer. The BMW was currently secured against a loan with the National Australia Bank, though the owner's details weren't accessible for obvious security reasons.

I was on the right track, and it was time to bring in the big guns.

I dialed Constable Fitzgibbons. Hopefully, he was still feeling well enough disposed towards me to do me a favor, off the record of course.

The good Constable answered on the third ring.

"Kane, one of these days you are going to be the death of me," he muttered. In the background, the busy hustle and bustle of the station filtered down the line.

"Hey Fitzy, still at the station? I thought you would have been off shift by now."

"I would have been if I hadn't spent the last hour being grilled by two very cranky detectives wanting to check your alibi."

"Ah, you've met the charming Detective Hart and her infinitely more personable partner, Detective Gibson."

"Not how I would have described them," Fitzy replied.

“Not to their face at least,” I added with a chuckle.

“I value my career,” Fitzy replied. “And I know when to shut my mouth. A skill you’d do well to acquire sooner rather than later.”

“You wound me, Fitzy. I thought we had each other’s backs.”

Fitzy sighed. “Sorry, it’s been a long night.”

“I know the feeling,” I replied, tapping my fingernails against the car. There was no point asking for a favor before I’d given him a chance to vent. “What did they want from you?”

“The pair of them were grilling me on your alibi for last night, just like I said. Why is it that two detectives think you're running around killing people on the Gold Coast? Normally you have a better relationship with the law than this."

"It's a long story," I replied, not wanting to admit to B&E on a call with an on-duty officer.

"Well, I've had a long night, so give me the cliff notes version," Fitzy replied.

In for a penny, in for a pound. "They may or may not have found me at one of the scenes, looking into the crime. At the time I was yet to be engaged by my client."

"No wonder they think you did it. What were you thinking?" I could almost hear Fitzy face-palming from a suburb away.

"I was thinking that someone is killing people in my city and blaming it on a ghost. I was wondering what I might be able to do about that. The fact they are treating my interest in the case as a reason to toss me into the pool of suspects is absurd."

"I told them as much," Fitzy replied. "And I told them where you were last night. So, hopefully, they'll leave you alone, but I'd recommend staying out of their way. At least until this matter is tidied up."

"I'd love to, but Mrs. Mooney asked me to investigate her husband's untimely death. Whether the good detectives like it or not, I'm on the case."

The phone went quiet. I knew he was just looking out for me, but I wasn't one to shy away from a case because things got a little hot.

"If you're not careful, they're going to toss you in holding for the night. I wouldn't be breaking and entering any time soon," Fitzy said.

"I'll keep that in mind. I appreciate you clearing up my whereabouts last night, but I was actually calling for a favor."

"Of course you were," Fitzy replied, "but it's going to have to wait. I'm just leaving the station. It's been a stupidly long shift. I'm going home and getting some much-needed rest."

"On the way out, I don't suppose there's any chance you could run a plate for me?"

Fitzy's sigh carried down the phone as his bag hit the floor loud enough to wake the dead.

"Why the hell not?" His fingers worked a keyboard in the background as he asked, "What manner of mischief are you up to now?"

"Well, don't be mad..." I began.

"But you're entirely ignoring my recommendation to stay away from this case?" he replied.

"Yes, but if it's any consolation, I'm not enjoying it," I replied with a grin.

"It's not at all. What plate are we running? Out with it."

I looked down at the brand-new plates that were meant to be on a BMW somewhere.

"And is this going to get me in any trouble with Hart and Gibson?" he asked.

I scratched the back of my head. "I really have no idea on that front. They won't share any information with me, and I have no way of knowing if they are ahead of me or behind me in the investigation. However, I found something I think might be interesting. Maybe if I throw them a bone they'll stop trying to toss me in jail."

"You'd have to have a bone first." Fitzy laughed.

"That is true. You tell me. Here's the plate."

I read off the plate to Constable Fitzgibbons and waited while he ran it in their system.

There was a long pause.

"Darius, are you trying to get me fired?"

"No," I replied, my ears perking up. "Does that mean you found something interesting?"

"Why have you got me running one of the victim's plates?" Fitzgibbons replied. "We know where their cars are and for all I know, Hart and Gibson will have an alert in the system for anyone looking into them."

"Good thing you are heading home for a sleep then," I replied, my mind racing at the possibilities. The Datsun's plates belonged to one of the other victims. "There's no reason to tell them about it until tomorrow."

"Darius, some days I can't decide whether I like you or whether I want to knock you on your irritating arse."

For this sort of lead, I was willing to get myself clobbered, not that Fitzy was likely to do that to me.

"Just give me some advance warning if you don't mind," I replied. "I really only have one good side and it would be a shame if you were to damage it."

"As if," Fitzy replied. "A good side? Who do you think you're kidding."

I laughed. I had that one coming.

"Darius, do you mind at least telling me why we are running Charlotte Stanley's plates?"

I wondered how much I should share. After all I could finally be ahead of Hart and Gibson.

"Because I found them somewhere they ought not to have been," I replied, wondering if this was why the two detectives were sitting on the garage in the first place. Was this why they were so confident the cases were connected? Maybe I wasn't ahead of them at all.

I needed to level with Fitzy. If the detectives got on his case, I didn't want him paying for doing me the favor in the first place.

"Charlotte Stanley's plates are attached to the Datsun parked in James Mooney's garage. Last time I checked, the two didn't know each other," I replied.

There was a long pause as Fitzy went quiet.

"So either our ghost has a sense of humour, or he's operating from a carefully crafted plan in which he knew he would be killing Charlotte and could use her car's plates as no one would be looking for them to slip into Mooney's garage and knock him off too," I said.

The front door of Mooney's office clicked shut and the hair on my neck stood on end. I was pretty sure I'd shut the door behind me. I certainly wasn't expecting any visitors, and no one knew I was here.

"Do you have any suspects, Darius?" Fitzy asked.

There was no way I was answering that one. Not before I was certain. "Appreciate your help, Constable, but I'm gonna have to be going."

"Darius, no."

"Feel free to tell Hart and Gibson about that little detail, see if it doesn't buy our way out of the doghouse."

I hung up the phone right as three men strode into the garage. Or perhaps more accurately, one businessman and two towering thugs that could have doubled as rugby linebackers.

I recognised the businessman.

Slipping my phone back into my pocket, I met the stare of the Gold Coast's Nightclub Kingpin, Benjamin Marino.

Hard Bargains. Saturday, April 22nd 1530hrs

WHEN YOU COME FACE-TO-FACE with a man you believe to be responsible for an ever-increasing number of murders, it is only natural to feel a little unsettled. The fact that he was trespassing on private property at the scene of one of those murders only served to heighten my sense of danger.

Most people lock up in dangerous situations. In my case, the Australian government had spent a considerable amount of money ensuring that I did not. In spite of the presence of Tweedledee and Tweedledum, either of whom was at least my height and just as wide, my mind was already racing to consider my surroundings and what might readily lend itself to being a serviceable weapon.

In a mechanic's workshop, weapons were not in short supply. A tool chest on wheels stood about four feet away. Doubtless it would hold hammers and spanners, all of which could prove deadly in the right hands, but it was something of a lucky dip. You had to open a drawer and hope you picked the right one. Each drawer cost you precious seconds and time would be at a premium.

My training told me there were no less than four flammable or explosive substances stored in the garage itself, including the aforementioned jerrycan laying only a few feet away. All of them would need to be considered in the event Marino or his goons opened fire.

When outnumbered, one was well-served to even those odds as quickly as possible. I considered a pre-emptive strike. Hit them before they knew I was a threat.

But before I committed to a course of action, I wanted to know why they were here. Right now, all I had were theories and conjecture. If I wanted justice for Wendy Mooney, I needed some real evidence.

Marino was wearing a suit coat over a blue, open-collared shirt, matching slacks, and expensive Italian shoes. By contrast, the goons seemed to have bought their outfits from a Lowe's outlet. Given how their boss was dressed, I was surprised that Hawaiian shirts and cream slacks were permissible work wear. Perhaps it was Marino's attempt for his goons to be less noticeable. Both had a pack of cigarettes and a lighter jammed in their shirt pocket.

The Hawaiian shirts were about as effective for camouflage as trying to hide a machine gun behind a fairy floss dispenser.

As I measured up the muscle, I knew that neither of them was responsible for Mooney's death. The site was too clean for either of these lumbering behemoths to have been involved, though I would have paid good money to see them try to squeeze their way out of the Datsun's boot.

"What do we have here?" Marino asked, his eyes never leaving me.

"I was going to ask you the same question," I replied, "given I have the key, permission, and cause to be here. I also know you aren't a client of the establishment. So what can I do for you, Mr. Marino?"

"Oh good, you know who I am. That ought to save us both some time."

He seemed to enjoy the sound of his own voice. That bode well. As long as we were talking, I wasn't having my skull caved in. I decided to use the opportunity to try and get some answers.

"What brings you here?" I asked again.

Marino shrugged. "We were in the neighbourhood and saw a new car out front. Our understanding was that the garage was closed. So we popped in to ensure nothing untoward was occurring in here."

"Concerned neighbours, isn't that lovely," I said. "Untoward like what? A murder?"

Marino gave me a smile that contained all the genuine friendliness of a coiled red belly black snake.

"Mr. Kane, I read the papers. I know exactly who you are. I'm also aware you've been engaged by Mrs. Mooney to investigate her husband's unfortunate demise."

I took a step away from them, just a little one, but it brought me closer to the tool chest should I need something to hide behind or use as a weapon.

"And how would you know that?" I replied. "I'm not in the habit of disclosing my clientele and I can count those who know on one hand."

"Mr. Kane, I have friends in the police force and your name has come up repeatedly of late. You are an interesting individual, and I make it my business to know about such individuals who operate in my town. Besides, you are standing here claiming you have a key and cause to be here. Where would you have gotten them but from the victim's wife?"

Marino smiled glibly.

He was right. It wasn't a particularly difficult leap to make. Far more concerning was his claim to have allies within the police force. If Marino had informants in the police department, his reach was considerable. No wonder he'd avoided prosecution so readily.

The part that bothered me was how I had come to be on Marino's radar in the first place. Sure, I was here in the building he wanted to buy. But he made it sound as if he'd known about me for some time. My mind wandered to the Crypt Killers, and I couldn't help but wonder if they had been a part of his operation? A nightclub owner with a narcotics connection. It was hardly a gargantuan leap.

"Well, I'm flattered, and I would love to stand around swapping small talk, but I really am very busy working the case."

"Marvelous," Marino replied, "because that's what we're here to talk to you about. The case."

The confidence in his voice irked me. He had the air of a man used to giving orders and having them followed for all the wrong reasons.

I feigned a smile. "You have information that might be of assistance? Pray tell, how did you come by that?"

Marino shook his head. "Oh, I'm afraid we know nothing whatsoever about Mooney's untimely death. But I did want to offer you an opportunity to save yourself some time and heartache by dropping this loser of a case. There's nothing to be gained by laboring a suicide, Mr. Kane. Your efforts only prolong everyone's suffering, and for what, a paycheck?"

"Everyone's gotta eat," I replied, ignoring his assertion. I wanted him to think we might be more alike than different, even though the thought sickened me.

He rested his hands on his hips. For all I knew, there was a gun tucked in the back of his pants. Carrying such a weapon was illegal in Queensland, but Benjamin Marino didn't strike me as the kind of man who cared much for those sorts of guidelines.

"Oh, it's just that such a high-profile case tends to draw the attention of the police, the mayor, people in high places, Mr. Kane. People in my circle of influence. You've already agitated several of them and poking around here is only going to serve to antagonise them further. Why not let sleeping dogs lie? Mrs. Mooney can grieve in peace, and we can all move on."

"I appreciate your concern, gentlemen, and your advice," I replied, nodding my assent.

Marino's smile widened.

"Unsolicited though it might be," I continued. "Between you and me, we both know that the property we're standing in is of vital importance to you and that you were engaged in an effort to purchase it from James Mooney. An offer he had rejected soundly before his untimely death."

"Not a criminal act," Marino replied. "I make real estate offers on an-almost daily basis."

"Most of them along Peninsular Drive it would seem," I replied, goading the beast.

Marino raised an eyebrow. "I see you've been doing your research."

"I'm very thorough," I replied with a shrug. "It's why my clients pay me the big bucks, but in this case, I'd do it for free."

Marino's fingers tightened into fists.

"Unfortunately, your thoroughness is starting to prove an inconvenience," he said. "The longer you dally, the longer Mrs. Mooney will take to consider my more than generous offer. I understand her need for closure, and your need for employment, but both are likely to become expensive inconveniences if we can't proceed sooner rather than later on our deal. As a result, I'm willing to make you an offer in the best interest of all involved."

I scratched at the back of my neck, mainly to test how the goons would react to my hands passing out of view. "Really? What offer would that be?"

"You withdraw from your investigation and let Mrs. Mooney know you found nothing of interest. In response, I'll increase the offer I made James by thirty-five percent to help Mrs. Mooney be more fully compensated for her husband's lack of income. I understand she's struggling with the insurers. I will see that cleared up also. Naturally, I will also pay you for your time to date, meeting your fee on Mrs. Mooney's behalf."

"That is generous," I replied with a nod.

Marino plowed on. "Mr. Mooney's good widow will be cared for, you will be paid, and I can continue my efforts to bring more affordable housing to Peninsular Drive."

"It is quite a compelling offer," I replied. "It could certainly save me a lot of time and effort." I pretended to buy in. I wanted to see how he responded when he didn't get his way. "Unfortunately, it would also require me to look the other way for someone who frankly has the most to gain from this little murder. And I don't know that I could sleep at night taking cash from the man who is most likely responsible for the death of my client's husband. No matter how quickly he settled my bill."

He groaned. "I was worried you might be an idealist."

“I’m many things,” I replied. “Blind, deaf, and dumb aren't among them. I’ll work the case until I find the killer. That's what I promised Mrs. Mooney and I'm a man of my word. So if you want to expedite that process, I would suggest that you gentlemen head on out and let me do my job. Unless you're afraid of what I might find."

"Mr. Kane, I’ve been very patient, but if you continue to suggest that I had anything to do with Mr. Mooney's unfortunate demise that will change.”

I studied Marino. For a thug, he was showing unusual control. His ability to not lose it in the face of obvious goading made me re-evaluate my previous conclusions. When you accuse most thugs of murder, they either laugh it off or get agitated. Particularly, if it's the truth. In contrast, Benjamin Marino was waiting on my every word.

My previous assessment that he was a spoiled party animal was off the mark. Perhaps that was his intention. It was possible that Marino purposely portrayed that image in the media so that people would underestimate him as I had. As I stared at those brown eyes, I saw behind them a cold calculating mind.

At the same time, I grew increasingly uncomfortable with the fact I was alone in a garage with three men who would have no trouble hiding my body, should it come to that.

"Unfortunate," I replied, buying time. “That's an interesting word because of everyone in James Mooney’s circle of influence, you stood the most to gain by his death. That's what the police would call motive. Frankly, I'm surprised they haven't yet come knocking on your door.”

"The reason they have not come knocking on my door, Mr. Kane, is that they know I'm an upstanding businessman with no connection whatsoever to this case. Whatever interest I have in this property, it’s hardly worth destroying my reputation by killing James Mooney. The upside isn't worth the risk. It's bad business."

"That isn't stopping you from purchasing now, though, is it?" I asked.

"I'm simply making the most of the cards that have been dealt," he replied. "If there were any evidence to the contrary, I'm sure the police would have already run it to ground. They couldn't care less about the property's sale."

"I guess that's why you tried to make it look like a suicide," I replied. "If it wasn't for all the wear and tear on the hoist, the police just might have bought it. Perhaps you thought Mooney was a pushover and didn't account for him going out with a fight."

Marino scoffed. "James Mooney was motivated by one thing—money. I have plenty of it and sooner or later, James and I would have come to an agreement. He could run his little dent repair business anywhere. It didn't have to be on my street. We would have found an arrangement that would have seen him out of here and the property in my hands. I had no need to kill him. If you're going to continue spreading this slander, you and I are going to have problems."

I stepped closer to the toolbox, spying a pile of rags on top of it that sparked an idea.

"Well, if I'm mistaken, why don't you depart and let me do my job? I will undoubtably find you are precisely as innocent as you've declared, and we can all move on with our lives."

"And while you form that conclusion, I could lose months," Marino replied. "Rather than be innocent until proven guilty, you'd have me be guilty until you're satisfied I'm innocent. It's hardly fair. Now why don't you simply take my earlier offer and save us all a lot of time by calling it a day?"

"Or what?" I replied. "You'll kill me too?"

Marino laughed. "Nothing quite so pedestrian as that, but I could just have my men hold you down while I work you over a little. Help you become a little more cooperative."

"Such restraint," I replied, eyeing the thugs. "Watch him boys, wouldn't want your saintly boss turning into a killer now, would we?"

Benjamin Marino took a step forward. "I never said I wasn't a killer. I simply said I'm not responsible for James Mooney's death. There is a difference you would do well to note."

The garage grew awkwardly still as we stared at each other. For their part, the thugs looked eager to carry out Marino's threat.

In the interest of my own well-being, I probably should have capitulated. Unfortunately, I wasn't particularly good at looking the other way.

"That call you interrupted was the Queensland Police Service. And when I don't meet with the good constable, he's going to come looking for me. He knows exactly where I am. You're on a timer, gentlemen. So get out of my way or give it a shot. There is no chance I'm going to take your blood money."

Marino shrugged. "Paranormal investigator, I should have figured you were crazy. When the police get here, I'll have two witnesses that say you attacked me without provocation. It will be difficult to work the case with both of your legs broken. Gentlemen, if you wouldn't mind."

Gentlemen. There was no chance either of them had *gentle* intentions with me.

As the nearest thug lunged at me, I darted sideways. My foot caught on the jerrycan full of petrol. The can tipped, rolling toward the workbench, spilling its contents across the floor.

The first thug came at me again. I scooped up a handful of rags and waved the fistful of them in his face like I was some discount matador at the world's worst bullfight. When he swiped at the rags, I punched him straight in the throat.

Tweedledee went down hard.

I went for his companion. He lashed out with his leg, sending me sideways into the tool chest. Grabbing it, I spun with the tool chest, turning a full circle before rolling it at the linebacker. The tool chest built up momentum and rammed into him, sending him to the floor. Stooping down, I delivered a right hook to his jaw, then yanked the shiny silver lighter out of his chest pocket.

Dragging the rags through the fuel, I picked up the jerrycan and jammed the rags in it. As I turned, I came face-to-face with Benjamin Marino and a 9mm Glock pointed right at my chest.

"Stop, now!" Marino said.

I was fast, but I had no delusions about racing bullets.

"Very amusing, Mr. Kane, but that's quite enough."

"I agree," I muttered. "I'll be leaving now. So you might want to step aside."

"I don't think I can do that," Marino replied. I couldn't help but notice his hand didn't shake at all as he grasped the pistol.

"Try harder." I looked down at my right hand where I had the thug's lighter pressed against the fuel-soaked rags. "Three feet is all you have, and that gun isn't going to stop me. We'll both go up in a blaze of glory and if by some unlikely miracle any of you survive, the arson investigation that follows will see the sale of these premises put on hold indefinitely. You can kiss your new development goodbye."

I took a breath to let the thought marinate. "Or you can step aside."

Marino stared into my eyes, seemingly trying to measure my resolve. "What the hell is wrong with you?"

"If you'd bothered to do your research thoroughly, you'd have discovered that before I was a paranormal investigator, I was a member of the Special Air Service Regiment. My specialty was munitions disposal. So before you consider pulling that trigger, or make any further threats, I want you to understand that if I perceive you to be a genuine threat, Benjamin Marino, you become a target."

The skin around his eyes tightened, but he stayed silent while I continued to talk.

"No matter where you are, where you go, or what you do, there is nowhere I can't find you. Every time you strut around your beach-front mansion or visit your mistress, you'll wonder if I can make the shot at that distance. I can. Every time you get in the car without checking underneath your seat, you'll wonder if today is the day you hear a faint click, before your world ends forever. You won't even see me coming. That much I can promise you."

Marino's fingers tensed around the trigger. He was a man used to getting his way who was now discovering, perhaps for the first time in his life, what it meant to meet an immovable object.

"Before you make a very silly choice, Benjamin, let me share with you a lesson I learned in Afghanistan."

"Oh yeah, what's that?"

"The more you have, the more you stand to lose," I replied. "Why do you think it's so easy for extremists to convince their people to strap bombs to their chests and walk into crowded markets, or charge military convoys and end their life all in the hopes they might bring one man's dream crumbling to the ground? You have been building an empire and if your finger tightens on that trigger one more millimeter, everything you've ever worked for goes up in flames with the both of us. Are you ready to pay that price, Marino? I am. Can you say the same?"

"Or?" Marino asked, his voice as strained as the vein running down his temple.

"Or..." I drew a breath. "You let me do my job. If you're as innocent as you say, then my investigation will find the same. The killer is accelerating their timeline already. Bodies are dropping faster and faster. Sooner or later, I'm going to catch them. When I do, James Mooney's name will be cleared, his widow will be cared for and have her reputation back. The garage will be unencumbered, and she'll have no need of it. Or you pull that trigger, and you won't have any need of it either."

Marino's eyes played over the jerrycan full of fuel. The scent of the petrol-soaked rags was so strong it almost made my eyes water.

I had no need to bluff. I was facing a man who had something to lose, and I'd shown him the price he would pay. I simply hoped he wasn't mad enough to test me.

Marino grunted as he jammed the pistol back in its holster at the small of his back.

"You have three days, Mr. Kane. I suggest you make the most of them."

I nodded as I stepped past him, jerrycan still in hand.

"Gentlemen, it's been a pleasure. I sincerely hope we never cross paths again. Understand, Mr. Marino, if anything should happen to me, I will be certain everyone looks squarely at you. You might have friends in the police, but I have brothers in the service. You never want to meet them."

I backed out through the office, keeping my eyes on the three of them until I felt the door at my back. I pushed it open and let it slam shut behind me. I ran like hell out of the building, taking the fuel can with me.

There was no chance I was leaving a weapon covered in my fingerprints behind. There was no telling what Marino might do with it.

Three days.

That was all the time Marino had given me, and I was still stuck chasing ghosts.

I couldn't shake the sinking sensation that I'd just made a lasting impression on a powerful enemy.

Sacred Sausages. Saturday, April 22nd 1630hrs

My heart pounded as I raced home.

Everything about the Casper Killer was utterly confounding. Until an hour ago, I'd been sure Benjamin Marino was behind it all. Now, having heard him out, I wasn't so sure. He was either the greatest liar I'd ever met, or he was innocent and simply trying to profit from Mooney's demise with a callous disregard for everyone in his way.

Right now, I had no idea which he was, and what was worse, I was now up against a very real deadline. While I doubted his motives, I was confident Marino would only be too happy to carry out his threats.

I'd lost my lead and angered an organised crime boss. Not a bad day's work. Winning friends and influencing people wherever I went.

I was already running late for the BBQ and bingo night at the church, but I'd promised Max an outing and I couldn't leave my partner in crime pining at home. Swinging by the house, I scooped up Max, and loaded him and a few of his favorite chew toys into the back seat before racing to the church.

My parents had been attending the Trinity Lutheran Church my entire life. While I hadn't attended a Sunday service in some time, I was always happy to man the barbecue at their social events. Pastor Nick had always been good to me.

The church itself had been around for decades. Made from grey weatherboard with a sturdy corrugated iron roof, the old building was surrounded by a freshly mown lawn on which dozens of tables were arranged. There had to be sixty or seventy people already milling about.

Saturday bingo night was something of a tradition. Most of the guests were closer to retirement than they were to my age, but a few younger families joined us. They would take any chance to get their children out of the house and wear them out in the hopes of getting a better night's sleep.

I pulled into the parking lot and caught my breath. Marino was far from the first to point a gun at me, but familiarity never made it any easier. Leaning over to Max, I gave him a good scratch.

"Now you be a good boy tonight, you hear me?"

His expression told me he had no idea what I was talking about, but I suspected he was conveniently forgetting our last visit here. Last month, he'd chased pigeons through the yard and tripped poor Mrs. Cleary. She hadn't come to any harm, but I still felt bad. Though not bad enough to leave Max at home.

I'd been promising him some playtime all week and I had the feeling he still hadn't forgiven me for leaving him with my parents while I'd visited Tempest in London. Not that he would have suffered with Mum and Dad; they would have spoiled him rotten.

I grabbed his leash and toys and lifted him down out of the car. As we crossed the lot, I could make out dad in his place at the caller's table. He enjoyed emceeing the event.

Off at the punch table, mum congregated with a group of her friends.

I headed for my mother. I knew better than to avoid saying hello. If she was waiting to ambush me with her hope for a prospective daughter-in-law, it was best to get it over with quickly.

"Hey, Mum, good to see you."

She threw her arms around me. "Darius, you came!"

"Of course. I said I would, didn't I?"

She shrugged. "I suppose you did, but then again you've been so busy lately, I worried you might have gotten tied up with a case."

I'd walked into that one, but I really didn't want to talk about work when I'd just been threatened by a thug. No need to alarm her if I could avoid it.

"Oh, that can all wait," I replied. "I wouldn't miss Bingo Night for the world."

As I spoke, my mind wandered back to my lunch with Mary, and I wondered if I hadn't made a mistake by leaving early. I'd hardly broken open the case and I'd almost gotten my skull caved in.

I'd found conversation with Mary fascinating and wished I was spending dinner with her. I was going to need to get her details off Glenda and give her another call.

Then there was Holly Draper. I still owed her a call and was no doubt going to have to fix whatever damage Glenda had done by mixing up the messages. I was still eager to find out what she knew about the case and in particular, what she knew about this morning's victim. The detectives hadn't said a word about it, nor had I seen any press coverage of it yet. Not that I could just show up there; two crime scenes in two days might be pushing my luck.

Better that I let them speak with Fitzy and clear my name first. Perhaps then they would be a little more amenable.

“Darius?” my mum said, putting her arm in mine. "Come with me, dear. There is someone I'd like you to meet.”

I let out a sigh.

"Please, Mother, not again. I don't think I can take another blind date.”

"Oh hush, Darius. One of these days, you’re going to learn to trust your mother’s instincts.”

I was pretty sure at this point that even my devout Lutheran mother would have sold her soul if she thought it would get her grandchildren any faster.

"I’m telling you it really isn't necessary,” I replied. “I don’t need help finding a wife.”

She didn’t listen, instead leading me over to a young woman that couldn't have been more than about twenty-five. The brunette was sitting on a section of garden wall in jeans and a tank top and peering at the underside of her nails. With two earrings in one ear and a stud in her nose, Saturday night bingo was clearly not her idea of a good time.

"You remember Christina, don't you?" my mother asked.

It took me a moment to place her. Her appearance had changed markedly from the last time I saw her a good six or eight years ago. Christina was Pastor Nick's daughter. She attended church almost as frequently as I did.

"Of course. Christina, how are you?" I asked, being congenial while trying to figure out my mother’s plans. I was too old for her by a decade at least. What was mum playing at?

“I'd be better if I wasn't here,” Christina replied, not looking the least bit excited to see me.

"Well, looks like they're about to get started," my mother said. “I'll leave you two to catch up.”

Dad’s voice came over the microphone, rousing the golden oldies into a bingo frenzy.

Mum made herself scarce, leaving me standing there alone. Christina stared at the ground as I shifted my weight awkwardly from one foot to the other. I would take Marino and his Glock over this anytime.

"Look," Christina began, “I'm sure you're nice but—”

An extra rejection wasn't what I needed today so I stopped her short.

"I don't know what they’ve told you, but I suspect we've both been lured here under false pretenses by our well-meaning, but perhaps oblivious, parents. Rest assured I'm not a party to their marital machinations. I have enough going on in my own life as is.”

Max barked his assent. He would happily monopolize my time if he thought it would get him a few more walks.

Christina let out a sigh of relief. “Oh good, it's not just me then.”

"No, my mother tries to do this to me as often as she can. Doesn't seem to understand when I tell her I’ll find someone on my own when I'm good and ready. I’m discerning, not desperate.”

"Parents.” Christina laughed. “They have this way of not actually hearing the words that come out of your mouth.”

"Isn't that the truth," I replied.

"I have been in a relationship for the last six months, but they're so busy trying to drag me back to church that they still haven't actually worked that part out yet."

"Why don't you just tell them?" I asked. "At least it would put an end to all of this nonsense."

Christina smiled but there was bit of pain behind it. "Oh, if it were that easy. Mum and dad are pretty uptight, you know. I doubt they'd approve."

"Perhaps," I replied, "but they're not oblivious. The world just isn't what it was when they were kids."

"I don't think they're that progressive," Christina replied. "Not progressive enough for me to bring my girlfriend home to meet them, anyway."

"Girlfriend?" I nodded slowly, seeing her dilemma. "That's why you haven't told them."

"Precisely. I don't think I'm quite ready for that discussion. I know they aren't."

I thought of what I knew of her parents. "Perhaps you're right, but you'll never know until you give them a chance."

She nodded weakly. "Maybe one day. But not today."

I sat down beside her. "Well, Christina, I'll tell you what I'm gonna do. We can sit here and shoot the breeze about whatever you like. Both our parents will think they have succeeded beyond their wildest dreams and perhaps they'll leave us alone for a few weeks. Then when we are done, we can both go our separate ways. In the meantime, we can both enjoy a conversation about anything other than dating and awkward small talk. How does that sound?"

Christina's smile broadened.

"That sounds pretty good to me." She broke off a twig on a nearby bush. "Dad says you were a decorated soldier, now you chase ghosts. What went wrong?"

I couldn't help but laugh. It wasn't what I'd expected, and I guess from her perspective my career choices had taken a bit of a dive. So I set about explaining the grind, glamor, and gossip of being the Gold Coast's only paranormal investigator. We spent the next forty minutes catching up, talking about everything that had changed since we last saw each other.

Across the lawn, her dad was setting up at the barbecue. A slender woman in her early forties with her hair pulled back in a ponytail was walking beside him carrying a tray of sausages.

"Well, Christina, it's been a pleasure, but I promised your dad I'd help man the barbecue. I'll see you around, huh?"

"Sure thing," she replied, ruffling Max's ears. "Thanks for the chat."

"Hey, would you mind watching him for me while I cook?" I asked, indicating Max. "Otherwise, he'll spend the whole time trying to sneak sausages off the plate."

I held out the leash for her.

"It would be my pleasure," she replied, scooping him up and sitting him on her lap. Say what you will about beagles, but the ladies love them.

Leaving them to play, I reported for BBQ duty as the blond woman headed for the bingo tables.

Pastor Nick was in his fifties with a balding pate and a slight paunch around his midsection. He had a ready smile and an easy-going manner that never changed, whether he was manning a barbecue or giving a sermon on a Sunday.

“Need a hand with those?" I called as I stepped under the marquee.

"Indeed, Darius. It’s a good turn out tonight. I don’t think I’ll be able to manage the BBQ on my own.”

I doubted that, but that was Pastor Nick - always able to make you feel like you were needed.

“Who was your friend?” I asked, nodding in the direction the woman had departed. I couldn’t recall seeing her around, but it had been some time since I’d last attended and the two of them looked rather close.

“Oh, that’s Alice,” he replied with a smile. “She’s been lending a hand around the place.”

“Since when did you get an assistant?” I picked up the tongs and started loading up the BBQ.

He chuckled. “Since I got old and bit off more than I can chew. Between my duties here and the youth shelter I’m pretty busy. Alice helps run the AA meetings each week, lends a hand at the shelter and even started a new initiative helping inmates improve their literacy before they’re released, makes it easier for them to find work once they’re out.”

There was a reason we jokingly referred to him as St. Nick and it wasn’t just because of the Santa suit he wore for the kids at Christmas.

The two of us made small talk while we cooked the sausages and onions. Once the sausage sizzle was under control, I helped butter the bread and prepped the sauces.

"I saw you talking to Christina earlier," Pastor Nick began.

The pastor was a good man, and I had no desire to lead him on. I also couldn't sell out his daughter's secret. That was hers to share if and when she was ready.

"We had a nice catch up. But if you have the same hopes as my mother, I fear you might be disappointed. For one thing, there is quite the age gap."

"Age isn't half the barrier you think it is, Darius. I've seen marriages with larger gaps stand the test of time, while newly marrieds the same age divorce in days. But I was never expecting the two of you to get together. That isn't why I bought into your mother's plan."

He was choosing his words carefully. The question was why?

"If that wasn't the reason, it means you had your own." It was a statement not a question. "What were you hoping for?"

The pastor turned the sausages.

"Lately, Christina has been quite distant. She has also made a number of changes in her appearance. No doubt you saw the new piercings."

I tried not to laugh. With everything parents these days were contending with, I thought it was adorable that he still found that to be troubling.

"I did," I replied. I was not volunteering anything until I knew what his concern was. Christina had taken me into her confidence and I didn't want to say anything that might cause her trouble. As I often chose, I shut up and let the pastor fill the silence.

"It's not just the piercings," he said. "She's been sneaking about. Several times I've caught her lying to her mother and me. We're not bad parents, Darius. We just care about our daughter."

"It's only natural," I replied, pushing the onions around the grill so they didn't burn to a crisp. "I'm just not sure what I can do to help."

"Well, you're an investigator, aren't you?"

"I am," I replied, "but my caseload is rather full right now."

There was no way I was taking this sort of case. Not for any money. Their problem was communication, not paranormal propaganda.

The pastor's face fell, and in it I saw an earnest dad who just worried about his kid.

I set down my spatula and turned to face him. "Look, pastor, I just spent the best part of an hour talking your daughter. She's a good kid. All I can suggest is that you do the same. Whatever is bothering her, I'm sure you can work it out together."

"I guess you're right," he said. "I'm sorry to trouble you. I know it must seem silly."

"It's no trouble," I replied, trying to reassure him, "but I try to restrict cases I take to situations I know I can help. I fear my interference might only place more distance between you and your daughter where none is needed."

"Let us pray that you're right Darius." He smiled weakly.

"From your lips to his ears," I replied, eyeing the grill.

"The cases you do take, Darius, aren't you worried if you spend enough time dabbling with the paranormal, you'll end up inviting it into your life?"

I smiled. "Still worried about my immortal soul, pastor?"

"It's quite literally my job," he said, matching my grin with one of his own.

"It isn't real, pastor. Ghosts, ghouls, vampires. It's all a farce scheming con artists use to bilk people out of their livelihoods."

"It's a big world, Darius. Just because you haven't experienced the supernatural for yourself yet doesn't mean others cannot or will not."

"My job isn't to change other's beliefs," I replied. "When I take on any case, I do it with the intention of helping them, no matter what they believe. If I debunk their superstitions along the way, that's a bonus, surely?"

"A noble pursuit," he said, "but one that is bound to make you unpopular with those who would use those superstitions for their own gain."

I was about to reassure the good pastor that I could handle myself when a white van screeched to an abrupt halt in the church's parking lot.

The manner of its arrival had alarms ringing in my brain. Retirees didn't screech into bingo night like the Blues Brothers parking the caddy.

If that was a member of the congregation, I'd eat my apron. The van looked vaguely familiar but white commercial vans weren't exactly rare.

The van doors slid open and out piled a dozen figures in black robes, their faces completely obscured by eerie masks.

The cult of Beelzebub.

And here I was hoping they would simply fade into obscurity after I set the police on them. Kidnapping and attempted murder was the sort of racket that merited the undivided attention of the Queensland Police Service. Or perhaps it would have if a serial killer wasn't dropping bodies every few days.

I supposed their high priest didn't enjoy being called Cinderella. Or maybe it was the fact I'd broken his nose. I scanned the cultists, but didn't see their leader's gold mask anywhere.

My pulse quickened. Why were they here? Surely, they couldn't mean to attack me in front of fifty witnesses.

The cultists started across the lawn, only they weren't heading for me. Hell, I didn't even think they noticed me manning the barbecues.

That was when it dawned on me. What if they weren't here for me at all? Their threat had mentioned those I loved.

They were here for my parents.

"Pastor, get everyone inside, now!" I shouted as I left the marquee. "Call the police."

"What is going on, Darius?"

His voice rose as the detachment of cloak clad weirdos made a beeline for his congregants.

"Heaven help us," he muttered.

"In my experience, Father, the good Lord helps those who help themselves," I answered as I set off to intercept them, still carrying the set of tongs in one hand.

Pastor Nick raised his hands.

"Everybody, inside, now!" he shouted, trying to drown out my father as he called the numbers.

"Snake's alive, it's fifty-five," my father said into his mic, seemingly oblivious to the danger heading his way.

Max barked as he noted the cultists presence.

They crossed the grass, heading straight for the caller's table.

"Dad, look out!" I pointed at the cultists as I raced towards my father.

He looked at me, then followed my frenzied gesturing to the closing cultists. His face twisted up in confusion.

Christina stood, her knees shaking as she watched the whole drama unfold. Max barked like mad.

"Call the police, Christina," I shouted, noting her father still hadn't picked up his phone.

The cultists ignored me entirely as they went straight for my father. Six of them scrambled onto the stage.

One of the congregants screamed. The shrill high-pitched wail shattered the illusion that this was part of some skit or fun.

The cultists ignored the chaos unfolding. Two of them grabbed dad by the shoulders.

"Look here," he said, trying to pull free of them. "I call the numbers around here."

He shoved one of the cultists backward off the stage.

"Dad, they aren't here to take your job. They are here to take you," I bellowed, racing down the stretch of grass between the tables.

"Well, I never," my father replied, yanking his other arm free. My father might have been lean, but he was tall and he had reach. The robed figure landed on his bum.

Max barked his angry protest as Christina tried to hold onto his leash. I looked at the tongs in my hand and cast them aside, before scooping up one of the folding chairs. I closed it and with a swing that would have done WrestleMania proud, I connected with the closest cultist. Only I wasn't acting. The blow caught him in the back, sending him screaming as he cartwheeled awkwardly off the side of the stage before landing in a heap.

A second cultist caught the chair before I could repeat the move again. As I tried to pull it free, his buddy punched me in the kidneys.

I grunted. “Cheap shot.”

Dropping the chair, I grabbed the first man by the front of his cloak and slammed him into his companion. The two of them went down in a tangled mess. I advanced on a cultist grappling with my father. He let go of dad and turned to face me.

Dad scooped up the cage full of bingo balls and brought it down over the cultist's head. The cage itself wasn't too heavy, and it stunned the thug more than doing him any real damage. But it was all the distraction I needed. Lunging forward, I tackled him to the stage.

The thud of our combined impact carried through the yard.

The cultist lashed out, kicking me in the groin with a blow so hard I could swear my family jewels were now located somewhere in my stomach. I couldn't breathe and simultaneously wanted to vomit.

But more than anything, I was mad. Mad that these nut cases were so consumed with their own delusions they were willing to ruin other people's lives in some demented attempt to usher in their promised dark Messiah.

I locked the pain away, pushing it down deep. Grabbing him by the front of his robes, I drove my forehead into his face. I hit him hard enough that I hurt. He gave a weak groan before his head hit the stage and he stopped moving completely.

"Run for it! It's that crazy detective," one of the cultists shouted.

Those that were still on their feet bolted for the van. Their compatriot, now out cold on the stage, got left behind. I tried to rise to my feet, but I could barely breathe.

As the van peeled out of the car park, dad scribbled on the table itself with a marker. Finally managing to find my feet, I realized he was writing down the license plate.

He put his hand on my shoulder. “What in heavens was that all about?”

I panted as I tried to catch my breath. “Just some left over Looney Tunes from my last case. It would appear they haven't yet had enough.”

My father stared at the cultist that was out cold. "I think he has. He’s not dead, is he?"

I thought I could detect his chest faintly rising with each breath.

“You hit him hard enough his body is here, but his brain is already in the next life."

"That's what he gets for kicking me in the balls,” I muttered. “Coward.”

Stooping down, I checked his pulse to be sure. He had one. Excellent. I would have been severely disappointed if I had deprived the police the chance to question him.

I checked his airway, making sure he wouldn't choke on his own tongue, and rolled him onto his side for good measure.

"Are you planning on giving him CPR?" Dad asked.

"No need," I replied. "He's still breathing. Which is more than I can say for his boss when I get my hands on him."

"Son," my dad warned, "let the police do their job."

My mother and the pastor rushed out of the church.

"Ian, Darius, are you all right?" Mum called. "Who were those dreadful men?"

"Servants of the devil," the pastor said authoritatively. "They practically reek of the occult."

I pulled over a chair and sat down beside my unconscious prisoner. "Close enough, pastor. Close enough."

"Darius, I warned you, didn't I?" He shook his head. "If you dabble with the devil, you get his mess. The good Lord—"

"Pastor, if the good Lord has an issue, I'll happily hear it from him, but as far as I can tell, I've just helped dispatch his competition."

"But—h"

"No *buts*," I replied. "The lot of them are deluded and dangerous. When the police arrive, we'll hand him over and we can all go back to our barbecue and bingo in peace."

"You mean to continue after all this?" Pastor Nick asked, surveying the mess.

"I haven't spent the last hour cooking to go home hungry," I replied.

Max gave an affirmative bark.

"So please, pastor, head inside. Reassure your congregation that all is well, and when our friends in blue arrive, I'm going to need an abundance of witnesses to state my actions were self-defense."

Pastor Nick cocked his head to the side. "Why would they think anything else?"

My mind wandered back to Hart and Gibson grilling me.

"Oh, just a hunch," I replied, looking down at the thug. I nudged him with the toe of my shoe. "The real question is, how long is it going to take you to rat out your boss?"

An Overdue Appointment. Saturday, April 22nd 1800hrs

If I got paid every time I had to wait for the police, I would be amassing the sort of fortune that would allow me to start launching rockets into space.

At least that was what billionaires seemed to do with their money nowadays. Unfortunately for me, no one was paying me to sit and wait with this idiot. Yet I had to do it all the same.

If I left, I would have the police beating down my door again. What made it worse was I'd closed the Masters case and sent my final invoice. The fact the cult of Beelzebub now had a personal axe to grind with me wasn't really Cali's fault. It was simply collateral damage for a case I'd taken.

Yet here I was, still dealing with it. I shrugged. No point getting upset about it. That was just the way the cookie crumbled this time. Instead, I used the time to try and process everything that had happened to me today.

I started with the interrogation this morning, the infinitely more pleasant lunch with Mary Baker, and my dalliance at the garage with Benjamin Marino and his thugs. All of it was enough to leave me at something of a loss when it came to the Casper Killer. I'd had my theories but speaking with Benjamin Marino had left me perplexed.

And if he hadn't killed Mooney, then he was unlikely to have killed the others as whoever had killed Charlotte Stanley had also been responsible for Mooney's demise. The number plate alone was evidence of that.

If it wasn't Marino, then he was the luckiest thug alive and simply benefiting from the damage caused by our seemingly incorporeal killer.

I'd gone from having a solid theory to nothing in a matter of hours and was back to dealing with the stupid cultists who seemed only too willing to bear out their grudge. I was going to have to find their self-styled high priest and introduce him to the constabulary. Perhaps Hart and Gibson might actually help rather than hinder me with a bona fide killer in custody.

Police sedans rolled into the church car park, disgorging a wave of constables that would have been immensely useful twenty minutes ago. Fortunately, the good detectives were nowhere to be seen.

I spent the next half-hour giving an account of what had happened and referring the officers to their colleagues who'd taken my statement the night Cali Masters was attacked. Like most, they were a little skeptical as I told them of the cult's intention to sacrifice an innocent person. It was the sort of bizarre crime that seemed wholly out of place in our time, but they heard me out, taking notes as I spoke.

When I was done, they turned their attention to the detained cultist on the stage. Having taken eyewitness accounts from Christina, my father, and the pastor, they concluded they had enough to work with.

"If you need anything else, here is my card," I said. "Happy to answer any follow up questions you might have. Taking these crazies off the street will benefit us all."

The officer, a young woman in her thirties, looked at the card. "Blue Moon Investigations. I've heard of you."

I wasn't sure whether that was good news or not.

After a lengthy pause, she smiled. "Fitzgibbons says you're all right."

"Any friend of Fitzy's is a friend of mine," I replied. "Thanks for taking this one off my hands."

The officer and her partner dragged the handcuffed thug to their car.

I'd had a few sausages while I waited, but I grabbed another two for Max to snack on. After loading my parents into their car, I sought out Christina–she still had my dog.

"Darius that was very brave," she said with a bit of a wistful look about her.

"It's not brave to knock a man out," I replied. "It's brave to keep trying to connect with your daughter, even though you feel like she's drifting away."

"So you talked to dad, huh?" she asked.

I laughed. "Your father is a good man. He might not be good at communicating it, but he clearly cares about you. Which is a lot more than many people have in this world. Give him a chance. He might surprise you."

She rolled her eyes. "He just wants to tell me how to live."

"Most parents just want to save their kids from the pain of mistakes they see others making all the time."

"I want to work things out for myself," she replied, patting Max.

"Nothing wrong with that," I said. "And when you do, give them a chance to accept you for who you are."

I held out my hands for Max, and Christina handed him over.

"Thanks for taking care of him. He's been dying to get out of the house."

"Anytime," Christina replied. "He's the best company here."

"I'll try not to take that personally," I said with a chuckle. "He is pretty great."

I sat Max on the back seat of my Ute and drove my parents home. Parking in the drive, I scooped up Max and followed them inside.

"You really don't need to spend the night on our account," my father said. "I'm quite alright."

There was no way I was leaving them alone with the cult of Beelzebub on the loose.

"The good Father was right about one thing. Those people were at the church because of me, and if they tracked you to the church, they can track you here. I'll be spending the night here until they are in custody."

My mother was still a little pale, but she managed a smile. It didn't quite vanquish the stress and worry lines at the corner of her eyes. I'd seen enough trauma in my time to know they needed something to occupy themselves with.

"Why don't you put on a cuppa, Mum, and the three of us can relax and catch up? We didn't get our bingo in so perhaps a game of gin rummy?"

"That's my boy," my mother said.

Gin had always been a compromise. My father loved counting games, but my mum loved cards. The three of us had been playing since I was a child.

My mother rushed out of the lounge room to put a kettle on as I set Max down. He spent enough time here that he had his own bed, bowl, and last summer dad put in a doggy door for him. The patio door still didn't shut quite right, but it was the thought that counted.

"So, son, how is the Casper case going?" Dad asked.

Not the distracting conversation I had in mind. *So, son, let's forget about those mad lads that want to bring in the dark messiah, and let's talk about your serial killing ghost.*

"Who said anything about the Casper case?" I asked.

How did he even know I was working it?

"You didn't need to," dad said. "A bunch of weirdos attacked us at church, and you barely gave them or the officers a second thought. Something else is on your mind. You're a workaholic, so it is most likely a case and I can't help but note the wording you used when dealing with your mother yesterday. The kind of dancing around you do when you don't want to lie but have every intention of going against her wishes."

I probably got my intuition from my dad.

"You know me pretty well," I said, making my way over to the dining table. "And the case has turned to pot, much like my day. My best lead seems to be miles off the mark, and I really have no idea who is running around killing people in the dead of night."

I didn't want to burden my dad, but perhaps it would take his mind off his almost kidnapping. Perhaps together we could uncover an angle I hadn't considered.

"Well, what have you got so far?" he asked.

I was just about to reply when a knock at the door interrupted us.

"I'll get it," my mother called, hurrying out of the kitchen.

My father's hands shook. It was a faint tremble, but I caught it anyway. He was thinking the same thing I was.

"Don't, Mum. It could be those men again." I rose from the table to follow her to the door.

My mother peered through the glass panel beside the door and shook her head. "It isn't. It's a woman."

I relaxed a little. As long as it wasn't the cultists or Benjamin Marino, I could live with it. I wasn't in the mood for any more excitement tonight.

My mother opened the door, revealing a woman in her late twenties. She was slight of build but lean like a runner. Her brunette hair was cut short at the shoulder. A set of gold rimmed glasses sat on her nose, and she wore a bag over one shoulder. The bag itself was stuffed with folders and paperwork.

"Hello, can I help you?" my mother asked.

I was half expecting a sales pitch. Which made me all the more surprised when the next words out of her mouth were, "I'm looking for Darius Kane. Is he here?"

My mother gave me a broad smile, and no chance to evade our guest. "Darius, it's for you. Do invite the lovely young lady in for tea. I've just put the kettle on."

My mother might have been willing to welcome in any potentially eligible woman that knocked on the door, but after fighting for my life twice in one day, I was less than eager.

"I'm Darius Kane, and who might you be?"

The woman was a good deal shorter than I was and had to look up to meet my eye. "Darius, a pleasure to meet you. I'm Holly. Holly Draper."

Holly Draper? The journalist for the Gold Coast Bulletin.

The shock must have been written across my face, because she said, "So you have heard of me? That's funny, because the impression I got from your receptionist was that you had no idea who I was and didn't want to talk to me."

I buried my head in my hands, groaning.

"You'll have to pardon Glenda. Sometimes she isn't giving her full attention to the job," I said. "I was supposed to meet you for lunch today, but she mixed up my messages."

Holly placed one hand on her hip and raised an eyebrow. "You expect me to believe that? Oh, Darius, you're going to have to do better than that. I do this for a living."

"I'm telling the truth. If you spent five minutes with Glenda, you'd understand."

Holly watched me intently. She wasn't buying it for a moment.

"Look, forget about Glenda. Why are you here? And how did you find me at my parents?"

"I'm an investigative journalist, and I'm good at my job," she replied as if that was somehow a complete explanation.

It was not, and I wasn't in a particularly trusting mood. "Go on."

"When I reached out to Wendy Mooney, she told me she hired you. At first, I was excited because I followed your progress on the Crypt Killers. I thought perhaps we could compare notes on the case."

"So you spoke to Wendy? That doesn't explain how you found me here."

"I was following up with the previous victim's next of kin, to see if I could establish common factors in their cases. By the time I got to Wendy, she'd already engaged you, and said if I had questions, I should speak to you. So here I am."

Score one for Wendy. Her keeping a lid on what she knew had brought Holly to the table. I'd been worried I would have to play hardball with her. Now I knew she had little on Mooney's case, but she could still be an invaluable connection to the other victims. It still didn't explain how she'd tracked me here.

"And how did you know I was here? This isn't my place."

"That wasn't tough. I have friends at the precinct who mentioned that little mess down at the church. Pastor Nick and I worked an event together a few years back. When I asked him where you'd gone, he told me you'd driven your parents home. And here I am."

"And he just gave you their address?"

She nodded calmly. "It was on their records, and I can be very persuasive."

"I'm beginning to get that impression," I replied.

"Darius, are you going to invite that young lady in, or are you going to keep her out there in the weather all night?" My mother's voice carried from the kitchen.

I knew what she was doing. As far as my mum went, any female company meant at least the opportunity for her to have grandchildren before she died. Female with a pulse, that was as discerning as my mother was right now.

She had a point, but not on the dating front. I wasn't going to get Holly to open up on the doorstep, and my Benjamin Marino angle had come up short. If my gut was right, that gangster was innocent. Well, not completely innocent, but innocent of this at least. I needed more information, and fast, before another body dropped.

I stepped to the side and gestured into the home. "Would you like to come in and have some tea? Perhaps we can compare notes about the case."

Holly Draper's lips turned up into a smile. "I'd like that very much."

We settled in at the dining table. My mother bustled about in the kitchen, and my father appeared to have gone to take a shower. After the excitement at the church, I imagined he needed a rest. I dare say it was probably the most exciting thing that had ever happened to him and not in a good way.

Holly settled her bag in front of her on the table. She rested an arm on it, almost guarding it.

"Where would you like to start?" I asked.

"Well, for starters, what was the mess at the church?" Holly asked. "Pastor Nick said something about a cult?"

"Disturbed miscreants from a prior case. Unrelated to the Casper killings, I'm afraid."

"How can you be sure? Holly asked.

I held up a finger. "I answered your question. Now one of mine."

If Holly Draper wanted me to put all my cards on the table, I was going to get answers of my own. Journalists were notorious for holding the best bits of any case back so that no one could steal their exclusive. I couldn't care less about the news coverage, but the smallest of details could be the difference between life and death for the next victim.

"Very well," she replied. "Ask away."

"What's in it for you?" I asked. Motive mattered here, just like any other case. "You managed to get it on the front page of the paper. That must have taken some clout, but it was more conjecture than fact, but I can see you are invested in the case. Do you have a personal tie to one of the victims, or are you after the scoop?"

"Does it really matter?" she asked.

"It does." I leaned back in my chair. Knowing what drove her gave me an indication of what I could expect from her. Someone tied to the victims was more liable to make an emotionally charged decision that could get us in strife. Someone chasing a promotion could be relied on to act in a predictable manner. Usually their own best interest.

"I don't have a connection with any of the victims. But I do care what happens in this town. A killer walking the streets is bad for everyone." She pushed her hair back behind her ear. "Naturally, this story could make a massive impact in my career too. Does that bother you?"

"Not at all," I replied with a grin. "You're honest. That counts for more than most people realise, at least with me. Aspiration isn't a crime, though at times our society seems happy to demonize it."

"Try being a woman," she said. "I have been passed over for promotion twice in the last three years. The first time I was too young. The second time I was told my work in the field was invaluable. But strangely neither of the men that were promoted were plagued by those same problems."

"People suck," I replied, "and you deserve better than that. Everyone deserves an even playing field."

Holly laughed. "Can I quote you on that one?"

"Sure, for all the good it's worth. I don't know that I carry much clout with your boss."

She cocked her head to the side. "After that mess with the Crypt Killers, you'd be surprised. You've made a little bit of a name for yourself, Darius."

I didn't know Holly Draper well enough to decide whether that was a genuine compliment or simply flattery in an attempt to get me to lower my guard.

"Speak for yourself," I said. "You were on the front page yesterday. No mean feat by any stretch."

"Yes, and if that was the extent of the battle, it would have been a nice win. But the second the paper printed, the detective running the case flew off her rocker. They have been putting pressure on my boss to pull the story from our website and exile me to the doldrums. If I can't prove I'm right about the killer, then my career prospects will grow grim."

"That wouldn't happen to be detectives Hart and Gibson, would it?" I ventured, not wanting to tip my hand.

"You've met them?" Her face fell a little. "Of course you have. Detective Hart has a way of getting what she wants. I should have known she'd get to you first."

She had reached that conclusion pretty swiftly. In a matter of moments, she'd relegated me to a camp filled with detective Hart's fan boys.

"That doesn't bode well for me," I said. "Hart getting what she wants."

Holly folded her arms. "Oh, and why is that?"

"Well, it would seem the only thing Detective Hart wants is to throw me in jail. As recently as this morning, she was treating me as a suspect."

Holly's eyes bulged a little. "You're kidding?"

"Not even a little bit. They woke me up this morning, banging on my door and demanding an alibi for my whereabouts last night. It turns out Detective Hart is not my biggest fan."

"That Detective Hart, her looks are exceeded only by her incompetence," Holly said. "Probably a good thing. If they weren't, I'm sure she'd be Commissioner by now. Relentless career climber, that one."

"I thought a little aspiration was a good thing," I replied.

"Aspiration is one thing," she said, "but I have it on good authority that Hart would sell out her own family if it meant she could advance her career. There isn't anyone or anything she wouldn't put out to pasture for a promotion."

"I was friends with a few of the officers that were going for detective the same year as her. Two of them were written up for minor infringements, often overlooked in the course of duty. The third she reported for sexual harassment."

I winced. Hart played dirty.

"What's more, she'd been verbally egging him on for weeks. When the idiot sexted her, he had no proof and she reported him. Not the brightest tool in the shed, but she almost got a good cop fired."

"No love lost between you two then," I said.

"Not since the moment we met," Holly replied, like that was all the explanation that was needed.

Reflecting on my less than stellar encounters with the detective, I couldn't help but agree with her.

“She’s the actual devil,” Holly said. “When we solve this mess, it will be a win. If we beat her to it, well, that will be priceless.”

“A little payback then. She calls your editor to cause you grief and you get the last word in the next issue that goes to print.”

“I’ll immortalize her,” Holly said with a grin, as she drummed her fingers on the table. “I am a little surprised though. You are the kind of man she normally ropes in and wraps around her little finger. I wonder why she's gone after you instead."

“You and me both,” I replied. “She's out for blood.”

I paused as I thought through Holly’s words. “What do you mean ‘kind of man?’ What does that even mean?”

Holly looked down at her fingernails. “Ah, nothing. She just has a type. That's all.”

I gestured with my hand, encouraging her to go on.

"You know, tall, handsome men. The kind that look good in a uniform and see her and think they have a shot. She has a whole little squad of constables eager to be the next Mr. Hart.”

Had she just called me attractive? For someone who had done nothing but strike out for months, I was having unseasonably good luck with compliments lately.

"The tea is ready," my mother called, carrying two saucers with teacups sitting atop them. She set them down on the table and proceeded back into the kitchen to grab the kettle and some spoons. She poured each of us a cup of tea, placed the spoons in, and smiled at Holly. "Mind that, dear. It's quite hot. Would you like milk or sugar?"

"Just sugar, please," Holly replied. "Two cubes, thank you."

I couldn't help but think my mother had been loitering at the kitchen and listening in on us. Her timing was just a little too crisp. She placed a small saucer with several sugar cubes on it on the table and hovered.

"Why don't you go and check on dad?" I suggested. "He was looking a little shaken up earlier."

My mother looked down at me, her facial expression indicating she would much rather hover over our shoulder. As far as she could see, this was the most visible progress I'd made in months.

"*Go!*" I mouthed while Holly was looking down at her tea.

Mom took her win and went to check on my dad.

"Everything okay?" Holly asked.

"Oh, he'll be fine. Fortunately, he has a strong heart."

"I mean your mum. You seemed in an awful hurry to get rid of her. What's that about?"

There were so many reasons, and I wasn't ready to embarrass myself, so I settled on the least damning. "Well, for one, I'd rather my mother wasn't aware that I was working the Casper Killer case. She has a tendency to worry."

"Isn't that sweet," Holly replied, sipping at her tea. "And the other?"

Like a runaway train hurtling down a mountain, it seemed utterly unavoidable. So I took it head on.

"If I let her linger much longer, I'm afraid she would start planning our wedding. I'm in my thirties, and unmarried. There is no greater sin a son could commit."

"Oh, she can't be that bad," Holly replied. "She seems sweet."

"You keep that in mind when she starts into you. If you take long enough to finish that tea, she'll be expecting you to have her grandchildren."

Holly laughed but it tapered off quickly, and an awkward silence settled in the dining room.

Smooth move, Darius. Mood killed. Mission accomplished. You have known the woman a matter of minutes and already you brought up marriage and bearing your children. There is a reason your past dates have gone poorly.

I tried to stop the train of self-destructive thoughts, but it seemed intent on steaming full speed through my mind.

I asked Holly another question, more to distract myself than anything. "In your article, you seem quite convinced the killings are connected. What makes you so sure?"

Holly looked at me, her lips drawing into a tight pensive line. She leaned back in her chair. "That's not how this works, Darius. You've had your question. Now it's my turn. If you want me to put my cards on the table, you're going to share too. What did Wendy tell you about James? And what angle are you working?"

Her reluctance didn't bother me. I could understand the hesitation. As far as she could see, I'd knocked back her invitation once thanks to Glenda's handling of my messages. Whether it was ineffective or intentional interference, the result was the same.

I'd always believed that trust could not be purchased, only earned. I leveled with her.

"When Wendy Mooney came to see me, she told me someone had been trying to purchase James' garage. I suspected it might have been motive to kill him when he didn't agree to the purchase. I did my research and discovered Benjamin Marino has been buying up most of Peninsular Drive to turn it into a series of apartment complexes. I figured when James didn't comply, he had him killed. And while I don't have a concrete connection to the other cases, it's not a leap to believe that a banker and a lawyer might have been involved in the development. Until this afternoon, I was wholly convinced Benjamin Marino was responsible for having Mooney killed. He may not have done the deed, but I was confident he'd given the order."

"You say that like a man who's changed his mind."

"Now I'm not quite so sure," I replied, crossing one leg over the other.

"What changed?" Holly lifted her teacup.

"I met the man," I replied "and while I'm confident he's been responsible for killing others, I don't believe he killed Mooney."

"How can you tell?"

"Right now, it's my gut. But I've met my share of killers, and I'm inclined to trust it."

I could always tell those who'd ended a life from those who'd merely thought about it. There was something different in the way they carried themselves, the way they laid out their threats. Benjamin Marino was a cold hard killer. Of that,

I was perfectly certain, but he seemed just as confused about Mooney's death as I was. And that struck me as unusual.

"I'm inclined to agree with you," Holly replied.

"Oh yeah?" I perked up. "Why is that?"

"While it's almost certainly an interesting angle, it doesn't explain the ghosts or the connection with the other victims. Marino doesn't strike me as the kind of man who needs to hide behind a veil of fear."

"Ghosts?" I asked. "I figured they were just speculation."

Holly shook her head. "We have multiple accounts of strange spectral forms at several of the sites."

I wasn't buying it. "The ghosts could simply be a distraction, to keep people busy."

"No, it's more than that," Holly replied. "If they were looking for a distraction, they would be causing mayhem in the streets, maximizing the terror. Whoever is responsible for the ghostly apparitions is using them as a tool, not to distract but to strike fear into the heart of their victims. These killings are malicious, cold, calculated revenge. That's why I know Benjamin Marino didn't kill James Mooney."

I leaned forward, picking up my tea. "Then who did?"

Holly tapped the folders sticking out of her bag. "One of the people he took everything from."

I nodded along. It made sense. After all, it was motive 101.

"There's only one problem. They're all dead or dying."

Grudge Bearing Ghosts. Saturday, April 22nd 1930hrs

Well, that was certainly going to complicate matters.

Dead people don't commit murders, and I wasn't buying the ghosts for a minute. Regardless of the mounting evidence, I still believed there was a flesh and blood killer behind this mess.

It also explained why she'd come looking for me. She'd hit her own dead end in the investigation.

"A motive without a killer is going to prove problematic," I replied, considering what I knew of Mooney. I'd been working the Marino angle so hard I'd almost forgotten the gossip Esmerelda shared earlier. "You're working the car accident angle."

"Exactly," Holly replied with a smile. "James Mooney blew the repair job and as a result his client plowed right into oncoming traffic. His client died, and the other victim was severely maimed."

"And you think that someone involved in that accident is responsible for Mooney's death?"

"I do."

Esmerelda believed the same, though she chalked up the killings to the unfinished business of the victim's ghost. I put more stock in Holly's conclusion despite the talk of a spectral killer roaming the town.

"The victim died, right?" I asked, wanting to double check the facts. Esmerelda was usually pretty good, but one could never be too certain.

"He did," Holly replied. "Complications caused by the accident. He was dead before the trial even began."

"The trial was brought on by his wife, if I understand correctly."

"Exactly. Her name is Victoria Burnham. Her husband Reggie was the love of her life. When he died, she pressed charges. The scandal forced Mooney to close his garage, but he was eventually found innocent by the jury. Now, years later, he opens a shop here and only a few months later winds up dead. Seems a little too coincidental for my tastes."

I folded my arms. "It's a good theory, but you wouldn't be this confident unless you had something. What makes you so certain the killer originated from that case and not something from Mooney's more recent dealings?"

Holly pulled folders out of her bag, fanning them out on the table and sifting through them. She picked up one of them and flipped it open. It was filled with copies of newspaper articles. The first one showed a vindicated James Mooney standing on the steps of the courthouse next to a man in a suit who seemed familiar, but I couldn't quite place where I'd seen him before.

Holly turned the picture so I could get a better look at it.

"What if I told you James Mooney's criminal defense attorney was Victor Sellers, the second victim?"

That was where I'd seen him before. He was in the dossier that had been sent over by Tommy. "Sellers was Mooney's counsel?"

"He certainly was," Holly replied.

That changed things. When I'd worked the Marino angle, I'd not been able to find anything concrete linking the victims to each other. All I had was supposition.

"And what about Charlotte Stanley?"

"I haven't figured that part out yet," Holly replied. "But I suspect she's connected to them somehow. Given her vocation, I'm betting her bank is involved in the case somewhere. Perhaps they lent Mooney the funds to muster his defence, or perhaps when the Burnhams lost they were unable to meet their own debts. They were certainly struggling after the accident. Perhaps the bank was financing the house?"

"Are you aware of the fact that the plates from Charlotte's car were used to check a vehicle into Mooney's workshop the day he died?"

Holly's eyes lit up. "You're kidding?"

"Not at all," I replied. "I only just made the connection today. I suspect Mooney's killer was hidden in the vehicle's boot. It was an old wrecker and didn't have its own plates. So they stole Charlotte's, figuring the police wouldn't notice their absence. After all, her death was an apparent suicide. What reason did the police have to scrutinize her vehicle when Charlotte died in the tub? Seemingly of her own negligence."

"So the same person who killed Charlotte put the plates on an old vehicle and smuggled it into Mooney's garage. But if they were in the boot, someone had to drop it off. So the killer isn't working alone," Holly said.

"That's what I figured. Shame James's cameras didn't seem to catch it coming or going. He seemed more worried about people creeping around the back yard than driving into the front lot."

"The killer is careful," Holly mused. "Comes and goes like a ghost."

"It makes for a catchy headline," I replied, "but Sellers was gunned down, and Mooney was strangled to death. Last I checked, ghosts don't have hands."

She cocked her head. "For a paranormal investigator, you certainly seem dismissive of the possibility."

"All the monsters I've met were human," I answered with a shrug. "Do you know anything about the fourth victim?"

"His name is Robert Minders. He died of an apparent heart attack in his home last night. What connection has he got to the case, do you think?"

I didn't even know where to begin there. I knew nothing about the man whatsoever. I would have to get Tommy onto compiling a dossier.

"Well, the police grilled me about him this morning. It's safe to bet they see a connection. We need to find out what it is. I have some friends on the force, but the detectives running the case know who they are so will likely freeze me out."

"Hart seems to be keeping the cards close to her chest," Holly said. "I think she sees a promotion in her future. I'll see if Gibson will talk with one of my colleagues."

I considered what I knew about the case so far.

"We have four victims and our killer is steadily increasing his pace. He is building up to something or working against a deadline we don't understand. Rushing increases the risk they will be caught. Why take that chance now?"

Holly took a sip of her tea. "I can't say for sure. I figured the police were ahead of us. I just can't work out how. They must know something we don't, and the killer is spooked."

Mulling over everything Holly had shared, I changed my approach. "You said Reggie Burnham died in the accident. What about the other vehicle? What happened to the driver there?"

"His name is Kevin Thompson. I checked into him too, but unfortunately, he is in respite care. The accident left him a paraplegic and his health has steadily deteriorated ever since."

I let out a sigh. Reggie was dead, and the other victim was unlikely to have the physical capacity to carry out any of these murders.

"Was Kevin married?"

"Long since divorced. His wife has no love for him despite his poor fortunes. I tried to reach out to her for comment, but she told me she wasn't interested."

When working down a list of those with an axe to grind over the accident, we were quickly running out of candidates. I could see what Holly meant. They were all either dead, or close to it. There was only one we hadn't discussed.

"That leaves Victoria Burnham," I said. "The woman who brought the case in the first place."

"That's where I keep ending up." Holly closed the folder. "But Victoria Burnham has been living in an aged care facility for the past five years. I'm pretty sure the nurses would have noticed if she was slipping out in the middle of the night to murder people."

"I think we ought to go have a chat with her anyway," I replied. "She has the most motive of anyone, and her first attempt for justice was thwarted. Perhaps Victoria has someone else doing the dirty work for her."

"You think she's really playing Sudoku in an aged home while brutally planning the murder of those responsible for a husband's death?" Holly asked.

I thought back to my last tour. "It's probably more interesting than bingo night. On my last deployment, we'd spent months searching for an enemy operative who was radicalizing local youths, ambushing our patrols, and masterminding numerous attacks across allied installations. We spent months kicking down doors, only to eventually discover it was a seventy-two-year-old man who played chess in the market all day. He'd been in front of us the whole time, hiding in plain sight."

"That's terrible," Holly whispered.

"Just a different kind of monster," I said. "One that can look you in the eye and smile, all the while planning your death. Victoria has the most motive. I think she's worth talking to."

"Well, it's after hours now. What do you say we head over together and visit her in the morning?" Holly asked, gathering up her folders.

"Sounds like a good idea to me." I badly needed a decent night's sleep, and I wasn't going to get it anywhere but here, where I could also keep an eye out for my parents.

"Great I'll come back in the morning. Say, nine o'clock? We can drive over together."

I nodded. "It's a plan. In the meantime, you should keep your head down. Whoever is dropping these bodies will think nothing of coming after you too. Have you got somewhere safe to lay low?"

"If you're trying to get me to spend the night, Darius, you're going to have to try harder than that."

I laughed. "You give me far too much credit, or not enough. I'm not sure which."

Holly laughed as she loaded her paperwork back into her bag. "Don't you worry about me, Darius. I'll be just fine. I'd like to think it goes without saying, but in case it doesn't, when we blow this thing wide open, the exclusive is mine."

"I wouldn't dream of talking to anyone else," I said, rising from the table.

"I'm serious, Darius. This sort of story makes and breaks careers. I've looked for this break for years, and now I'm this close." She held up her hand, her thumb and pointer only an inch apart.

"Holly, I'm a man of my word. When we catch this killer, you will be able to tell the world how you were the first to join the dots."

"You don't want the credit?" she asked.

"I'm not greedy. There's enough glory to go around. Besides, this can be a harsh gig. It would help to have the Gold Coast Bulletin's rising star on my side now, wouldn't it?"

"I suppose it would," she replied, slinging her heavy bag over her shoulder.

"Are those all for this case?" I asked. "Or do you just pack a few extras in case you have to thump a wayward mugger?"

Holly grinned. "It's this case. Everything I have looked at so far."

"Do you mind if I borrow some of them? I just want to make sure I'm caught up before we kick off in the morning."

Holly considered the request before reaching into her bag and drawing out a spiral bound folder. She slid it onto the table.

"I'm trusting you, Darius. Don't go rogue on me."

"I wouldn't dream of it," I replied. "You still have more than enough in there to lay me out cold."

My mother entered the room. "You're not going, are you, dear? I was just about to fix some supper."

Mum was at defcon four. We'd already eaten at the church, but she was willing to make another meal just to keep Holly and me talking.

"That's very kind of you," Holly replied, "but I really must be on my way."

My mother smiled to try and hide her disappointment. I took the chance to walk Holly to the door.

"I'll see you in the morning," I said with a smile as I held the door open for her.

"Nine AM sharp—don't sleep in," Holly said over her shoulder as she headed for her red convertible.

Holly Draper seemed to be doing all right for herself.

"I wouldn't dream of it," I called after her. Sleep and I tended not to spend too much time together.

No sooner had the door closed than my mother cornered me in the hall.

She was all smiles. "She seems lovely."

I didn't have the energy to enter into the grandchildren debate with my mother. My day had begun being interrogated by the police. I'd been cornered by a mobster and attacked by cultists. Right now, I wanted nothing more than to put my feet up and binge read Holly Draper's research until I dozed off.

"She's absolutely delightful," I replied to my mother, "but she's a work colleague and that was the first time I met her. If you start stalking her, I'll just go ahead and book myself in for a vasectomy."

My mother's eyes bulged. "You wouldn't dare."

"Just try me," I replied. "We'll see."

Mum shook her head in disbelief. "I was just making sure you'd noticed. You can be a little dim when it comes to women, Darius."

"Thanks, Mum, I can always rely on you to bring me back down to earth. How is dad doing?"

"A little shaken up, I'm afraid. But he's called it a night and gone for some rest. You should do the same."

"I think you're quite right," I said, picking up the folder off the table.

I'd eaten enough at the church that I wasn't really feeling particularly hungry. No doubt if Holly had stayed for dinner, Mum would have put on a three-course meal, but as I looked closer, I realized even she was pooped, and likely a little relieved to see Holly head home. She could use the break too.

I bent down and gave her a kiss on the cheek. "Thanks, Mum."

"What's that for?" Mum asked, her brow furrowing.

"Always keeping an eye out for me," I replied. "Now let me return the favour. You head on upstairs and get a good night's rest. I'll stay on the couch and make sure no unexpected guests stop by."

"You'll do no such thing," she said, raising a finger. "I've already made up the guest room. There is a fresh set of sheets and a towel."

"Okay, okay," I replied, trying to placate her. "I'll see you in the morning."

Mum headed up to bed and I had the house largely to myself.

I looked down at my watch. It was a little after eight. I made a round of the house, checking all the doors and windows just to be certain. None of them had been left open, but given the way the killer entered a number of the crime scenes, I wasn't confident that would stop them. Fortunately, I figured the Casper Killer had little idea I was on his or her case.

I was more worried about the cult of Beelzebub.

The real danger would come tomorrow when we confronted Victoria Burnham. If nothing else, it would serve as an announcement that we were hunting for the killer. If Mrs Burnham was pulling the strings, we were inviting retribution.

In the guest room, I kicked off my boots and went for a quick rinse in the shower. The hot water felt great on my aching muscles. I had some fresh clothes I'd left here for emergencies, and I changed into a set of shorts and a t-shirt before flopping down on the bed.

I skimmed my emails. There was one from Tommy. I opened it first. It had his bank details, so I took a few minutes to send over the funds for the work he'd already done. Hitting reply, I let him know I'd sent the money. I also asked him to investigate the fourth victim, Robert Minders, and any connection he might have to the others.

Setting my phone on the bedside table, I grabbed Holly's folder. Propping myself up on one hand, I started to read.

I've always loved to read, mainly legal thrillers and military fiction, but every now and again I'd find myself drawn into a fantasy world and would binge read the entire series. Time was something that I'd always ended up with a bit of on deployment. Once off duty, there wasn't really a great deal to do but loiter around the base. So I'd taken up my old love of reading.

I leafed through Holly's notes on Charlotte Stanley. There was nothing particularly new there. The bank was still my leading theory. I knew she was involved, courtesy of her recycled plates being used at Mooney's garage, but I was still a little unsure as to why she'd been targeted.

Victor Sellers had represented James Mooney, and the papers included in the folder seemed to credit Sellers with most of the glory for that achievement rather than Mooney's innocence. It seemed even the papers were of the opinion Mooney was guilty, but Sellers' fine legal mind had persuaded the jury otherwise. In the margins beside the print, some handwritten scrawl read, *firm's footage shows semitransparent ghostlike being, but no clear view of the gunman.*

Well, that was news to me. No wonder Holly was so insistent. They had footage of one of the ghosts. The security camera at Sellers' parking structure had, in fact, caught something on camera. I would have to ask Holly about that tomorrow. I wondered if she had a copy of it anywhere. More importantly - how had she gotten it out of a firm full of lawyers? She must have won someone over.

When the folder got to James Mooney, the notes on the accident itself were prolific. It included a profile for both Reggie and Victoria Burnham as well as Kevin Thompson. There were pages of medical reports detailing Reggie's injuries as a result of the accident, as well as an obituary after he'd passed.

Victoria's profile also made interesting reading. Now retired, she had spent most of her life working in the public sector, employed by the Department of Births, Deaths, and Marriages.

The picture showed a studious old woman with glasses, set next to an artist's depiction of her sitting in court behind the prosecution. She was a wafer-thin old woman, and the longer I looked at her, the more I was convinced she couldn't be carrying out the killings herself.

Had I made a mistake dismissing Benjamin Marino so quickly? Or had Victoria Burnham hired muscle? Where had she found someone with enough talent to carry out four clean murders in such quick succession?

Kevin Thompson's profile was even more interesting. Apparently, he'd been a locksmith in his day, which I found fascinating given how our killer seemed to come and go from locked crime scenes with ease. Were he not confined to a wheelchair, he would have been my lead suspect in a heartbeat.

I flipped through numerous medical records, including a series of x-rays, and wondered just how Holly had managed to acquire those.

She had connections, no doubt about it. Clearly, she'd had similar concerns to mine, as she'd run that particular lead into the ground. The sheer volume of medical records was impossible to ignore.

Kevin Thompson was about as likely to be the killer as Santa Claus. As I read on, I found a note that the divorced Kevin did have a son, Tyler John Thompson, though in brackets after it was simply the word: *deceased*.

Perhaps that explained his ex-wife's estrangement.

Kevin's wife was indifferent, and his son was deceased. It was difficult to consider who else might have as great a motive as Victoria Burnham.

I flipped back to the old woman's profile and stared at it.

Was the mastermind behind the Casper killings really a seventy-two-year-old in a nursing home?

Morning Mischief. Sunday, April 23rd 0840hrs

I WOKE UP TO the sound of a spoon clinking against a bowl in the kitchen. Letting out a massive yawn, I stretched my weary muscles.

It had been a long few days, but it always was when I was working a case. I had a definite tendency to burn the candle at both ends, and my nightmares didn't particularly encourage me to get a good night's sleep.

Wandering out to the kitchen, I found my dad sitting at the counter, finishing off a bowl of Weet-Bix.

"Morning, Dad. How are you this morning?"

"Much better after all that excitement yesterday." He set his spoon in his bowl. "A good sleep is just what I needed."

"Sorry about that," I began, but he cut me off.

"What do you have to apologize for? Those maniacs are not your fault."

“Well, that’s not exactly true,” I replied. “They are a leftover issue from an old case. I thought I’d seen the last of them, but it appears not. Don’t worry, I'll see that they are dealt with. Those men won't bother you or mum again."

My dad nodded. "They caught me off guard last time. If they come back, I'll be ready.” His jaw had a grim, determined set to it. He wasn’t joking. My father taught me how to shoot a long time ago. After the cultists attacked my parents at the church, he had no doubt relocated his shotgun somewhere a little closer to hand. If the cultists did make the mistake of coming back, they would be in for a world of hurt.

I couldn’t wait for the cultists to act though. As soon as I got through with the Casper Killer, I planned to start hunting the high priest. I wasn’t going to stop till his whole little cabal was in custody.

I didn’t have long before Holly would arrive, so I quickly loaded a few Weet-Bix into a bowl, piled on some sugar and milk, and sat down at the kitchen bar beside my dad.

"Much on today?” he asked.

"I'm just going to run down a new angle on the case," I replied. "Hopefully we can identify this Casper Killer before he causes any more mayhem. Four bodies in two weeks makes him the most dangerous serial killer we've had in some time.”

"Just watch your back, son," my father replied. “Don't be afraid to call the boys in blue to watch it too."

I answered between mouthfuls. “That's the plan, Dad, but if I can work out who he is, he’s going to need to watch his back."

"That's my boy.” Dad slapped me on the back as he got up and headed for the back door.

"More work on the patio?" I called after him.

"It's not going to finish itself."

I looked at the beam still resting on the back patio. "I'll take care of that beam tomorrow. Just do the rest of the cuts and we'll have it up before you know it."

"Sounds like a plan," my father called back.

There was a beep from the front yard, and I looked down at my watch. Five to nine already. She was early. I threw a few more spoonful's of Weet-Bix into my mouth, wiped my face with a paper towel, and grabbed the folder off the bench.

I found Holly Draper sitting in the driveway in her red convertible.

"You're early," I called, approaching the car.

Holly grinned. "What can I say, I'm just excited to be working with the Gold Coast's pre-eminent paranormal detective."

There was a cheekiness to her grin that made me smile.

"Your sarcasm is noted," I replied, reaching for the door handle, "but for the record, I'm the Gold Coast's only paranormal detective. I've cornered the market."

"Get in," she said. "You're not one of those men who has to drive everywhere are you?"

I sank into the seat. "Not at all. In fact, I've always wanted a chauffeur."

Holly pointed a finger at me. "Don't go getting any ideas, mister. I expect you to earn your ride."

She backed out of the driveway and took off down the street. As we hurtled towards the end of my parents' suburban street, I couldn't help but think how deceiving appearances could be. Holly Draper looked like a timid bookworm, but beneath the surface there seemed to be an iron backbone and a hunger for adrenaline. Neither of which I would have expected at a glance.

I tapped the folder. "Your research is extremely thorough."

"You read it all?" Holly asked.

"Every word," I replied. "As they say, knowledge is power. You must have quite the network of sources."

Holly nodded. "Some more willing than others, but most people return my call these days. I've spent years building relationships in this town. To be honest, it kinda shocked me when your receptionist fobbed me off."

"I hope you're not still holding it against me," I replied as we wove through the Gold Coast.

"I dunno. I might find it in my heart to forgive you, if you prove useful today."

"Oh, I think you'll find I hold my own." I laughed as my phone buzzed. I looked down. It was an email from Tommy. I scanned through it as we drove.

We reached Golden Greens Aged Care in good time. Parking in the visitor's car park, we headed inside. A woman in her late fifties manned the front desk, typing busily at a computer.

"Can I help you?" she asked, glancing up at us.

"We're here to see Victoria Burnham," Holly Draper answered.

"You'll find her in room 212."

"Thank you very much," I replied, before heading toward the lifts.

"Gotta sign in first," the woman called, tapping a folder on the front counter.

Holly hastily scrawled her name and signature. I took the pen when she was done.

The woman went back to typing and doing her best to ignore us. In the column for who we were visiting, I put in Victoria's name. Then I flipped back through the register looking for other visitors. If Victoria Burnham was masterminding murders, someone had to be communicating with her, and I doubted they were doing it over the phone. I flicked back through two weeks' worth of the log but couldn't find any other visitors for Victoria.

Holly watched me work and I kept searching until the receptionist looked back up at me to see what was taking so long. I set down the pen and gave a big smile.

"All done. We'll see you on the way out."

We headed into the lift and as the doors shut, Holly nodded approvingly. "Checking the visitor's log. Slick move. See anything interesting?"

"Not particularly," I said. "But as far as guards go, that one pays about as much attention as Garfield the cat on a good day. It's not a far cry to believe someone could be signing in with an assumed identity. I considered using one myself."

"Why didn't you?" Holly asked as we reached the second floor.

"Because if we're right and someone is in fact working with Victoria Burnham to murder those responsible for her husband's death, then we could be stepping into the crosshairs."

"That's why I used a fake number and address," Holly replied.

"That's why I didn't," I replied. "If we ruffle Victoria's feathers, our killer might come looking for me. With any luck, we can catch him before the killer goes after another victim."

Holly raised her eyebrows. "You're not serious. You're intentionally baiting a serial killer?"

"Better me than an unsuspecting victim," I replied.

"Do you have no regard for your own well-being?" Holly asked, clearly questioning my sanity.

"I have considerable confidence in the blood, sweat, and small fortune the military poured into training me. I'll take my chances."

"One of these days, your luck is going to run out," she replied.

"Well, we better both hope it's not today. You wouldn't want to get caught in the line of fire, would you? Room 210, wasn't it?"

"212," Holly replied. "This way."

She pointed down the corridor.

As we entered the room, we found Victoria Burnham sitting up in her bed, propped up by a stack of pillows, watching the TV which appeared to be muted. On top of the TV cabinet sat a series of birthday and get-well cards. Some of them were recent. Judging by the ages scrawled in the handwritten messages, some had been there for years. On her bedside table was a photo of a man, presumably Mr. Burnham, and beside it rested a stack of newspapers. Four of them.

Victoria Burnham was supposed to be in her early seventies but, from the deep wrinkles and pallid complexion, I concluded she mustn't be well. Time seemed to weigh heavily on her as she sat fully dressed on top of the covers. Her hair was mostly grey, and her blue eyes followed us as we entered the room.

"Mrs. Burnham, my name is Holly Draper. This is Darius Kane. I was hoping we could talk to you for a few moments."

Victoria Burnham looked down at her watch, an old and inexpensive timepiece, before cocking her head to the side as if considering our request.

"Sure thing, dear. I am not going anywhere."

There was only one chair, so I left it for Holly. Instead, I leaned against the TV cabinet.

"Holly Draper..." Victoria mulled over the name. "You're that reporter that writes for the Bulletin."

"I am," Holly replied. "You read the Bulletin?"

"Every day, dear," Victoria replied smoothing the edge of her blanket as she pulled it higher. "I like to keep track of what's going on in the world."

"Well, that's why I'm here," Holly said. "I'm writing an article, and I've actually got a few questions that I'd love to ask you."

"Questions? For me?" Victoria asked, her voice showing a hint of surprise.

"Yes. In the course of writing that article," Holly said, tapping the paper with the front-page article I'd read in Paradox the other day, "I became aware of your story. And your connection with the late Mr. Mooney."

"Horrible man," Victoria muttered, her countenance changing in an instant. "His negligence killed my Reggie."

"I know, and maimed poor Mr. Thompson. Just a travesty what happened to him," Holly added.

"We tried to take him to court, you know," Victoria replied, "but they found him innocent. Can you believe that?"

"A travesty of justice," Holly said, leading Victoria along to soften her up.

Victoria tapped the paper. "Seems karma got him in the end."

"It would appear so," I replied. "Tell me, Victoria—May I call you Victoria?"

"Of course," Victoria said with a big smile. "Anything for a handsome young man like you."

"I'm sure you say that to everybody," I replied with a smile. "Tell me, do you keep in touch with Mr. Thompson at all? The other victim from the crash."

"Oh, from time to time," she said. "But he hasn't written in over a year. He took his son's death very hard."

I nodded as my theory continued to form. "How did he die? The son?"

"Drug overdose," Victoria shook her head somberly. "Why do you ask?"

"No particular reason. I looked into it, but couldn't find any details of his death. Nothing in the papers, or online. It came and went in a flash, almost as if it never happened."

"Well, it was a terrible tragedy," Victoria said, her knuckles turning white as she gripped her blanket. "Poor Kevin hasn't been the same since."

"Did you know him well? The son?"

"Oh, we met a few times," Victoria replied. "He used to bring his father's letters. Kevin wasn't big on emails and computers, you know."

"We haven't been to see Mr. Thompson yet," I said. "We figured we'd speak with you first."

"You're going to speak to Kevin? Why? What has he got to do with anything?"

I looked at Holly who remained silent. I took that as permission to continue my line of questioning.

"Well, Mrs Burnham. I'm not a reporter, but I'm something of an investigator. I've been looking into these cases," I replied.

"These cases?" Victoria asked, her face twisting up in confusion.

"Yes, and judging by the dates on the papers on your bedside table, you have more than a passing acquaintance with the matter."

Holly narrowed her eyes on the papers.

"Whatever are you talking about?" Victoria asked, a tired tone in her voice.

"Four papers, four victims. The most recent paper is yesterday, the day Robert Minders died. The one beneath it isn't the day before as you might expect but instead is from several days ago."

It was the day after James Mooney had died. Holly's article was printed on the front page.

"I'd hazard a guess it announces Mooney's death. The other two correspond to the earlier victims, Charlotte Stanley and Victor Sellers. The real question, Victoria, is what do you have to do with this case? Are you simply collecting trophies of all those who have wronged you? Or is there more to it than that?"

"I don't know what you're referring to, and I think it's just about time for breakfast, so if you'll excuse me, I'll be getting on with my day."

There was no way I was leaving. Not now that we had her talking.

"You know exactly what I'm talking about," I replied. "James Mooney was the man responsible for your husband's death. Victor Sellers was his lawyer. Charlotte Stanley worked the finance, and Robert Minders was the jury foreman responsible for acquitting James Mooney."

Holly's face fell. She hadn't worked that out yet. I'd picked up that particular tidbit from Tommy's email in the car this morning. I'd been saving it for this very moment. Holly's surprise was worth its weight in gold.

Score two for Tommy.

"As far as I can tell, Victoria, there are only two people alive who have an axe to grind with this collection of victims. You, and Kevin Thompson. So if you don't know anything about it, we best be going to speak to Kevin. I wonder what he'll say."

"Good luck with that," Victoria replied. "He barely speaks these days and doesn't know a thing."

"And you do?" Holly asked,

"I, uh," Victoria stammered as her regal composure melted.

"You obviously aren't carrying out these murders, but I'm betting you know who is?" Holly asked. "How many more people have to die before it stops?"

Victoria's mouth twisted into a snarl. "All of them."

"They are already dead," I replied. "The banker, the lawyer, the shoddy mechanic, the jury foreperson. It's over, Victoria, and sooner or later the police are going to connect you to it. It's only a matter of time."

Victoria laughed. "I only have months left to live. Those bastards ruined my life and before I leave this world, I will be even with them. He'll see to it."

"Who will see to it?" Holly asked.

Victoria clenched her jaw shut, realising she had said too much.

"Who?" Holly demanded.

"TJ," I replied, reading the cards off the top of the TV. Almost all of them were signed the same.

"TJ stands for Tyler John, doesn't it? Tyler John Thomson. Kevin's son."

"He's dead," Victoria spat, her voice full of venom.

"So you said," I replied as a familiar itch started at the back of my neck. It tended to happen when I was onto something. "The only problem is he died last October, six months ago."

I picked up the right most card on top of the TV. "But this card came on your birthday. Two months ago, and four months after TJ is meant to have died. TJ is not dead at all, is he, Victoria?"

"But," Holly interjected, "I've seen the death certificate."

"Me too. It's in your folder. Victoria's seen it too. Haven't you, Victoria? I don't know how you did it, but I suppose a career spent working at births, deaths, and marriages made you enough friends to get it into the system. TJ is our ghostly killer, and he is going to keep dropping bodies until we stop him, isn't he?"

"You'll never catch him." Victoria laughed. "You're already too late."

She looked at the TV that had cut to a Channel 9 news exclusive. The breaking news banner at the bottom of the screen read Ghosts Terrorise Australia Fair. Australia Fair was a giant shopping center in the heart of the Gold Coast. I stared in shock at video footage showing translucent ghostlike creatures hovering through the food court. Another angle showed one chasing shoppers through the mall. Terrified shoppers were running everywhere.

I stared at the screen. Every police officer, paramedic, and first responder would be heading to sort out that mess before all hell broke loose.

"He's going after another victim," I said.

"But why now? Why show the ghosts in public when he's tried so hard to avoid the scrutiny before?" Holly asked.

"Because he needs a distraction," I replied. "He's saved his hardest target for last, and he's realized the police know exactly who it is. After all, there is really only one person left to blame. I mean, he could try and kill every single juror but I'm sure the police started scooping them up after Robert's death yesterday. Too many coincidences to overlook. No, there will only be one person left—the judge that presided over the case. Isn't that right, Victoria?"

She said nothing, her snarling lips drawn tight.

"Sorry for your loss, Victoria, but this isn't how you make it right. We're going to put an end to this. Come on, Holly. Let's go."

"Go where?" Holly asked, still catching up.

"Wherever Judge Saunders is, that's where TJ will be heading."

We raced out of the room, leaving a furious Victoria Burnham seething in her bed. She wasn't going anywhere and while we could have tried to prevent her calling her accomplice, stopping her would do us more harm than good. Part of me was hoping she would call TJ and warn him off. Now that we knew who we were looking for and that he was very much alive, TJ's time was limited and dwindling. If we could scare him into going to ground, it gave us the best chance of saving the judge's life.

As we raced down the hall, ignoring the orderlies shouting for us to slow down, Holly called the judge's chambers.

She shouted into her phone, "Well, I suggest you keep trying. If you reach her, send her to the police now. Her life is in danger. I'm going to need her address."

When Holly hung up the phone, she looked at me. "The judge's aide says she is out playing a round of golf. She does it every Sunday morning and should be finishing up soon."

"Let me guess, the Glades Country Club?" I asked, already confident I knew the answer, but wishing I'd put it together hours ago.

"How do you know?" Holly asked. "Could you hear the call?"

"Nope. I just know that our killer already cased it. There was a valet stub in the boot of the Datsun in Mooney's garage."

The stub wasn't a piece of junk after all. I dialed the country club to inquire after the judge.

Except the judge had already left to head home for the day. I let Holly know.

"If he's not killing her at the country club, why the valet ticket?" Holly asked.

I thought about the question, and the answer clicked. "He's in the boot. Just like at Mooney's garage."

"I've tried the judge's mobile," Holly replied. "She's not answering. It goes straight to message bank."

"He must be blocking the signal somehow," I said. "He has all this mess to distract the police. He's going to kill the judge when she gets home."

"Not if we do get there first," Holly said as she clambered into her convertible. I jumped into the passenger seat and didn't even get my belt on before she tore out of the car park.

I only hoped we could get there in time. Judge Saunders' life depended on it.

Judge, Jury, Executioner. Sunday, April 23rd 1100hrs

BASED ON THE ADDRESS her PA gave us, Judge Saunders' home was only about fifteen minutes away. Given when the judge left the country club, she would be almost home.

If my theory was right, her life expectancy could be measured in minutes. There was no time to waste.

I would have called the police, but with ghosts ravaging the largest shopping center on the coast, their resources would already be stretched thin.

Ghosts. It was hard to believe, but even I had started to relent when staring at the translucent shades on the TV. They certainly looked real enough, and the panicked responses of the shoppers around them only served to amplify their presence.

I would need to look into them but right now, Judge Saunders had to be our priority. We were her best chance of survival.

"Not long now," Holly said as she blasted along the Gold Coast highway. If she didn't get a ticket out of this, I'd be amazed.

Fortunately, the police had their hands full enough as it was. I was grateful for the distraction. We couldn't afford to be pulled over by the traffic branch while trying to save the judge's life. I didn't want to call Gibson and Hart just yet either. I wasn't ready to have Detective Hart get in our way. Besides, given everything Holly had told me, I doubted my new partner would be keen on bringing in my favourite detectives before we had this in the bag, and we knew what we were dealing with now - TJ Thompson.

He's young, clearly disciplined, and very dangerous. The one thing he was not was incorporeal. And when we came face-to-face, that was an advantage he would sorely miss.

If we could save the judge, her reputation and influence would shield us from the detective's ill will.

Of course, if we failed, we would be up a particularly brown creek without any means of propulsion.

As Holly drove, I checked and rechecked my theory. The last thing I wanted was to be the boy who cried wolf. If I broke into the judge's house and TJ wasn't there trying to kill her, there would to be hell to pay.

Kevin Thompson had been a locksmith. And while his wife was out of the picture, his son wasn't nearly as dead as we'd been led to believe. I was sure Victoria had pulled those strings.

Did Kevin's parents even know he was still alive? Or was this something Victoria and TJ had masterminded together? The death certificate was a particularly good forgery and the amount of effort it would have taken to fake the other aspects of the incident were impressive. Then again, Victoria and TJ had eight years to plan their revenge. Watching his father's condition deteriorate while being unable to help must have been devastating.

No doubt TJ traced his misfortune back to James Mooney and his apparent negligence. Looking at the murders themselves, they all made more sense now.

Charlotte Stanley's death had been quick and relatively painless. Sellers, on the other hand, had been gunned down and left to bleed out in the car park of the firm he'd built securing freedom for alleged criminals. Mooney's strangulation had been up close and personal. TJ would have been close enough to watch the life drain out of James Mooney.

Minders was a heart attack. I was sure the police would find some sort of poison or panic induced catalyst, perhaps a ghostly visitation.

What did TJ have in store for Judge Saunders?

Clearly, TJ had learned his father's trade. His ability to slip through locked doors no doubt proving invaluable as he carried out the various murders. The added deception of being smuggled into Mooney's workshop in the trunk of a car was testament to both his discipline and single-minded focus.

Unfortunately for him, it had also left us the crucial key I'd almost dismissed as garbage: the valet stub to the Glades Country Club. The Datsun had been a test run for slipping into the Judge's secured residence undetected.

The judge's weekly round at the country club. It was the one appointment TJ could reliably assume she would keep. It was also a far more viable target than the courthouse which was adjoining a police station. Getting into the judge's home, inside a secured estate, would have been difficult given the perimeter, but TJ had planned his attack meticulously. If my guess was right, he was tucked in the boot of the judge's car right now, being driven right into a garage by the woman he planned to kill.

There was a callous calculation to his plan that was almost impressive. A single-minded, dogged determination to perform every detail. Each murder provided the police little or nothing to work with, whilst being carried out close enough together that they didn't have time to play catch up. He clearly understood police procedures and how long it would take them to work the scenes and run their investigation to ground.

With Minders' death, I had no doubt the detectives would have put together the links too. But now TJ had the police responding to a near riot at the mall, leaving him the perfect opportunity to make his final move.

Holly and I were the one element he hadn't accounted for. After all, I didn't work like the police. I was less concerned with evidence in a court of law than I was with solving the case. All I needed was to prove James Mooney's death wasn't a suicide. I didn't need to convict TJ, so I wasn't stuck building a case for the prosecution.

I just needed him.

Holly hit the causeway, heading out to Ephraim Island, and there she picked up speed. Ephraim Island is a wealthy community built on an island in the middle of the bay between the mainland and South Stradbroke Island. It was mostly apartments, but there were a series of expensive homes on the northeastern shore, one of which Judge Saunders owned.

Holly slowed to a less conspicuous pace as we rolled past luxury apartments. Rounding the final bend, we spotted a police car sitting out the front of the judge's home.

“What do you want to do?” Holly asked, nodding to the car.

“We don't have time to try and win them over,” I replied. “Pull up at the neighbour's place and let me out.”

Holly rolled past the squad car and pulled into the neighbor's driveway, a large hedge blocking the corvette from the officer's view.

I leaned closer to Holly. "Give me five minutes and then try to bring the cavalry. Make sure they know I'm inside. I don't need to be shot by the good guys."

"Five minutes?" Holly asked. "That isn't much time."

"It's all we've got," I replied. "He'll be biding his time, but he won't wait long. Sooner or later, the police are going to realize the mall is a distraction. We need to go now."

I slipped out of the corvette and closed the door gently. Holly pulled out of the driveway and drove a loop of the estate.

Slipping through the edge of the hedge row, I raced down the nature strip between the two luxury homes. I didn't have time to knock on the front door, and I couldn't afford to alert TJ to the fact we were onto him.

At the end of the nature strip, I was met with the beautiful crystal blue water of the bay. The judge certainly wasn't slumming it here. But she did have a ten-foot-high wall intended to keep unwanted visitors out.

Leaping, I grabbed the top of the wall and pulled myself up. I've climbed worse in my time and there was no barbed wire or other unpleasantness along the top of it. I'd slowed a little since leaving the SAS, but I could still move when the occasion required.

Reaching the top of the wall, I rolled over it and dropped into the yard with a finesse younger men would struggle to match.

I just hoped the neighbours weren't looking out the window at that particular moment.

Scanning the yard, I planned my approach. The row of trees would block most of the view from the house. The structure was an expensive two-story mansion with a balcony protruding off the second floor that granted spectacular views of the bay. I suspected that was the master bedroom.

My heart pounded in my chest. If I was wrong about the judge being the next victim, I was going to have a hell of a lot of explaining to do. Breaking into the bedroom of a sitting judge, a female one at that, was the sort of career suicide I didn't need.

However, if I was right, the judge was as good as dead. If TJ could strangle a man like Mooney, who was in his prime, an older woman wouldn't stand a chance.

I just had to trust my gut and pray I was right. I eyed the second-floor balcony. It was higher than the fence, and I didn't like my chance of reaching it unassisted. Fortunately, a barbeque station built beneath it offered the boost I needed. I climbed atop it and reached for the elegant stainless-steel rails.

A scream cut through the morning air.

The judge. It had to be. Redoubling my efforts, I grabbed the rail and pulled myself up, clambering over it. I raced across the balcony. Testing the door, I found it locked.

"I suppose that would have been too much to ask for," I muttered as I grabbed the stainless-steel chair from the outdoor table setting. Putting power into my throw, I sent the heavy steel chair through the door, sending glass everywhere. Following so close behind, the glass was still falling in my wake, I reached the inner door and tore it open.

There was a secondary scream. Now inside the house, I could pinpoint its location. Sprinting along a wide corridor, I shoulder barged through a door and into the Judge's bedroom.

There I found Judge Saunders dressed in a heavy cotton bathrobe, her hair done up with a towel after the shower she'd just taken.

All five foot five of her slender frame were rooted to the spot, but she wasn't staring at me.

No, she was staring at a translucent white ghost hovering in the air before her. Its ghostly hand pointed at her.

"Guilty," a raspy voice declared. The scratchy tone reverberated through the bedroom like a hiss.

A chill ran down my spine.

It was a ghost.

At least, it certainly looked like how I imagined a ghost might appear. But it didn't react to my presence at all. If this really was the shade of Reggie Burnham plaguing the living, surely he would have something to say about me bursting through the door to interrupt his revenge.

But it didn't. Which meant it was a program. In spite of my racing heart, and cold sweat, I dismissed what I figured was some sort of technological distraction.

"Judge, we have to get you out of here," I called over the rasping voice.

The judge turned to me, realizing I was there for the first time. Even the manner of my entrance didn't seem to have registered with the ghost in her face. For a moment, I feared Her Honour was going to have a heart attack, and I couldn't blame her. She was standing face-to-face with a ghost.

"Who are you?" she gasped, looking at me and the glass remnants of the door I'd broken on my way in. "What are you doing in my house? Get out, before I call the police."

"They're right outside. My task is to get you safely to them," I replied, my eyes searching the room. TJ had to be here somewhere, no doubt enjoying the scene his spectral haunt was causing. There was a sadism in terrorising his victims before ending their lives that I only now was beginning to comprehend.

I spotted a small squat cube resting behind a vase on the judge's writing desk. It had clear line of sight to the ghost.

"Guilty," the ghost rasped again. I crossed the room in three strides, picked up the cube, and hurled it at the wall. It sailed through the air and the ghost jumped about all over the room as the projector spun wildly.

"Guilt—" the voice rasped as the cube hit the wall and shattered, fizzling out before it could finish its sentence.

"What the...?" The judge muttered as the ghost vanished.

I turned to speak to the judge.

The bedroom door burst open. A man close to my own age came charging through it. He was wearing a balaclava, khaki slacks, and a tight grey t-shirt that struggled to contain his well-muscled form.

"You had to interfere, didn't you!" he bellowed as he charged like a wounded bull.

I reached for the vase as he raised a pistol. I was expecting it to be pointed at me, but instead he leveled it at the judge. Clearly his vendetta was worth more to him than me. I hurled the vase of sunflowers at TJ. It smashed into the pistol as he pulled the trigger. The shot went wide of the judge, punching through a window.

Before he could correct his aim, I was on top of him.

The judge yelled as I wrestled with TJ's gun hand.

In the heat of a struggle, most people try to wrestle the gun away. This fights against the natural strength of the wrist and pits your effort against the greatest resistance. Instead, I pushed with his wrist, twisting the gun down and away from the judge, pointing it at TJ's own stomach.

"Give up," I said. "Or pull that trigger and go out like Victor. Gut shot is a bad way to go."

"He deserved worse," TJ grunted. "I'm not done."

With a herculean effort, he turned, trying to bring the pistol to bear on the judge who stood transfixed by the struggle.

TJ's finger tightened on the trigger. Throwing all my weight behind it, I twisted his wrist.

A singular gunshot rang out.

Judge Saunders gasped as a blotch of red formed on TJ's shirt.

"I tried to warn you," I replied, shaking my head in frustration.

He'd taken the only shot he had.

"No jail for me," he whispered. A faint smile crossed his lips as he coughed.

I yanked the gun free and turned to the judge. "Call the ambulance."

Judge Saunders stood still, rooted to the spot.

"Your Honor!" I snapped, breaking her reverie. "The ambulance, now, please."

Judge Saunders nodded and went for her phone.

The colour had drained from TJ's face. I lifted his shirt. The angle of the shot would have carried the bullet through his lung. There was no telling just how much damage it might have done, but from the rapidly draining colour on his face, I figured it was mortal.

"Give me the towel," I called to the judge, pointing at the towel on her head.

The judge unraveled the towel and handed it to me. I pressed it against the wound. I needed answers and I doubted TJ was going to live long enough to make a statement.

"Impressive work, faking your own death. That's commitment," I said, trying to keep TJ talking.

"I needed them all," he groaned. "I promised."

"So Charlotte Stanley, that was you?"

He smiled. "She foreclosed on dad's house. She had it coming."

"Sellars? Mooney? Minders?" I asked, ensuring the judge was listening too. I wanted a witness.

"Yes, scumbags, the lot of them."

"Minders was just doing his civic duty," I replied.

TJ laughed. "Sellars got to him. The three of them were all dirty. If you have enough money, you can get away with murder."

He groaned, his face twisting up in pain. "Well, not from me, you can't."

"Why the judge?" I asked, nodding toward Judge Saunders. "She was just doing her job."

"All of them, that was the deal." TJ grunted. "She insisted on all five."

"She who? Victoria?" I asked. Was the old widow's hatred really so blind?

TJ's face contorted. "No, not Victoria. She had no part in this. It was..."

TJ's voice grew weak as his hand gripping mine trembled.

"She who?" I demanded. If someone else was still out there, I needed to know who they were. And what was her stake in this?

TJ leaned forward. "The Djinn. Her plan, five bodies, no prison, that was the deal."

He hadn't pulled the trigger by accident. TJ had done it on purpose.

"Who is she?" I demanded.

TJ went limp in my arms. I'd seen enough men die to know he was no longer with us. His last words played through my mind over and over. Her plan? The Djinn? Who was she?

Confucius once said that when planning your revenge, you ought to dig two graves. TJ's desperate search for vengeance had cost him his life. The Casper Killer was dead. But he'd taken four people with him.

"He's dead?" Judge Saunders asked, hovering nearby.

"He is. I hope you caught all that," I said.

"Every word," she replied. "He was the Casper Killer?"

"Indeed, his name was Tyler John Thompson. You once sat a case against the man responsible for injuring his father. A mechanic by the name of James Mooney."

Judge Saunders nodded. "I remember the case. It was a mess. The police must have figured out the connection, because they parked that detail out front yesterday. Didn't tell me why though. A warning would have been nice."

"I'll let you take that up with them, Your Honor. They aren't my biggest fans at the moment."

"Who are you?"

I'd just wrestled a man to death in her bedroom and she had no idea who I was. "Your Honour, my name is Darius Kane. I'm a private investigator. I apologize for the manner in which I entered your home. But when we discovered his plot, I couldn't reach you on the phone, so I had no other choice. Don't worry, I'll pay for your door."

"The door is the least of my problems right now."

There was a pounding at the door downstairs. Holly must have prevailed on the police finally.

"That ghostly apparition, it looked so real." The judge shook her head.

"Holographic projection. Intended to distract you while he snuck in and killed you. It's how he's managed to kill so many without leaving a trace. The victim has always been so terrified, they never fought back."

"Well, it appears I am in your debt, Mr. Kane."

"Call me Darius, please," I replied. "I'm just doing what I can to help Mooney's widow, Your Honour. If you wouldn't mind letting the police in, I'm sure they have a lot of questions for us both."

She nodded and made her way out of the room. I sent her first for two reasons. Firstly, her security detail were far less likely to shoot her. And secondly, I wanted a look at the hi-tech projector TJ had been using. The quality of the projection was more advanced than anything I had ever seen.

I gathered up what was left of the ghost projector. It was remarkably compact in size, but the technology was advanced, and unusually had no markings on it whatsoever.

If TJ was broke, how had he afforded this sort of tool? I fished through the bits and pieces. There was some broken circuitry, a shattered lens, and a few other components I didn't recognise. If the Djinn helped him plan his revenge, perhaps she also provided him with assistance. But why?

The curious cat inside of me couldn't leave a question unanswered. I took one of the microchips and slid it into my pocket, ensuring there was enough debris left for the police to believe it was still all there.

"Darius Kane, always sticking your nose where it doesn't belong."

"Detective Hart," I replied, recognizing the air of superiority in her voice.

I turned and found her wearing the heck out of a tight black pantsuit. I could certainly understand how she got her way. If she didn't think I was a serial killer, I'd have at least thought about braving her personality long enough to take her to dinner.

"Right on time," I replied, as her mouth rose into a smile. "In time to miss the hard part and take the credit."

Hart shook her head. "I'm just flat out trying to keep you from getting yourself killed. One of these days, I fear I'm going to show up at a scene and find your body. You're lucky the officers outside didn't shoot you on the way in."

"I'm touched," I replied, placing a hand on my chest. "I didn't know you cared."

Detective Hart looked at me and nodded to the door. "We need to talk. Now."

Maestro. Sunday, April 23rd 1230hrs

HART LOOKED LIKE SHE was going to burst a blood vessel.

A steady stream of police officers were making their way inside the room, so I pointed to the hallway and gave her my best smile. "Sure, detective, why don't we step into my office?"

Hart followed me out and as I turned, I noticed the hint of bags beneath her eyes and furrow of her brow.

"I do hope you aren't going to try and pin this mess on me," I began. "I've had quite enough of that already. Besides, I have a witness. Judge Saunders saw everything."

Detective Hart shook her head, her emotions torn somewhere between laughing and crying. "No, nothing like that. The judge has already been quite emphatic about the role you played in there. So you got him after all?"

"Yeah," I replied, trying to read the detective. "A ghost, I guess, in the loosest sense of the word. Meet Tyler James Thompson, a name you might recognise from—"

"The case against James Mooney, eight years ago," she interrupted. "That's the angle we'd been working too, but everyone was dead, incapacitated, or incapable of the murders that were piling up. Any idea how he pulled that off?"

"Victoria Burnham worked at Births, Deaths, and Marriages. I suspect she helped him fake his death and file the false paperwork." I set my hands on my hips. "I was almost too late. The judge could have been killed because you lot spent more time chasing me than working together."

"No need to salt the wound," Hart replied. "Gibson is still downstairs taking flak from Saunders. Whether you like it or not, Darius, you don't have a badge. We can't just go giving you information on an open case."

"Right now, I'd settle for you not trying to arrest me, whenever we cross paths," I replied. "I doubt this is the last case we'll both be working."

"I think I can manage that," Hart replied. "Baby steps."

It wasn't much but it was a start. If I could win her and Gibson over, I would have one less thing to worry about.

"So how did you work it out?" I asked. "The connection between the victims."

Hart leaned against the balcony rail. "Well, Charlotte was an odd crime scene. It didn't add up, but not enough to be sure it was foul play. Her sister mentioned she'd been complaining about ghosts though and that struck us as odd. When the security footage in Sellers' garage showed an apparition approaching him before he was gunned down from a different angle, we had a tenuous link but nothing concrete."

"Until Mooney died." I crossed my arms, watching the crime scene techs at work clearing the judge's bedroom.

"When Mooney died, we joined the dots fast," Hart said. "But there was no way of knowing if the killer was done. The person responsible for the accident was dead. Minders took us by surprise. When he struck, we put a detail on the judge and went looking for the other jurors, not sure where he'd strike next. When the mess started at Australia Fair, we figured it couldn't be a coincidence, so we headed straight here."

"I'm surprised you made it here in such good time. I wonder if he realized his distraction would be a beacon. I guess he figured he'd be out of here before anyone knew what had happened."

"But the detail out front," Hart replied. "Unless..."

I looked out over the water and pointed. "He'd have gone that way."

"That's a heck of a swim back to shore." Hart looked sceptical.

"He sat in the boot of a car for hours and was more than fit enough to make it."

"It's a fair theory." Hart turned to take in the shattered balcony door, the bullet hole in the glass, and the fragments of broken door everywhere. "Is this sort of mess what we have to look forward to if we work with you?"

"Work with me?" I tried not to swallow my tongue. "That's what you call it, huh? Accusing me of murder, hindering my efforts. Shutting me out of the investigation. That's you working together? Heaven help me if I was to get in the way."

She flashed me a little smile. "You have no idea what I do to those who get on my bad side."

After talking to Holly Draper, I think I had a fair idea, but I wasn't going to say that out loud. I just reminded myself that behind the detective's enticing smile was a cold calculating mind. But the smile was awfully distracting.

Geez, Darius, maybe you should listen to Carl.

I surveyed the damage. "Believe it or not, this is me on a good day."

She shook her head. "How did you figure it out?"

"We visited Victoria Burnham. I saw a birthday card signed TJ from her last birthday, months after he was meant to be dead. When I saw the news, I knew he must be going back. The judge was my best bet. When we called her secretary, she said the judge was at golf. That was when I realized what he was up to.

"Mooney was a test run for the judge. When I was crawling around that Datsun, I found a valet stub for the Country Club. I figured TJ was going to try and slip into the boot and ride home with the judge."

Hart's eyes grew wider and wider as I spoke. "Very clever, Darius. You'd make a pretty good detective, you know?"

I raised an eyebrow. A compliment seemed almost out of character for the ornery detective.

I was on guard; her shift in character was a little too quick for my tastes. Sure, I'd been exonerated but she'd given me hell.

"That sounds dangerously like a compliment. What gives? You were ready to toss me in a cell yesterday."

"Only because you kept showing up at our scenes," she said. "And I wasn't sure what to make of you. What would you have done in my shoes?"

It was a fair point. Wrong, but given her job and the fact she was constantly confronted with the criminal element of society, it was a little more understandable.

“I’ll give you that,” I replied, extending an olive branch. There was no point antagonizing her when she was making an effort.

“So if you don’t mind, I’d like to start over.” She held out her hand. “I’m Olivia.”

Olivia. It had a nice ring to it. I reached out my hand to shake hers until I realised it was still covered in blood and pulled it back.

"I'm sorry.” I mimed a handshake. “Rain check?”

“Sure. Why not tomorrow when you come down to the station to give us your statement?” Hart said.

It was going to take time to think of her as Olivia.

"You don't want it now?" I cocked my head to the side.

"I suspect we'll be busy for hours yet, and the news crews will be here any minute. Why don't you swing by the station tomorrow?”

“Sounds like a plan.”

Hart flicked a thumb over her shoulder. “I need to get back to this mess. Behave yourself, huh?”

“No promises,” I replied with a grin.

I followed Hart back inside and helped myself to the judge’s soap to wash the blood off my hands in the bathroom sink. As I left, the crime scene techs were locked in conversation with Hart. I gave her a nod and slipped out of the room, using the normal entrance this time.

Detective Gibson hadn’t made it much further than the front door. Judge Saunders was there, and from the looks on both their faces, he was enjoying it about as much as being slow roasted over an open fire.

I left them to it and headed for the front door.

"I wouldn't go out there, if I was you, Darius," Gibson called after me. "The media are swarming like vultures. That Draper lady is already here."

With all the goodwill I'd just built with Hart, I didn't have it in me to tell him she'd driven me here. "Nothing I haven't seen before. If it's all the same to you, I'd rather get home. I have a dog to walk, and a patio to finish."

Judge Saunders stepped sideways into my path. "Mr. Kane, I really can't thank you enough.

"My privilege, Your Honour. Just doing my part."

"You did considerably more than that," she replied, "and I won't forget it."

I wasn't entirely sure what that meant, but having a judge well disposed toward me certainly couldn't hurt.

I wandered down the front steps to the driveway. A bevy of police waited there holding camera crews at bay. I searched their ranks and found Holly looking a little miffed.

"Mr. Kane, a word please," one reporter called. "This is Peter Sears from Channel 7. We spoke after the Crypt Killers were apprehended."

I smiled. "Of course, Peter. How are you?"

"Well, thank you. Do you have a moment to talk about what transpired here?"

"Peter, I would love to," I replied, watching Holly's face for a reaction. She looked fit to commit murder. "But unfortunately, I've promised an exclusive to the Bulletin. It was Holly Draper who was instrumental in cracking the case and saving Judge Saunder's life."

Peter looked like he'd been shot. It seemed he'd expected this exclusive too, based on our history. I threw him a bone and made good on another promise. "I can say I wouldn't have solved this case without the invaluable assistance of Esmerelda from the Paranormal Palace. It's almost like she can see the future. If you haven't been yet, you're doing yourself a disservice."

That sound bite was all they would have to play on their channel tonight and if nothing else, it was bound to keep Esmerelda happy. I slipped through the crowd and made for Holly Draper and her red corvette.

"I thought you were going to throw me under the bus there," she said with a smile.

"I'm a man of my word," I replied. "It's your story. Whenever you want the exclusive, it's yours."

We headed for my parent's home, stopping in a park to record a brief interview for Holly to run with, before she dropped me at their driveway.

"I'd love to stay and chat," she said with a grin, "but I've got a story to write."

It was almost lunchtime on a Sunday morning. I couldn't help but admire her work ethic.

"We can talk anytime," I said. "Go knock 'em dead."

My parents were out but I grabbed Max and his leash, and took him for a well-deserved walk. With the Casper Killer dealt with, I just wanted the afternoon to recharge my batteries. Max and I stopped at a dog friendly cafe, enjoyed lunch, and walked all the way to the Spit. Its dog friendly beach is one of my buddy's favorite places to play. Running in the surf and sand, he was adorable. It lasted until he mistimed a wave and got bowled over.

I plucked up my soaked little beagle, carried him to the beach shower, and then we headed home.

Evening was coming quick, and I was considering my dinner choices when my phone dinged.

My heart fluttered a little when I recognised Mary Baker's number. The text read simply, *Dinner? My place. 7:00pm.*

It was a little more intimate than I was expecting. I texted back asking if I should bring anything.

A bottle of wine, something that will pair well with salmon.

The message was followed by an address just outside Surfers Paradise city limits.

I'll see you then, I replied, trying not to seem desperate. I had a little skip in my step as I made my way to the front door. The good doctor's company was just what I needed. With any luck, Carl's advice would prove unnecessary.

Life was looking promising indeed.

Max wagged his little doggy tail enthusiastically, seemingly echoing my good mood.

"Things are looking up, buddy," I said as I fixed him dinner.

It was almost six o'clock, so I showered, slipped into some smarter dress slacks and an open collared shirt, and headed for the good doctor's house, stopping to buy a pricey bottle of Chardonnay, largely on the assumption that the staff at the 'Bottle-O' knew what they were talking about.

I punched Mary Baker's address into the GPS and made my way to her house.

It was a small home. There was no car in the driveway and the front door was open.

My gut twisted a little. No one left their door open around here. It wasn't that sort of town. I grabbed the Chardonnay and headed for the house.

As I reached the door, my blood ran cold. An eerily familiar symbol was scrawled across it: a large red circle with a pentagram inside it. The paint wasn't even dry yet.

The cult of Beelzebub.

My heart raced as I charged into the house.

How could they know about Mary? It didn't make sense. Here I was protecting my parents and they'd gone after someone I met hours ago.

"Mary?" I shouted, searching frantically.

If the deluded zealots had harmed a hair on her head, I would kill them all.

But the house was empty. Actually empty.

Not a sign of life in it, including furniture.

I halted in the kitchen doorway, my heart racing. The kitchen had a simple table, set for two. One of the plates had a piece of paper on it with a typed note. I picked it up.

Apologies for the deception, Darius. I was dying to meet you. I do hope you'll stop getting in my way. I'll take a rain check on dinner. The Djinn.

In my mind, I could hear TJ's dying words.

I lifted my eyes to the opposite chair at the table. There was a black dress and blazer draped over it. In the blazer's pocket were a set of wire rim glasses, and on one corner of the chair sat a striking red wig that was remarkably lifelike.

It was everything Mary Baker had worn to lunch with me yesterday.

Only she wasn't Mary Baker at all. I'd eaten lunch with a sociopath responsible for the deaths of four people. Five, if I included TJ.

"Five bodies, no prison, that was the deal," TJ had whispered.

What deal? What had she promised him? Revenge? Why? What did she have to gain from his revenge?

I scooped up her outfit, the note, and my Chardonnay and headed for my car. As I did, I stopped at the door, staring at the cult's adopted iconography.

"Why was it here?"

And then it hit me: the words of the high priest. "She switched the knife."

That was what he'd said. At the time, I'd been too busy to give it much thought. Now I wondered if he wasn't referring to the Djinn.

Was she behind that mess also? The kidnapping of Cali Masters, the sacrifice, the knife. She was toying with them, too. Why?

And why tell me by plastering their iconography on the door?

That's when it clicked.

She was playing with me.

Here I was with my Chardonnay ready to celebrate, when the brains behind the Casper Killer was still out there.

The Djinn.

I looked down at the disguise in my hands and knew I'd get nothing from them. She'd left them for me. Given how clean each of the crime scenes were, I doubted I would find so much as a hair follicle on any of them.

Whoever the Djinn was, she was clever, calculating, and dangerous.

And I was so far behind her machinations I couldn't even see her in the distance.

I climbed back into my car and slid the key into the ignition.

As I did, I realized her mistake: pride.

She'd been so eager to take a victory lap, so eager to display how she could pull my strings like a puppet that she'd made one mistake.

Just one.

I now knew she existed.

The End

About the Author

Dear Reader,

Welcome to Blue Moon Australia. I know it's a little journey across the pond for many Tempest Michaels fans, but one of the things Steve and I got excited about when planning this series was just how different the setting is from the gothic British feel of the original series (which I love).

So, you're in for salt, sand and supernatural suspense, set around some of the most picturesque beaches in the world. The Gold Coast.

I hope you're as excited as I am. The next four books are going to take you on a wild ride and leave you guessing until the very last page is turned. Who is the Djinn? Why is she gunning for Darius? What price will he have to pay to unmask this deadly villain... buckle up it's going to be a fun ride. I've included a glossary of some of the more eccentric Aussie terms in this novel and a peek into Book 2 Sirens and Sea Monsters below.

Outside of the Blue Moon universe, I also write urban fantasy where the magic is rather real, so if you're in the mood for a little action, mystery and magic while you wait. Check out my other titles. They are good, clean fun, just like this one.

Until next time, all the best.

Sam Stokes

Email: samuel@samuelstokes.com

Want to see my other titles? Head to my website

https://www.samuelcstokes.com/

Or sign up to my newsletter where you'll receive free prequel books, exclusive short stories, giveaways, and so much more. My newsletter is the place to go to never miss sales, new releases and special merch. Copy the link below into your browser.

https://www.books.samuelcstokes.com/jointhevips

If you enjoy social media, I have a growing group of readers who love to hang out, share their favourite reads, funny animal pictures, and torment me about when my next book is coming out.

www.facebook.com/groups/scstokesarcanoverse/

Glossary

At the end of each of my books I try to include a glossary of any Australian slang or unusual pop culture references I might have included. I like to include a few of these to give you an authentic Aussie feel, and the pop culture references, well, they're just a little fun. If I missed any, be sure to let me know.

Slang

Arvo – Short for afternoon. 'I'm going to pop over this arvo' is the sort of phrase you'd hear on a daily basis.

Ute – Short for utility. It is the Australian equivalent of what Americans would refer to as a truck (albeit perhaps a little smaller than the US variant). Darius' tank is a ute.

Snob – Used commonly as a replacement for snub. 'Julia totally snobbed me the other night'.

Pop Culture References

Scrooge McDuck – The popular Disney character. This reference was born out of my childhood cartoons and my career as a tax accountant.

Barney Stinson – The unrepentant womanizer from How I Met Your Mother. I've watched and loved every episode. If you haven't, I envy you, you have some hilarious tv ahead of you.

What's Next for Darius?

Darius Kane is Australia's only paranormal investigator. The police don't like him, the local crime kingpin wants to kill him, and there's definitely something sinister watching him from the shadows.

The Gold Coast has its share of weird and unexplained, just like everywhere else, but when a local swim coach goes missing, Darius finds his attention drawn to the waves ... or, more accurately, what might be lurking beneath them.

He's still sweeping up the mess left behind by the gang of sacrifice-happy cultists, and needs to get the police off his back, but with a stack of bills and more than one paying customer, the mermaid case simply cannot be avoided.

It might sound like a joke, but when his first venture into the surf leaves him needing stitches, things get real fast.

Like it or not, investigating the cases no one else will touch comes with a side of unavoidable danger and once again Darius is going to have to fight for his life if he wants to survive the truth.

Get your copy by copying the below link into your browser

https://mybook.to/aus2sirensseamonsters

Free Books and More

Want to see what else I have written? Go to my website.

https://stevehiggsbooks.com/

Or sign up to my newsletter where you will get sneak peeks, exclusive giveaways, behind the scenes content, and more. Plus, you'll be notified of Fan Pricing events when they occur and get exclusive offers from other authors because all UF writers are automatically friends.

Copy the link carefully into your web browser.

https://stevehiggsbooks.com/newsletter/

Prefer social media? Join my thriving Facebook community.

Want to join the inner circle where you can keep up to date with everything? This is a free group on Facebook where you can hang out with likeminded individuals and enjoy discussing my books. There is cake too (but only if you bring it).

https://www.facebook.com/groups/1151907108277718

Printed in Great Britain
by Amazon